ADVANTAGE

By

Robert David

This book is a work of fiction. Places, events, and situations in this story are purely fictional. Any resemblance to actual persons, living or dead, is coincidental.

ISBN: 1-4107-2823-4 (e-book)
ISBN: 1-4107-2824-2 (Paperback)

This book is printed on acid free paper.

1st Books - rev. 03/19/03

Acknowledgement's

www.bluediamondlightbody.co.uk

with many thanks

for showing me how.

And to my family

Thank you for all the support and guidance.

Authors note-

I hope you will enjoy this book, it is made up of a mixture of fact and fiction given from my own perspective as an inperfect being in an inperfect world. Which is which is up to you to decipher.

CHAPTER 1.

It was a cold night in July, which really wasn't that remarkable considering this was North Dakota, one of the northern most points of America .

Two men were trudging Along the road, they were talking, their voices carried on the wind alerted the wolf of their presence.

It would have smelled them coming but they were approaching from down wind .

It ducked down a hare hole just as they passed by.

The two men continued on, the wolf in the mean time leapt out and continued to dig at the chicken run fence.

"This is a depressing little town!".

Thought Arthur Katskill for the second thousand time that day

"The only Advantage" he thought on,

"The town of Vantage has; is the beautiful mountain reservations that surround it".

"Still I've enjoyed most of the last 22 years of my life in this town ".

"I just don't want to spend the next 22 here!".

"Spend the next 22 what? ".

Asked his father from the mini kitchen behind the counter.

Arthur hadn't realised he spoke aloud,

"Oh nothing, just thinking aloud" he replied.

Arthur had been working as a salesman in his fathers camping shop for the past year now after leaving school without achieving much in the grade department.

It wasn't that he was unruly or stupid.

He just didn't get any of it done; for Arthur Katskill school was a form of neurosis followed by brief flash of light and freedom.

Now in his fathers shop almost a mental paralysis had set in;

his mind felt heavy, slow and old.

It had been that long since anything new had happened, if it did he was sure he wouldn't be able to cope.

Now Arthur being the reasonably intelligent person he was, did realise this was not the correct or even a healthy state of mind for a young man or an old one for that matter in which to live his life.

He just didn't quite know what he could do about it.

So far he'd made enough money to buy an old battered 4x4 and had about a thousand bucks in the bank but still no idea if it was enough or of where to go.

"Soon" he thought "Soon".

"Those pesky wolves don't give up do they John?".

asked Mary Silverton, Johns wife for the past thirty years.

“No they bloody don’t!, still only lost one last night, not so bad eh? said John”.

“Your very chipper this morning aren’t you” said Mary.

“Its that fine coffee you make-its enough to make the dead smile” answered John.

“I swear you could charm your way into politics with a mouth like that, why you ever bothered with farming I’ll never know” he’s wife replied.

“Its the only way your dad would let me marry you!-I remember what he said (he scrunched up his face and gesticulated wildly with his finger stabbing at the air) -Its the farm you marry boy she just comes with it!”.

“He said no such thing you pig!” said Mary feigning indignation.

With that Mary stormed back to the kitchen.

Johns laughter followed her as she went.

“Ill get you for that one”.

She called back laughing despite herself.

“What you up to today?” she asked.

“Not a lot just got to fix the fence and Ill be off to meet Mike, he’s tractors thrown it’s cam and we’re going to tinker.”

“Oh, OK then, have fun wont you, dinners at 7”.

“OK see you later then babe”.

Called John as he left the house.

Kate had been on road all night.

"I'm exhausted" she thought.

"Ill stop at the next town for a bite and see if I can find a cheap room somewhere".

Her car, an old Buwick pulled steadily up the winding road on to Vantage.

"What a beautiful place!".

She thought looking out the window at the majestic scene below, the mist was just rising of the lower slopes revealing the heavy woodland below, driving through that mist had been a nightmare the previous night.

"I think Ill stay here a while if possible you never know I just might get some work done!".

She told her car.

Which by the way was called Harry and in her opinion was far more reliable than any other man she'd had the miss-fortune to meet so far.

Now Jack, there was one she wont forget in a hurry no matter how hard she tried to.

He'd seemed so nice so perfect for the first couple of months then she'd started to notice the underlying imbalance's of his character, he was so pig-headed so arrogant and so narrow minded, that it made him irresistibly sexy!.

It was an intoxicating mix and a great experience but one destined to end in tears (on her part at least).

"Oh well' live and learn" she thought.

With past memories of Jack buzzing around her brain Kate Rivers (23) a free lance writer drove into the small town of Vantage.

She stopped at the towns only bar/inn an old looking place with a battered sign that read “BOBS HOLE” and went inside; the bar was sickly sweet with warmth and stale beer.

“How can you say that McMiyers isn’t playing well,” Said a voice as she entered. “he’s already put 5 in this season and you can tell he’s only just warming to the game”.

The voice belonged to the bar man, a strong looking man in his 40’s.

He was speaking to a scruffy looking guy sat at the corner of the bar.

“I’m jus’ stating facs Bob, he’s never got over that leg injury from last year”.

“Sorry to interrupt.” Interrupted Kate, both men eyed her suspiciously.

"I need a room" she offered.

Bobs demeanour changed immediately.

"Ah a customer a, well Ive got a single- how long do ya' want it".

"Oh just a couple of nights" Kate replied.

"It'll be 16 bucks a night then, lill miss".

Kate bite her tongue, Jack used that term when being sarcastic.
"Thank you" she said .

The room was small with a lino floor which was flaked and faded but the bed was soft and warm.

She collapsed on it without undressing and fell immediately into a deep sleep.

She was standing in a woodland it was dark , creepy and misty with a humidity you usually find in a rain forest not a woodland like this.

There was a noise close by, something was moving towards her, something big.

Overcome by a primal fear she began to run, she could hear it getting closer.

A strange thought came to mind

"Why can you never run fast enough when your dreaming, the faster you try the slower you seem to go".

She began to panic, branches were slapping her about the face as she went slowing her even more, it was getting closer she could feel its chilly presence behind her almost gloating, savouring the taste of her fear.

She awoke, her clothes and the bed linen were soaked with sweat.

She got up and stumbled to the bathroom, looked at herself in the mirror.

"That was too real!". She told her refection and began to undress.

20 mins later she was showered and dressed in fresh jeans and T-shirt, it was six o'clock p.m.

She'd slept most of the day and was beginning to feel hungry.

"I wonder what the food's like here" she thought.

She went downstairs, the room was packed and smoky.

She approached the bar and ordered a cheeseburger, fries and a large brandy from the rather sparse menu and sat at the only empty table.

Which happened to have a good view of the main bar area.

Sipping her drink she decided a little people watching was in order, she loved to watch people in new environments and make notes in her pad, you never knew just when notes like this would be useful.

The scruffy man from earlier was sat in the same place, red-faced and talking loudly to a elderly man in a thick red woolly jumper.

She couldn't make out what he was saying over the general din, although he seemed by his gestures to really care that he was understood.

"Sport talk" she thought.

She continued to look around, there didn't seem to be anyone of her own age in the place.

"Great" she thought "Ive come to a retirement village."

Just then a slight dark-haired woman somewhere in her mid to late 40s came over with her order.

“The room OK?” she asked.

“Yes its fine” said Kate.

“I’m Jane, Bob’s wife if there’s anything else dear don’t be afraid to ask” said the woman.

“Thank you” said Kate “I wont”.

Jane left the order on the table and headed back to the bar.

Kate watched her walk away and turned to her meal, it looked quite good with only a marginal puddle of grease that she would soon hide with a more than what is generally considered to be a healthy dose of ketchup.

“All my minerals in one go” she thought and set about her meal.

Just as she was finishing her fries a young man seemed to appear next to the table

“May I join you?” he asked.

His voice sounded familiar some how, even with the slight Canadian twang.

She looked up at his face, it was nice, she thought not exactly handsome but open and friendly with no visible scars.

“Sure” she said.

Arthur finished work at 6:30pm he had a bad day

“To much thinking can really bring you down”.

He thought, the fact they had only two customers all day hadn't helped matters either. "I'll see you at home dad, I'm going for a beer" he said.

"OK but don't be to late you know your mother worries" said his father.

"OK" Arthur replied.

With that Arthur left the shop and headed down to Bob's, the chill wind felt invigorating against his face and he started to relax.

By the time he reached Bobs he was feeling the simple joy of going for a drink after a bad day, that he felt sure was shared by people everywhere who felt they were stuck in boring employment.

It was a true pleasure entering the warm noisy bar with its familiar smell of stale beer, sweat and fried food.

He made he's way to the bar, asked Jane for a beer and turned round to survey the room, "Usual crowd" he thought.

Then he saw her, she was sat at a corner table eating ketchup with a side order of fries and writing in a note book.

"Wow" thought Arthur "who's that!".

He stood there for a moment drinking in the lines of her legs visible in tight blue jeans, the swell of her hips tapering towards her waist and the beckoning firmness of her breasts sitting there high on her chest.

Leading the eye towards her muscular neck supporting a face of full lips high cheekbones and dark blue eyes, not forgetting the long auburn hair, tied up at the moment but Arthur could all to easily imagine running his hands through it.

Jane placed his beer on the bar "Two bucks please Arthur" she said, snapping him out of his trance.

Jane peering over his shoulder smiled.

"she's alone you know!" she said casually.

Arthur could feel his neck and ears start to burn, he past Jane the money and said "Thank you", a little too stiffly.

"No problem" said Jane, still smiling she walked to the other end of the bar.

Arthur stood still and taking a grip on himself thought, "You don't know if you don't try" and headed towards the table.

As he sat down, Kate noticed the look of relief on his face and warmed to him instantly.

She studied his hands as they went through the usual questions and answers these situations always bring.

“Where you from?” he asked after her name.

He couldn’t help staring at her eye’s while they spoke, they were such a rich vibrant blue he immediately thought of children with those same eyes.

He shuddered inside and pushed the thought away.

“Kentucky originally” she answered, she was still looking at his hands and could feel him staring at her eyes.

Every time she looked up he would glance away only to stare again as soon as she looked at his hands.

They were nice hands, elegant yet strong with long spatulate fingers.

“A small town” she went on “Much the same as this one excepting the weather”.

“So why are you here?” he asked.

“I’m trying to write a novel, this past year travelling round the states is all for research and ideas” she replied.

“How’s it going?”.

“Not bad Ive got loads of interesting notes, it’s just a matter of how I put them together, thankfully Ive not got that far yet!”.

“Thankfully?” he prompted.

“That’s where the real work starts” she added.

They talked on like this for hours, discussing their pasts and present aspirations, the next thing they knew Jane and Bob were putting chairs on tables and the bar was empty.

“I’m gonn’a have to break you up now kids it’s well past closing” said Jane.

“Oh, aright then” said Arthur.

“Are you doing much tomorrow?” asked Kate

“Working I’m afraid, I can meet you for lunch if you like?”.

“Here?” Kate asked.

“No there’s a dinner on the south-side of town. Don’t tell Bob I said this” he whispered conspirativly “but the foods a lot better there!”.

“What time’s good for you?” she asked.

“Noon?” he offered.

"It's a date then" she said.

With that she stood, leaned over and kissed him gently on the cheek, smiled said "Good night" then left the bar.

On her way up to her room she wondered if that was a good idea, the contact felt great but she couldn't help but wonder if it was too much, after all she only just met him and she knew only to well what small towns can be like for talk.

Thoughts of Jack assailed her.

"Right, Ill play it a little cooler tomorrow!" she said aloud as she entered her room.

Arthur was elated he couldn't believe it, all this time in this small town wondering what he was going to do and where he was going.

Then completely out of the blue, he meets this beautiful girl right here in his home town! “Incredible” he thought “and if I’m not mistaken she liked me to”.

The world had taken on a wonderful rosy glow as far as Arthur was concerned, he floated down the street to his car.

With thoughts of her spinning in his mind, he drove contentedly home.

Luckily his parents had gone to bed, so he wouldn’t have to listen to his mum moan about his time keeping, at least not until the morning.

The morning came, as did the expected lecture.

“Arthur you could at least call when your going to be late” said his mother.

“Sorry I lost track of the time” he offered lamely, he had neglected to tell his parents why he had been so late.

"Well next time do try to call, you know I worry about you" said his mother.

"OK mum" said Arthur starting to feel a little guilty.

"Well we really should be going" said his father, in an attempt to diffuse the situation.

"Ok then, have a good day boys" said Mrs Katskill.

Arthur's mother Helen Katskill also had to go to work, she worked in a clothing shop at the mall in town.

30 mins later the Katskill family parted and went about there respective days.

The morning dragged on for Arthur, dispite the fact the shop was busy, if anything the clock seemed to be going backwards.

His father could tell something was up but couldn't quite put his finger on it, Arthur seemed jumpy, a little on edge and he kept looking at the clock.

Finally it read 12:00 and Arthur grabbed his coat and headed for the door.

"Back in an hour dad" he called over his shoulder as he left the shop.

Albert turned to answer but Arthur had already left.

"I wonder what's up with him?" he thought.

Arthur ran around the corner towards his car and almost straight into Mrs Combe coming the other way pushing her grandson James gurgling away in his buggy.

"Oh, sorry Mrs Combe" said Arthur red faced.

"That's aright, how's your mother Arthur? I haven't seen her for a while, hope her knee's feeling better" she said warming up for a good gossip.

"Oh she's just fine, her knee's a lot better now, but I really must be getting on Mrs Combe, I cant talk right now, sorry, bye" said Arthur making his escape.

"Nice boy" thought Mrs Combe as Arthur ran on.

"bit highly strung though, he more and likely slow down as he matures" she said to James who gurgled in reply, they continued up the road.

Arthur reached his car, skidded to a halt and pulled his key's out of his pocket dropping them right next to the drain.

"Slow down" Arthur thought to himself.

"I'm acting like a teenager".

He took a deep breath and reached down for his keys, slowly and very deliberately he opened the car and got in.

Thankfully it started first time and he drove to the south side of town.

Kate had spent the morning exploring the town, she was surprised at the number of amenities there was for such a small place.

It had a mall, a cinema, a library, an indoor pool and a gym.

She noticed she kept looking at her watch and dispite herself smiled.

"Here we go again." She thought.

At ten to twelve she parked her car and entered the Dinner.

She took a table at the far end where she could watch everything that was going on.

A waitress approached her table, she was a pretty thing, petit about 16 with a “bob” haircut and a name badge that read simply “J”.

Kate guessed her name must be very un-cool, and “J” was the only alternative.

“What can I get you?” asked the girl

“Just a coke for the moment, I’m waiting for someone” Kate replied.

“No worries!” said the girl and scooted off.

It was 12:20 by the time Arthur reached the Dinner.

Kate hadn’t noticed, she was engrossed in a dispute a family were having two table’s away.

Arthur entered the Dinner and looked about, he spotted Kate at the far end sipping a coke and scribbling furiously at her note pad.

At that moment she glanced in his direction and waved, Arthur smiled and made his way towards the table.

As he sat down Kate put her note pad in her bag and turned to face him.

“Well, how are you?” he enquired

“Good” she replied.

“This towns bigger than it looks” she added.

“You think so?” he said.

“Yeah I didn’t expect to see a mall here”.

“That’s where my mother works”.

“Oh, which shop?”.

“Kit-bag, the clothing shop”.

“I didn’t go in that one”.

The waitress came back and they ordered an extra large pepperoni pizza and another coke for Arthur.

As is sometimes the way with a second meeting they both felt a little awkward, at first their conversation was a little jumpy it didn’t quite have the same easy flow as their previous meeting.

They hopped around from subject to subject until they found a common ground and once again found that open space between them where they could talk freely without the worry of being miss-understood.

This way they began to see and assess the deeper layers of each others psyche.

Kate liked what she saw, he was very much like Jack on the surface, but without the stubborn narrow mindedness that really brought things to a crunch with him.

She could also see he liked her scattered way of thought, the way she would lay a subject out like a map before her and pick out the bits she felt were of use to her.

This particular aspect of her persona had really annoyed Jack who'd preferred a more sequential method, generally arriving at completely obscure and unreasonable conclusions.

Their meal arrived and they continued to talk whist eating, another thing they found they had in common was a love of food.

They both seemed to visibly brighten whist eating and their conversation became more rapid and fluid, frequently interspersed with that kind of natural bubbly laughter that seems to come from nowhere.

Arthur asked Kate if she thought there might be something other than pepperoni on the pizza and Kate snorted with laughter blowing coke from both nostrils and immediately looked watery eyed, red faced and very embarrassed.

This struck Arthur as hilarious and he began to giggle uncontrollably which then set Kate off again.

Arthur thought she was excellent, he loved the way she would lean towards him conspirativly when telling a joke or sharing a point of view, she had a way about her. Her energy was so vibrant and never seemed to stay anywhere for long, but wasn't at all flighty.

She seemed to have a natural stability that matched his own but she also had an underlying wildness about her that was reflected in her chosen way of life.

“Besides” he thought “she’s sexy too.”

At this point it would be safe to assume Arthur was completely hooked on Kate, he was well aware of the dangers of this.

A few times in the past he’d felt an initial connection like this with someone, shown it to soon and of course scared them away.

“This time” he thought “I’ll play it cool, learn from past mistakes; and make room for entirely new ones!”.

He added as an after thought.

At this point Arthur happened to glance up at the clock.

“Oh no!” he exclaimed.

It was 1:30, they’d been there for over an hour!.

“What’s up?” Kate asked

“I should have been back at work half an hour ago!” he replied.

“Oh” said Kate.

“Can I see you tomorrow?” Arthur asked standing up and putting on his coat.

“Yes, where?” said Kate (“still a little too enthusiastic!” she thought,

hearing herself as if for the first time)

“There’s an interesting site nearby, an Indian burial ground and a cave come shrine.

I haven’t been up there for age’s but it’s pretty amazing, bit of a local curiosity really.

Do you want to go up there tomorrow?”.

“Sounds good, what time?” said Kate intrigued.

“Ill pick you up at 10:00, I’m not working tomorrow.

Better be going else I wont be working ,period!”.

Arthur dropped a twenty on the table for the food and hurriedly left the dinner, Kate watched him go.

“Nice butt” she thought.

CHAPTER 2.

The next morning was fresh crisp and bright, one of those picturesque Christmas days that you never get at Christmas.

Yesterday Arthur had been forced to tell his father about Kate on returning to the shop 45 mins late, his father had just smiled and said

"I was beginning to wonder!".

This morning Arthur was feeling bright and alert, he couldn't remember when he last felt so good.

He got up early, which is extremely rare at the best of times, showered and put together a picnic lunch of thick ham sandwiches some of his mums fresh home made fruit cake and a four pack of bud, jumped in his car and drove into town.

Kate sat in the bar drinking coffee and eating a breakfast of buttered toast and an over coating of jam.

"Well" she thought "I'll need the calories to keep warm."

She was looking forward to today, not only was she going on a date with Arthur but she was really looking forward to seeing this place.

She had always held a lot of respect for native Americans and their traditions although she'd never actually met any.

She liked what she knew of their beliefs and social structures, they seemed a lot more in touch with their environment and they once lived a very balanced existence, as opposed to the generally materialist western way of life.

That was until the "colonists" civilised (killed) them and appropriated (stole) their land. Kate did hold some strong opinions on this subject, it opposed her deep sense of right and wrong and seemed to make her angry whenever the subject arose.

She thought it best to change her line of thought and consulted the new entries in her notebook.

She'd wrote a lot about Arthur, this came as somewhat of a surprise to her, she hadn't quite realised she'd thought about him that much.

Arthur entered the bar, he saw Kate almost instantly, as usual writing in her note book.

He couldn't help wondering if he was mentioned in it.

"Hi" he said "are you ready to go".

"yep" she replied finishing her coffee and standing.

She picked up her last piece of toast and followed him out.

"I thought we could take my car" said Arthur

"The trail can get a little tricky in places and it's a 4x4!".

"Sure" Kate replied "how far are we going?".

"Its about eight miles to the site but the trail will take us at least two hours.

Although there's some excellent views along the way".

They drove south out of town and took a side road to the east.

It was a beautiful day the sun shimmered on the small lakes along the way making them appear to be lakes of jewels not water.

The sky was the deepest, most strongest blue Kate had ever seen and the snow on the higher slopes looked like crystal.

"Its magnificent" she said at last.

"I know, its the one thing this area has going for it!" answered Arthur.

"I wondered about that, why is Vantage out here? there's no other town for miles" asked Kate.

"It was originally an out-post for trappers at the turn of the 18th century, a sort of trading post.

That was before the gold rush came then the town boomed there's lots of mineral deposits in these mountains that are still mined today.

Although its not so much gold that's mined these days, more Iron and denser metals.

There's also the logging and not forgetting the die hard farmers.

Its quite industrial really.

The only thing that stops it all getting out of hand is sites such as the one we're going to visit today."

"So there's lots of sites around here?" asked Kate.

“There’s four that we now of but there could be more that we just haven’t found yet, they run in a line straight though these mountains and are protected by law”.

“What kind of sites?” asked Kate.

“The one we’re seeing today is a burial ground with a cave shrine, almost like a chapel.

The others are different. A few are shrines but some are unidentifiable, their meaning’s have been lost over time.

There are some native people still living in this area but if they know what these place’s mean there not letting on”.

“I can hardly blame them really!” said Kate her bile rising.

“I know what you mean” Arthur replied and they settled down to a comfortable silence.

A little later they reached the site, Arthur parked the car under a tall Elm.

“Here we are” he said and got out.

Kate followed suit “which way now?” she asked.

Arthur took his pack out of the trunk and indicated to a path leading off to the right.

“That way” he said.

They walked up hill for about 10 mins admiring the trees and foliage along the way, the path quite suddenly it seemed opened to a large clearing.

“This is the burial ground, the cave is a little further up” said Arthur.

There were poles sticking out of the ground dotted about the area some appeared to have been placed recently others had the look of age about them.

The poles themselves looked quite unique they were painted brightly with blues and greens also bound with red string and dangling with a varied assortment of feathers.

“Are people still being buried here?” asked Kate.

“I don’t think so” replied Arthur

“but these dream-poles are placed here regally by the descendants of the tribe. I think it’s a respect thing like bringing flowers”.

They began walking along the edge of the clearing towards the cave, they didn’t speak any more, a warm sense of stillness had enveloped them.

After a moment they reached the cave, there were small decorated cards and little gifts of coins and dried flowers peppering the wall just inside the entrance.

Kate looked at some of the cards, people had written little messages on them, one read-

WITHOUT HOPE THERE IS NO STRUGGLE,

WITHOUT STRUGGLE THERE IS NO GROWTH,

WITHOUT GROWTH THERE IS NO HOPE,

ANON.

It was surrounded by small painted flowers and light spiral designs in green and blue and smelled of rosemary.

She showed it to Arthur, he took it read it and smiled.

Kate replaced the card and entered the cave, she was at once mesmerised with the place.

She couldn't help but feel connected, it felt like coming home.

She felt alive, everything seemed to jump out at her almost as if it were an integral part of her being that until this moment she'd some how forgot.

It seemed incredible, almost like forgetting you had arms.

Arthur felt it too he felt strong and centred, focused and more at ease than he'd ever felt.

He'd been here before and had felt the calming stillness but never had this sensation here before, he looked at Kate and felt a deep understanding that two people can feel at times when they truly connect.

She looked at him and smiled.

Inside the shrine it was pretty bare there was a sort of stone plinth at the far end on which sat a large flat wooden bowl filled with dried flowers, also there was a very subtle but intoxicating aroma of wood smoke that seemed to seep from the very walls.

“Can you smell that?” Kate asked

“Yes its very sweet you can almost taste it” replied Arthur.

“there’s a good feeling here as well, its warm I feel at home”.

“I know what you mean” replied Arthur still smiling, he stepped closer to her as he spoke and lightly took her hand.

She jumped at the contact and returned the gesture with a light squeeze.

Before they knew it they were kissing ,it felt natural and slow, later Kate would remember it as her best kiss yet!.

At last they broke apart and stood looking at each other with silly grins, Arthur was the first to laugh and Kate soon joined him.

After that they felt compelled to leave, they left the shrine laughing together, holding hands they walked to a fallen tree on a patch of grass in the sun and sat down.

Arthur emptied his pack and passed Kate a beer.

“The energy here’s amazing, I wish I felt like this whilst I’m writing, Id never be able to stop.

I can see everything so clearly, it all makes sense; the mistakes I made in the past, the things in my life that have led me here to this point.

It all seems so unreal almost like a dream”.

Arthur put his arm around her shoulders.

“I know what you mean, I feel it to more so in your presence Ive come up here a lot in the past especially when I was younger, Dad used to bring me here and to the other shrines in the area” he said.

“What are the other places like” asked Kate.

“As I said earlier, there not all like this and you get a different feeling at each site, some can be quite ominous” Arthur replied.

“What do you mean by ominous” asked Kate.

“I not entirely sure, there’s one site in particular that fills me with an anger so intense I cant stay there for long and as soon as I leave the feeling seems to just drop away leaving me confused and tired.”

“That sounds scary!” said Kate.

“It is, but lets not dwell on it, just talking about it gives me shivers”.

“Okay, what did you bring to eat then?” said Kate smiling.

Arthur laughed,

"Just some sandwiches and some of mums cake" he said.

With that they settled down to eat.

They revisited the shrine on their way back and again felt the same warmth as earlier.

They reached the car by late afternoon and collapsed into it, Arthur drove them back down the track and they spoke about their childhood's as they went, a little about their parents and stories from their school days.

Before they knew it they were entering the town, it was about 7pm by now and they were both beginning to feel hungry and decided to go to Arthur's for dinner.

He phoned ahead to let his mother know he was bringing home a "friend" and they drove over.

As they entered Arthur's parents house Kate couldn't help noticing the contrast between this and her own home life she could tell there was a lot of love here.

Not that there wasn't at her own home its just that it seemed more open here more central to these peoples lives.

She put it down to the isolation of living in this environment and smiled to herself.

Arthur's parents were wonderful they embraced her immediately which at first she found a little overwhelming but soon warmed to it.

They made her feel like one of the family and listened intently whilst she spoke about her travels around the states.

They all sat down for dinner which consisted of fresh steamed vegetables salmon and wonderful pan fried new potatoes accompanied with a very nice white wine.

They talked and laughed for what seemed like no time at all but in fact was about four hours.

At last Arthur's parents announced they were going to bed and said good night.

Arthur led Kate to the lounge and passed her a large brandy, they sat in front of the fire and listened to the sultry tones of Janice Joplin speaking periodically until at last they fell asleep on the big old leather couch.

Arthur was the first to wake, he eased himself off the couch gently removing Kate's head from his shoulder and stood looking at her.

Her hair had cascaded over the arm of the couch, as he watched she stirred, snuggling further into the couch.

Arthur decided to make breakfast, he entered the large kitchen and set about preparing the eggs.

Just as he was pouring the mix into the pan he was startled by an arm encircling his waist.

“What you making?” asked Kate.

“Scrambled eggs and toast, hope you like eggs?” replied Arthur.

“Yeah, there isn’t much I don’t like!” said Kate “anything I can do?”.

“You can make the coffee and butter the toast, if you like” said Arthur.

“Aright, where’s the coffee?” said Kate.

“Under the machine, in that cupboard” said Arthur pointing.

A little later they where happily munching away, Kate as usual had an exceptional amount of sauce.

Arthur chose not to mention the obvious health connotations of this and instead asked Kate what she would like to do with the rest of the day.

After much deliberation they decided to go to the next site in line with the last one they had visited the day before.

This had been at the south-western most point of the line, they decided over the next few days to work their way along the line.

If Arthur could convince his father to give him the time off.

That was the first order of the day, Arthur poured two cups of coffee placed them on a tray and headed slowly up the stairs arranging sentences in his mind all the way.

He came down some time later, Kate glanced up from the magazine she had been reading and asked

"Well what's the verdict?".

Arthur's eyes had a heavy downcast look about them.

“OH” said Kate “Still we can see another site today at least”.

Arthur smiled

“How’d you feel about camping over the next few days?” he asked.

“They said yes then?” asked Kate

“Yeah they must really like you!”

“ofcourse” replied Kate with a smile.

“Why camping?” she asked in a more serious note.

“It’ll be easier to go from one site to another that way and we wont waste time going in and out of town, also my dad owns a camping shop so we’ll have all the best gear.”

“Sounds good” replied Kate “when do we go?”.

“Give me today to get the gear together and we’ll set off in the morning” Arthur replied.

“Okay” said Kate “I need to do some work anyway, what time shall we meet tomorrow?”.

“Ill pick you up at 7:00am” replied Arthur. “I need to go to the shop, I can drop you off at Bobs on the way if you want”.

“Ok” said Kate and with that they set off into town.

“See you tomorrow then!” said Arthur outside Bobs, they embraced and Kate quickly went into the bar.

Bob stood behind the counter smiling at her.

She said hi and went to her room.

"No prizes for guessing what he was thinking" thought Kate and she settled down to make her notes of the previous day, she smiled to herself as she wrote.

CHAPTER 3.

Kate was dreaming-

She felt an unlimited freedom, it felt like being caught on a breeze but at the same time anchored somehow to the present.

She didn't so much as see, it was more like feeling but not with a sense of touch or emotion, more with the mind in its most sublime form roving around where she knew herself to be.

As if she where outside herself but not disconnected, just moving in ever increasing circles, gathering information with every turn.

Connecting to the purest thought, thought in conceptual form transcending the need for language and structure, this connection at the most fundamental level of her being.

Attuned directly to the very building blocks of her soul causing her whole being to vibrate at an incredible rate until suddenly stopped.

She finds herself back in the flesh, she can feel her blood rushing through the vessels of her body a tangible sensation almost as if she were physically immersed in her own bloodstream whilst still in touch with the revolving sphere of her consciousness.

She opens her eyes, her surroundings swim into sharp focus.

She's in a cave of some kind the opening before her yawning, revelling the boughs of trees against an opaque sky.

Its dawn, she moves towards the entrance, her movements are strange, unfamiliar, not natural but at the same time more natural than ever before.

To move any different would upset this feeling of oneness, this sense of flow and balance.

She feels like liquid steel, with a strength of presence unparalleled by anything she'd felt previously, almost omniscient.

She felt like a god, she reaches the entrance and steps beyond. Not a cave but a hole in the ground, a burrow.

Puzzled she looks round taking in every detail with a glance, there's a noise in the distance, just beyond the cusp of hearing, its getting louder and clearer, she strains to hear.

Its a voice calling, it sounds familiar.

Memory crashes in, she can hear her name and someone touch's her shoulder, her perception explodes, fragmenting leaving a blinding light.

Then for a fraction of a second, nothing.

She wakes, Arthur is standing over her, his hand on her shoulder.

“Your a heavy sleeper” he said.

“I was worried when you didn’t hear me knocking so I asked Bob for the key, are you okay? you look pale!”.

“I’m fine-what time is it?” asked Kate irritably Arthur glanced at his watch

“Quarter to eight”

Kate looked down at herself she was still fully dressed and her note book was next to her on the bed

“I must have dropped off, I didn’t realise I was so tired last night, in fact I don’t remember last night, I couldn’t have slept all day yesterday as well”.

"Bob said he hasn't seen you since I dropped you off yesterday morning".

"That's really weird,- must be all that driving Iv done recently catching up with me at last?"

"I suppose" said Arthur looking doubtful and a little worried.

"Never mind, are you going to leave so I can get dressed then?" asked Kate

"Oh, sorry" said Arthur "Ill wait downstairs then" with that he left.

Kate got undressed and stepped into the shower, the hot water was a blessing.

“That was really strange” she thought “and that dream, it all seemed so real I wonder what’s going on? should I still go on this trip?, if not why not?

I mean really, it was only a dream after all, wasn’t it?”.

She resolved to go but intended to keep her eyes and ears open at all times.

For the moment it was best to shut these thoughts from her mind and get on with the mundane.

She washed her hair and pulled on some clothes, chucked her remaining clean clothes in a bag and went down stairs.

Arthur was sat at the bar sipping a coffee and talking to Bob.

As Kate got closer she released he was telling Bob where they were going, Bob seemed to be only half listening.

“I suppose he not that interested in much other than sports” thought Kate, with a second thought she added “That’s a little judgmental, I don’t really know him, maybe his just heard it all before”.

As she got closer she could hear a radio somewhere behind the bar, playing very low but she could make out the unmistakable tones of

commentary, she caught Arthur’s eye and smiled.

“Sleep well lill-miss?” asked Bob, turning her way with a slimy grin,

“Our Arthur been keeping you up?, has he”.

“Just a coffee please” smiled Kate, Whilst indicating a table in the far corner to Arthur.

“Sorry about him” said Arthur as they sat down

“Don’t worry about it” replied Kate, Bob brought over the coffee and Kate gave a curt “Thank you”, Bob returned to the bar and turned up his radio.

“Child” thought Kate.

They drank their coffees whilst Arthur spoke about the route they were going to take.

Kate decided not to mention her dream and Arthur decided she looked and sounded well enough not to mention her unusually long sleep.

Arthur paid for the coffees and they left the bar.

The 4x4 was parked right outside the door and looked packed full with all kinds of gear.

"Do you really think we'll need all this stuff for a few days?" asked Kate

"You never know, its always better to be over prepared than under" replied Arthur, they got in and set off.

The route Arthur had chosen led them north out of town along the main road for about 7 miles until they took a sharp turn right on what seemed an invisible path before the 4x4 pushed the smaller foliage clear.

The car bumped its way along for about half a mile until the track opened up, revelling it to be more used than it would appear albeit still quite rough in places and the 4x4 proving essential.

Kate asked Arthur where they would be camping.

“Lake stillgood’s just a couple of miles ahead, we’ll drive round to the far side and make camp the sites will be more accessible that way”.

“Sounds good!” replied Kate “how big is the lake?”.

“Its fairly big, about 2k across and 1k wide, -you can see it over this hill”.

As they reached the crest of the next hill the lake came into view, it was a stunning sight, reflecting the mountain peaks, a couple of miles in the distance and the clear pristine sky above.

As they drove closer along the track the lake seemed to shimmer and

sparkle reflecting a million suns.

Before reaching the lakes edge they took a track leading to the right that would take them around the other side.

They drove on with the windows down breathing the crisp mountain air savouring its freshness, they reached their campsite just after noon and set about pitching the tent.

Arthur did most of the work for the simple reason that he seemed to know what he was doing.

"Working in my fathers store has its advantages" he said as Kate looked on,

"As I can see" she replied "Shall I set up the stove, I'd like to think I made a contribution of some kind!."

"Yeah, its in the red hold all, knock yourself out!" said Arthur smiling.

Kate dug a small hole in the soft earth and set the little kerosene stove in it, she then collected some large pebbles from the lakes edge and set them around it.

By now Arthur had set up a very impressive tent and unloaded most of the contents of the 4x4 into it.

“My first apartment wasn’t that big.” said Kate looking at the tent

“Its the best one we do in the shop” Arthur replied

“Its incredibly well insulated and extremely strong.

Also that’s a breathable water proof fabric that keeps the interior cool in hot weather and traps heat when its cold!”.

“Are you trying to sell it to me?” asked Kate with a hint of laughter in her voice.

“Sorry, Ive worked in that shop far to long!” said Arthur a little sheepishly.

Changing the subject Kate asked

“Do we have time to see a site before it gets dark?”.

“Yeah there’s one about a mile away over that rise” said Arthur indicating with his arm” Shall we go”?.

Kate promptly agreed and they set off.

As they walked Kate slipped her hand in Arthur’s and gave it a squeeze which Arthur unconsciously returned.

“Its odd” thought Arthur “Iv only known this girl a few days and I already feel so comfortable around her, I wonder if she feels the same?-

I’d like to think so but you can never really be sure, she might be this open around everyone she meets.”

“Still I think Ill just try to enjoy the moment and not think to much.”

“Your quiet” said Kate interjecting on Arthur’s thoughts

“Sorry” said Arthur “I got lost in thought. I don’t go there very often!”.

Kate laughed and asked about the site they were going to.

“Its nothing like the other one, There’s a stream running through the woods up here and the site.

There’s also lots of strange carvings of animals in human like postures and some that are totally unrecognisable they also seem to be in very specific positions”.

“What kind of positions?” asked Kate,

“Its hard to explain” said Arthur “imagine a spiral made out in the shape of a triangle then cut it in half from the apex down through the base, well the statues are laid out two to three a side and base, over an area of about 300 yards and the stream runs through the middle, has done since I can remember anyway”.

As Arthur finished Kate noticed the first of the statues, whatever it may have been.

The stone was cracked almost completely in half and had been for some time guessing by the extent of the wear and lack of detail.

“I wonder what happened to this!, it looks like its been struck by lightning” said Kate examining the stone.

“Always a possibility, about half of them are in this state. The rest are more interesting” said Arthur.

With that they walked on, a couple of moments later they came across another statue, this one seemed to be in better shape.

On closer inspection they found it to be an eagle, its wings spread open in an almost welcoming gesture atop the lower half of a human torso and legs. It looked very strange, almost as if it couldn't decide which to be.

Due to the age of the thing and the formidable mountain weather the detail of how these two forms were incorporated was unfortunately lost as well as a large part of the wing from the right side.

None of which though could detract from affect the splendour and artistry of the masonry.

A few steps further on took them into a large clearing with statues clearly visible in the late afternoon sun.

"There's loads of them!" exclaimed Kate.

From where they stood they could see about thirty standing stone's of all different shapes and colours.

They stood in silence for a moment drinking in the gurgling sound of the stream and the magnificent site before them it was very surreal almost like an old mythical legend, it looked as though any second now a group of fairies or goblins were about to jump from the under growth and parade around the stones in some bizarre celebration.

Arthur and Kate began moving around the stones.

Arthur was right, about half of the stones were unrecognisable due to some damage befalling them decades or more ago. That was the strange thing

all the damage both Arthur and Kate surmised even though they declared themselves no expert's seemed to have happened around the same time, although how long ago that was- who's to know.

The stones themselves were extremely interesting they all seemed to incorporate animal and human forms.

“I wonder what they mean?” asked Kate

“Iv no idea, but they must have held a pretty strong meaning for the people who built them-you can see the effort that’s been made in putting this all together.

Apparently none of the stone used is local either, the closest source for these types of stone is a few hundred miles west of here by the coast!” Arthur replied

“That’s incredible, it must have took years to do, I wish I knew why”.

They stood pondering this for a moment, neither of them could come up with a reasonable conclusion.

Kate wondered over towards one of the statues.

This one was another bird of some kind, possibly an owl and again was also half human and made of an unusual pink and white stone.

Kate suddenly felt a wave of warmth rush through her body, it felt as though it emanated directly from the stone.

She swayed where she stood, Arthur was by her side in a flash.

"Are you OK?" he asked

"Yes I think so" Kate replied

"What happened?" asked Arthur.

"I'm not quite sure. I felt a wave of heat hit me like…I don't know Ive never felt anything like that before.

It was almost like an invisible wall, it came straight through me and just for a second, no less than a second. I don't know how to describe it, I felt larger somehow, as big as the planet.

It was very strange, but not unpleasant!" said Kate.

Arthur put his arm around her shoulders and they walked towards the next statue.

Dusk was just settling in, the stones began to take on (if this was possible) an even eerier atmosphere.

They were standing on the bank of the stream admiring a large statue of a man/bear in a dark blue stone.

Arthur suddenly noticed something new about the statues he glanced around at the others to make sure and smiled,

Kate noticed his movements.

“What is it?” she asked.

“Do you know Iv been here hundreds of times and Iv only just noticed that all the statues face towards the centre!”

"Wow, They do don't they!" said Kate looking around "I wonder why that is?"

"Its to focus the energy towards the centre" said Arthur.

"How do you know that?" asked Kate surprised.

"I don't really know, when you asked it just sort of popped into my head".

Kate looked at Arthur he seemed taller somehow and stronger.

He looked as if he could withstand a hurricane.

He smiled at her and said "so do you, you look more defined and healthier"

"I feel it, my body feels more substantial and I don't think my minds ever been this clear.

I feel new, this is amazing Iv read about experiences like this but never thought Id ever actually experience it my self “.

“I know” said Arthur “Ive been here loads of times and never felt anything like this, although Ive always known these sites were special but its almost as if Ive been waiting for you, to connect like this!.

I know that sounds weird, but its not it feels right”.

She looked him in the eyes, it was like staring into the depths of her own soul.

“I agree” was all she could manage.

With that she turned and walked out of the clearing back towards the lake.

Arthur stood still for a moment and then followed her.

As he walked back through the trees he had a very heavy feeling in his chest.

His stomach was doing back flips.

"Was that wrong?" he thought "It didn't feel wrong, it felt right oh no!

Ive blown it! no, she said she agreed.

It couldn't have been wrong, then why did she walk away.

It was to much must have been.

I couldn't help it I just opened my mouth and it all poured out".

Arthur broke the crest of the hill leading towards the tent and was immediately stuck with a deep sense of fear and panic, he couldn't see Kate anywhere, his heart started to race.

He could feel the blood pumping in his temples, he felt dizzy like his head was about to explode.

Then he saw her head poke out of the tent, and felt a wave of relief flood through him.

As he made his way towards her she smiled and said

“So what have we got to eat then?”.

Arthur burst out laughing.

“There’s some packs in the car, I’ll get them for you”.

CHAPTER 4.

Arthur gave Kate the food and they set about putting their meal together,

Arthur emptied one of the freeze dried packets into a pot added some water and set it on the little stove. Kate began cutting bread and opened a bottle of wine.

Arthur thought she was being very mechanical in her movements.They spoke no more than was necessary and he wondered if she was thinking about what he had said.

He thought he would wait it out and let her mention it first, if at all.

He was quite thrown by the whole thing himself and needed time to take it all in.

They ate in relative silence until their second bottle of wine sometime later at which point Kate's mood lightened and she seemed more her own confident carefree self.

This of course set Arthur more at ease and they began to talk and laugh more comfortably, in the bluish glow of the camping lamp as night set in.

A little while later Kate said she was going to turn in.

Arthur decided to do the same but said he would wait until Kate got herself comfortable, she thanked him and said she wouldn't be a moment.

Arthur settling into his own sleeping bag a few moments later, turns out the lamp and wish's Kate a good night, she leans over kissing him softly.

Arthur returns the kiss and holds her close savouring her scent.

In the darkened tent, Arthur could feel her smile.

She reach's down and unzips he's sleeping bag.

Arthur does likewise and finds her naked.

They continue kissing as Arthur stroking her back runs his hand over her thigh whilst gently kissing her breast.

She in turn stroke's he's face whilst caressing his chest lightly with her fingertips.

She moves down him pulling roughly at his pants, he wriggles until they come off.

Their legs encircle each other tingling where they touch.

For the longest moment they remain like this, savouring the contact and the warmth,

He rolls on top of her, holding her tight, she returning the gesture kissing harder now tasting him.

She welcome's him and he move's forward gratefully, neither of them prepared for the intensity of their joining overcome with emotion of the purest form this had to be love, they move in unison a perfect rhythm.

There was no end to the high's they reached with every pinnacle of pleasure there lay another beyond until suddenly in a torrent of joy they stop every sinew of their bodies taught as they culminate their union together.

Sated, they lay there holding each other in silence neither wanting to move until sleep finally found them…

The wolf howls at the moon.

A call anguished in its desire, knowing how unattainable that desire is.

Yet also knowing that soon the blessed sun will arise giving pause to the pain, staying the madness.

Channelling the need.

Turning the desire to that of the flesh, the wolf begins to hunt its instinct's alight the tide of the sense's turn, a gentle breeze brings the scent of pray.

The wolf following the scent greedily moves silently through the night, but the wind playfully changes.

The pray senses a presents.

Like a man before God. Absolute terror engulfs the small creature, it cannot move its minute brain urging it to flee but the coldness of its bones rooting it to the spot.

The wolf tense with excitement tasting the fear moves in for the final stroke savouring this moment he leaps and brings the game to a close...

Kate woke early, she left the tent as quietly as she could, so as not to wake Arthur and stood by the lakes edge enjoying (dispite the cold) the fresh crisp air and the wonderful panorama of the mist rising off the lake in the hazy early morning light.

She felt great, she knew last night wasn't a mistake, it felt right - Arthur felt right.

She crossed her arms around her body and exhaled, this was the first time in age's she'd felt this content.

This had been an amazing trip so far, who'd have thought they'd have such a great time together.

"Well, life's full of surprises". She said out loud.

The view seemed to smile at her and she couldn't help smiling back.

Arthur woke shortly after and climbed out of the tent, he immediately placed a pan of water on the stove and set about making coffee.

Kate sat beside him and pecked him on the cheek.

Arthur smiled at her and kissed the top of her head. They snuggled down together and drank their coffee.

After awhile Arthur said “Its a fairly long walk to the next site, we’ll have to set off soon or we wont make it before the afternoon”.

“OK” replied Kate “Ill just get some comfortable clothes on and we’ll go, shall I bring a coat?”.

“Probably a good idea, it might rain, Ill put some lunch together whilst you’re getting ready”.

With that they set about their tasks.

Half an hour later they were walking through the woods enjoying the explosion of life around them.

Their coats proved unnecessary as the day turned out to be bright and clear.

Butterflies and midges were swarming around in the shafts of golden light breaking through the canopy above, the wild flowers were glowing under foot and the grass seemed the richest green.

They didn't speak much, they were both were just enjoying the walk and each others company.

They reached the site by early afternoon.

Arthur seemed apprehensive for the last hour or so and no matter how hard

Kate tried she'd not been able to dispel the underlying mood.

He'd been laughing at her jokes and replying when she spoke but there was no real humour in his tone.

Kate was beginning to think he was having second thoughts about what was developing between them, so she thought she would come right out and ask him what the problem was!.

"Its not you" he replied.

"Do you remember after our visit to the first site I said that not all the sites make you feel that good , and that one in particular made me feel really angry!, and I couldn't stay there for long, well this is that site".

"Oh" said Kate feeling a stab of fear in the pit of her stomach and suddenly feeling very heavy.

"What's actually there then?" asked Kate

"Its similar to the first site in that there's a cave shrine, its very dark though it doesn't get much sun. Also there's lots of strange markings on the walls almost like aboriginal cave paintings, you know the kind of thing swirls and spirals plus people carrying spears and hunting but there not hunting animals like the aboriginal stuff, it seems their hunting other people!".

"That is horrible, but couldn't it just represent a war or something" replied Kate.

"I don't know" said Arthur "But you'll see for yourself now we're here!".

They entered the clearing and found themselves at the beginning of a ravine.

They were walking directly on the bed rock in the shadow cast by the rock faces either side.

"Where's the cave?" asked Kate

"Straight ahead where the rock faces meet at the end of the ravine" said Arthur looking pale.

"How are you feeling?" said Kate looking concerned and a little pale herself

"I'm fine!" Arthur replied a little curtly.

Kate chose to ignore his tone

"If he wants to deal with what ever bothers him about this place on his own that's fine by me!" she thought, the resentment she felt reminded her of Jack.

They reached the point Arthur had indicated, the mouth of the cave yawned menacingly before them.

Arthur took two torches out of his back pack and passed one to Kate, she took it wordlessly and entered the cave Arthur followed close by.

Kate saw the first of the markings on the wall to her left it was of a man drawn in black standing before a faded orange spiral holding what appeared to be a long spear, on the other side of the spiral was another man with two spears sticking out of him at right angles.

Kate thought the image wasn't as bad as Arthur had made it seem when he spoke earlier, she glanced over to find him studying a carving on the opposing wall.

Arthur caught her eye and gave her a weak smile just visible in his torch light.

She'd never noticed before how thin he was.

She dismissed the thought and wondered further into the cave.

Arthur watched her walk on, he was looking at a carved image on the wall it seemed to represent a meeting of some kind, there were about twenty people standing in a circle with a fire depicted in the centre.

The fire strangely enough was coloured a sickly green and all the people were wearing very elaborate head-dresses or cloaks that seemed an attempt to hide the shape of their bodies.

There was also an unusual image floating above the fire, there was a circle with a line through the centre horizontally and a line vertically with three prongs opened above it, and above that a very crude nasty looking eye.

There was a scraping noise coming from the direction Kate had gone, Arthur turned and walked towards the sound.

He approached Kate from behind making her jump as he neared.

"What are you up too?" he asked

"Not a lot , I'm just trying to clear some sediment off this wall to see the rest of this image". Said Kate impatiently.

Arthur peered over her shoulder to get a better look, there was a man standing with legs apart giving him a very masculine demeanour, which at first glance looked wrong and sent a chill up Arthur's spine that Arthur found repulsive, he dislike the image instantly.

Kate on the other hand was entranced by the picture she seemed to be drinking it in whilst she crouched scratching frantically with a small rock at the area around his right arm that was obscured by the sediment, in his left arm there was an unusual item it looked like an animals claw but was far to large to be that. Arthur surmised it must have been a weapon of some kind that had been modelled on an animals claw.

Kate was getting frustrated, she couldn't get the last piece of sediment off.

At last she stepped back and threw the rock she'd been using at the wall, a fragment splintered off and caught Arthur across the cheek drawing blood, he jumped back letting out a yelp of pain.

"WHAT ARE YOU DOING STANDING SO CLOSE, YOUR LUCKY THAT DIDN'T TAKE YOUR EYE OUT!" exclaimed Kate angrily.

Arthur looked at her in shock clutching his face, anger rising like a torrent within him.

"IF YOU DIDN'T THROW THAT STONE IT WOULDN'T HAVE HAPPEND IN THE FIRST PLACE, YOU STUPID COW!".

Kate stared at him

"HOW DARE YOU CALL ME THAT, YOU BLOODY WEAKLING, WHY DON'T YOU JUST CURL UP AND DIE!!!" with that she stormed past him and walked back towards the entrance.

Arthur stood still he couldn't believe what they had just said to each other.

"oh hell!" he thought.

At that moment he had the strangest feeling someone was laughing at him,

“that’s odd” he thought calming down, with that the feeling seemed to lift and he followed Kate out of the cave.

She was sitting on a boulder near the entrance with her head in her hands sobbing quietly, Arthur a sense of calm settling over him once again sat beside her and placed his arm around her shoulders

“Are you OK, I’m sorry for what I said” said Arthur gently.

Kate raised her head her eyes were all puffy and sore looking.

“I’m sorry too, I shouldn’t have thrown that stone in the first place and your not a weakling, I don’t know where that came from”.

“Its OK, its not really us, its this place I warned you it just seems to feel you with rage and I don’t think your a cow” said Arthur smiling kindly at her

“Ive never felt like that before.

I mean Ive been Angry but look at your face and it was my fault and I didn’t even care I was so angry at you and you hadn’t done anything, Arthur I’m so sorry” she started to cry again and Arthur held her close.

“It doesn’t matter, I know you didn’t mean it, -did you?” he said smiling

“Come on cheer up, lets head back to camp it looks like we may need our coats after all!”.

Kate looked up, the sky was really starting to darken, it look like it was going to start pouring down, soon!.

“Let me do something about your face first” she said

“Aright, there’s a first aid box in my bag” he replied.

Kate cleaned the wound and put a elastaplast on it, it wasn’t really that bad.

They began walking, pretty soon Kate was feeling a lot better about the days events.

They began to discuss what they felt had effected them.

It all began to seem less important as they put more distance between themselves and the site.

It wasn’t long before the heavens opened and they were trudging along through the mud.

The rain was intolerable, it felt like they’d been walking for hours and they could hardly see where they were going , after a while Arthur turned to Kate with a wry smile.

“We’ve got a small problem!” he said

“What’s that then?” she asked

“Well I’m sorry to say it but I think we’re lost!”

“What!” exclaimed Kate “How can we be lost?”

“We should have been there by now.

I’m not even sure of the direction we’re going in.

The compass doesn’t seem to be working right either the needle keeps spinning, it must be the mineral deposits in these mountains but Ive never had this problem in the past!” said Arthur.

With that there was a crack and flash of lightning.

“It all looks so different and its going to be dark soon!, What are we going to do?” asked Kate

"Well we have to find shelter to wait out the storm" replied Arthur.

"We'd better keep moving or we'll get too cold"

"It's too late for that" said Kate.

They walked on for another two hours by this time it was dark.

Kate kept slipping and nearly falling over in the mud.

She was cold hungry and tired she was beginning to wish they had stayed in bed.

"You really know how to show a girl a good time!" she called out, Arthur turned and gave a reply but it was drowned by a roll of thunder.

Just then he gestured up ahead, Kate's heart gave a leap of joy!, they must have found the camp.

As they got closer Kate saw this wasn't the case.

What Arthur had found was a cave, it looked small but at least it would be dry.

They crawled in and found it was just big enough to stretch out in, they cuddled up for warmth and settled down to a cold night, dispite which they were soon fast asleep.

They woke early the suns rays just peaking over the mountains tingeing the sky a subtle mauve, they left the cave and stretched in an attempt to bring some life back into their bones.

Arthur looked at his compass the needle was once again resting on north he took a bearing and showed it to Kate, they had been going in completely the wrong direction.

"We're closer to the last site than we are to camp, do you fancy going there first" said Arthur

"Yes aright then, we may as well I suppose" Kate replied.

Along the way they passed through a clearing and stopped short, on the ground before them lay a scorched area of turf about twelve feet in diameter.

"What on earth could have caused that!" exclaimed Arthur

"You know what it looks like don't you?" said Kate

"No, what?" asked Arthur

"Well, it looks like a corn circle!" exclaimed Kate.

"What you mean as in U.F.Os!" said Arthur.

"That's what most people think they are!, and what with your compass going wrong last night it sounds like a typical U.F.O sighting! we should probably report it" said Kate.

"I suppose but first lets go see the last site." said Arthur.

"Sounds good, I cant wait to get back and write all this up" said Kate.

They set off in the direction of the site and arrived a little before mid morning.

The site itself sat in a clearing at the foot of another ravine but this place wasn't empty, there were three men two of which were dressed in white decontamination suites and one in a normal grey business suit, it was safe to assume he was in charge.

Arthur and Kate approached the men cautiously.

"I wonder what this is all about?" said Kate

"I don't know, but lets find out!" said Arthur as they neared the men.

CHAPTER 5.

The three men stopped talking when one of them saw Arthur and Kate and gestured to the others, the man in the business suite strode towards them and met them half way.

“Hello, are you out for a walk?, its a nice day for it eh?. Did you park on the road nearby?” said the man

“Eh, no we” Arthur began,

Kate interjected her suspicion aroused,

“That’s right” she said “What are you doing here?”

“Oh we’re just conducting a geological survey of this area, I’m John I work for Highcliff holdings we’re a mining corporation stationed a mile north of here”.

“What kind of survey are you doing, you know this is a protected area don’t you?” said Arthur affronted “and why are those men wearing those suits?”.

“Just a precaution, and the survey’s just to see if a deposit we’re following comes this far south, well we must get going they don’t pay us to stand around and talk all day”. Said John seeming to get a little jumpy.

He called over his shoulder as he walked away,

“COME ON GUYS, TIME TO GO!”

The two other men picked up two heavy looking case’s and set off at a jog after him.

“That was strange” said Kate as the men moved out of ear shot.

"was it just me, or did it seem as though we just interrupted what ever they were really doing here?"

"No, I think your right, I don't trust that man we may have put pay to their plans for the moment but I get the feeling they'll be back, lets have a look inside" said Arthur indicating the cave with a nod of his head.

They entered the cave but neither of them could concentrate on their surroundings, there didn't seem to be any sign of damage or clue as to what the men had been doing but the place certainly didn't feel anything like the other sites they had visited previously it seemed dead, somehow flat and dull.

There were some interesting drawings on the walls, there were bright and pretty swirls of colour and image's of people standing beside structures of some kind that almost represented temples or pyramids with what appeared to be struts supporting them above the ground plus the same animal/man pictographs of second site.

Kate and Arthur didn't stay in the cave for long as they were starting to feel hungry and so they headed back towards their camp.

A couple of hours later they were nearing the third/negative site when they heard an argument raging, it sounded like the man they had met earlier shouting at someone who was obviously not backing down.

Kate suggested they try to sneak up and see what was happening.

They got close enough to see with out being seen, the man (John) from earlier was standing in front of the cave holding what appeared to be a recording devise he was pointing at the cave and shouting at one of the men who was standing just inside.

"WHAT DO YOU MEAN WE CANT USE THIS PLACE ITS JUST AS STRONG AS THE OTHERS"

“I SAID ITS TO VOLATILE THE PULSE IS ERRATIC” answered the other man,

“WHAT DO YOU KNOW YOUR ONLY A TECHNICIAN YOUR NOT PAID TO THINK YOUR PAID TO DO WHAT I TELL YOU TO DO!!”.

The third man stepped into view and spoke before the other man could retort.

“Listen to yourselves your not behaving like scientists, you sound like children. I think its safe to assume this place is different from the others, we’d better get moving if we want to cover all these places today”.

“Your right” said the man in the charge “Lets get out’ta here!”.

At that all three men set off in the direction of site two.

“What do you make of that then?” said Arthur

“Well I don’t think their doing any normal kind of survey -I think their up to no good!” Kate replied.

“I think your right, we’d better get moving though Id like to get back to our camp before they do!.

They reached the camp an hour later and by some stroke of luck they had beat the men there.

Kate began putting something to eat together whilst Arthur got some beer out of the 4x4 and passed one to Kate.

They could hear voice’s coming towards them, the men breached the crest of the hill and stopped looking at them in shock.

They then walked towards them “Ah, its you two!” exclaimed John

“Hi there” said Kate trying to sound surprised

“Are you still following that deposit?, it must be huge!” said Arthur with a smile.

“Eh, no we’ve come to check the lakes water, it all part of our companies environmental policy”.

“Oh that’s good” said Arthur thinking this man thinks fast on his feet,

Kate spoke up

“Its a long hard walk , especially in those clothes, would you like a beer?”.

One of the men in white move forward to accept but John quickly interjected.

“No thank you, we really mustn’t drink on duty”.

"Oh go on, its unlikely you'll be caught way out here!" said Arthur

"Well you've convinced us, if you can spare them" replied John looking for all the world like a trapped animal.

The three of them accepted a beer each and sat down.

"So your camping then!" said the taller of the men in white (The one who'd calmed things down between the other two earlier.)

"That's right" said Kate we've been out here a few days now!".

"Have you noticed anything odd since you've been here?" said the other man in white, John glared at him.

"How do you mean?" said Kate in her most innocent tone

“Well like in the weather you know, stuff like that” said the man glancing nervously at John.

“Well now you come to mention it” said Arthur.

“What!” said John looking worried.

Arthur looked at him reproachfully but continued.

“My compass was playing up last night, it kept spinning in all directions, Iv never seen anything like it!”

“Really!, that is odd, although it was probably due to the electrical storm we had last night.” said the man.

“Yeah, probably” said Arthur

“Well we must be on our way!” said John standing up “Thanks for the beer!, come on you two”

“Yes thanks for the beer” the two men said in unison as they rising to their feet.

The three of them began walking along the lakes edge towards the second site, without a second glance at the water.

Arthur and Kate ate double rations that evening whilst they spoke on the days events.

“What on earth are they up to out here?” asked Arthur

“Ive no idea, what ever it is it can’t be legal, else they wouldn’t be so secretive about it!” answered Kate

“Do you think its got anything to do with that burnt piece of ground we saw?” asked Arthur.

“Maybe but I think their meddling with the energy of the sites as well” said Kate.

“Yeah I wonder what that equipment their carrying does?” said Arthur.

“By what they were saying when they were at the third site it sounds like a kind of measuring devise, I think we should stick around for a while and find out!” said Kate her eyes growing with excitment.

“I agree” said Arthur “Tomorrow I think we should drive round to Highcliff holdings and see if we can find out what exactly there up to!”

“Sounds good” replied Kate.

By this time it was dark and they both agreed to turn in early.

The next day they rose early and loaded their equipment on the 4x4 and set off around the lake to pick up the track that would take them to the main highway and back towards Vantage.

They passed through Vantage by mid-morning and stopped (at Kate's request) for a bite to eat at the diner on the south side of town.

"It feels like such a long time ago, we were last here" said Kate as they entered the diner.

"It's true, a lot has happened since then" Arthur replied.

They sat at the same table as last time and looked at the menu.

"Do you think it feels strange being back in town now after all that's happened?" Arthur asked.

"It certainly does, everything seems to be moving so fast and out of sinc!" Kate replied.

The waitress came over to take their order, it was a different girl this time Kate noticed, this one was wearing a badge with the name “Kaley” on it.

“Are you ready to order?” the girl asked

“ER, yeah I’ll have a bacon and tomato sub sandwich” said Kate.

“I’ll have two pieces of spicy chicken and a beer please” said Arthur.

“Oh, I’ll have a beer too please” said Kate.

“No problem” said the girl “Wont be long” with that she walked away.

“Where were we?, oh yeah it’s, defiantly strange being back amongst people after the experiences we’ve had. But now I almost feel as though I'm disconnected from it all in some way. I don't know if this makes sense but I really feel different, not just from how I was before we left.

Fundamentally altered somehow, you know something deep within me has changed and although it feels strange right now I know its a positive change.

I really don't think I'm ever going to be the same again and I know one thing for certain- I don't want to be!." said Kate.

"I know exactly what you mean my mind feels less restricted in comparison to how it felt before. I'm the same person but I'm certainly more complete than I was before if that makes any sense. Those sites have unlocked some kind of doorway or area of our minds that have been closed to us up till now. Now these areas are open I want to explore them!" said Arthur.

"That's exactly it, the urge to explore!, that's what I want to do!" replied Kate beaming.

“What shall we do about the burnt ground we saw do you still want to report it?” asked Arthur changing tact.

“To be honest I don’t fancy walking into the sheriff’s station and telling them we think there was a U.F.O around last night, we didn’t see anything and other than the ground we saw we haven’t any real proof”. replied Kate

“I think your right it could be rather embarrassing, best to let that one go for the time being”.

The waitress came over with their drinks and put them on the table.

Arthur took a swig of his beer

“It’s amazing isn’t it?” he said.

“What?” asked Kate .

"The way your whole life can change in a matter of days, if your open enough to that change.

Just think if you went to those places and all you saw was the basic place and received nothing of the energy you'd live a very flat and dull life".

"Dull being the operative word" added Kate.

The waitress came over with their food and they settled down to enjoy it.

Kate put very little ketchup in her sandwich.

"That must be a first!" said Arthur watching her with a smile

"It is" she replied.

When they finished eating they got in the 4w4 and set off out of town.

A little while later they took the same road going east as they had done when they visited the first site.

“What are we going to say when we get there?” asked Arthur

“I don’t know!, we’ll have to think of something” said Kate.

“We could say we’re going to see the forth site” said Arthur. “That’ll work if we don’t see John again”.

“Well if we do it’s no real concern of his whatever we do!”said Arthur, there was a tinge of irritation in his tone.

“I don’t like him either!” said Kate

“He’s very suspect isn’t he?” said Arthur.

“Yeah, I wouldn’t trust that man as far as I could throw him said Kate.

They passed four farms on the way, they looked like desolate places.

“That must be a hard life” said Kate peering out the window at one of the farms.

“I wouldn’t really know, the farmers around here tend to keep themselves to themselves”, said Arthur.

As they neared Highcliff holdings the air seemed to be buzzing.

There was a kind of high pitched noise like the ringing in your ears you sometimes get after listening to loud music.

“Can you hear that?” Asked Kate.

“Yeah, I wonder what’s causing it?” said Arthur.

As they came round a corner they found themselves facing a checkpoint of some kind. There was a gate house and two men holding automatic weapons standing either side of an automatic chainlink gate.

The men were wearing blue and white uniforms similar to that of military police.

"Now I'm really curious!" said Kate as they approached.

One of the men waved them to a halt and stepped closer to the drivers side of the car, the other man trained his weapon on them.

"What's your business?" said the first man to Arthur

"Oh we've come up to see the cave shrine near here" said Arthur

"Well you've come to far the site's about a quarter of a mile south of here".

"Oh thank you, we'll head back then", replied Arthur.

The soldier stepped back but the other one kept his weapon on them while Arthur made a turn, as they were about to drive away another car was coming towards them Arthur pulled to the side of the road to let them pass but the other car swerved into their path and skidded to a halt.

"What's he playing at!, OH" said Arthur

"OH" prompted Kate, then she saw for herself.

John was getting out of the other car, he was looking even more stressed than the last time they saw him.

He called over one of the guards and stepped up to the 4x4.

"What are you two doing here!" he said rather gruffly

“We were going to check out the site but overshot it and found ourselves here” said Kate flashing her best smile.

“Don’t give me that!, you were there yesterday, why would you go back today”.

He turned to the guard

“Arrest them!” he ordered.

The guard pointed his weapon at them and told Arthur to throw the keys out the window, Arthur looked at Kate he tried to smile at her, she nervously returned the gesture.

He turned off the engine and threw the keys out.

They were pulled roughly from the car handcuffed and lead into the complex, the complex itself was made up of two oblong shaped two story buildings on opposite sides of a courtyard with a squarer three story building directly opposite the entrance.

They were lead towards the latter it appeared to be the administrative building where as the others gave nothing away of there function.

“What do you think your doing, this is a free country you know, we only made a simple driving error said Kate.

You’ve got no right to do this!” said Arthur trying not to let any fear show in his voice.

“Oh you’ve made an error aright!” said John getting himself more worked up by the moment.

“Do you think I’m stupid I saw your vehicle parked in town earlier, I know your up to something.

Who do you work for?, don't bother, I'm taking you to the supervisor he'll sort you two out!".

They were taken into a large office on the top floor of the admin. building, the walls were covered with ordnance maps and aerial photographs of the area.

Behind the desk sat a large man with a bald head and friendly face, he smiled as they entered but the smile didn't reach his eyes

"What have you brought me here John?" he said, his voice had that unmistakable southern twang to it.

"These are the two I mentioned in my last report sir, I just caught them trying to enter the complex!"

"That's a lie!" said Kate "We were not trying to get in we were going the other way when he showed up,(she nodded at John) we only made a simple error in overshooting our destination!".

The supervisor told the guards to take off the handcuffs and wait outside, he also told John to leave. John looked as though he wanted to object but left without comment.

"You'll have to excuse him, his been under a lot of stress lately, my names Jack Tiller I'm the supervisor at this installation.

I'm really am sorry for my colleges behaviour, please wont you have a drink".

He motioned towards a rather extensive mini-bar in the corner of the office.

"Don't mind if I do!" said Arthur

"Excellent!, what's your poison" said Jack

"I'll have a whiskey with a splash of soda" said Arthur

"Rocks?" asked Jack

"No, thanks" Arthur replied

"And you?" said Jack looking at Kate, his look made her feel dirty but she said she'd have a large brandy no mixer.

Jack then offered them a seat in the small chairs facing his desk and sat in his rather larger chair behind the desk took a swig of his drink and putting it down he steeple's his fingers and peers over them rather condescendingly.

Kate decided to go for it

"What are you doing up here then?, I thought this was a commercial complex I didn't realise it was a military installation"

“Oh it’s not at all military, but I can see why you’d think it was” said Jack punctuating the latter half of his sentence with a hollow, humourless laugh.

“No we just take on a few military contracts from time to time”.

“What kind of contracts” said Arthur getting in the swing of things.

“Oh I’m afraid I’m not really at liberty to say” answered Jack “but (he continued) I can tell you there’s no danger in what we’re doing up here”.

“Well that’s something anyway” said Arthur.

“I’m pleased I could be of assistance, but I’m afraid I’m going to have to ask you to leave now as I must really be getting on Iv a lot of work on today.”

"You mean we're free to go?" asked Kate

"of course, why wouldn't you be?" Jack said looking at her expectantly.

Jack saw them to the door and told the guards to escort them back to their vehicle, he also asked John to step in his office.

As they were lead across the courtyard Arthur noticed the buzzing had stopped, Kate was looking in all directions to try to get an idea of what they were up to here but it all seemed very quiet, whatever they were doing they were doing it indoors.

"Well, what on earth do you think your doing bringing them in here?" demanded Jack all pretence of friendliness gone from him, his face had taken on a remarkable resemblance to a beetroot, an image only enhanced by his baldness.

John stood ashen faced and looking very small in front of the door

“Their up to something, I know they are!” was he’s only defence.

“Lets just for the moment assume your right, do you really think that if they were up to something it’s such a great idea bringing them in here?, especially at the moment when we’re getting such unexpected results!, eh you could have brought the whole thing down on our heads you bloody fool!.”

John shrunk into himself even further at this.

“I still think we should keep an eye on those two” he said meekly

“Well if you really think that’s wise get one of the military personnel onto it but for gods sake tell them to be discreet, and I want you to take no further action in this matter without my prior knowledge, is that understood?”.

“Yes sir!” replied John.

“Good now lets get back to work, have we got the sat’s from last nights testing yet?”

“Yes, their in the lab sir.”

“Well go and get them!, do I have to do every thing every thing around here?”.

As the guards walked them to their car Kate tried talking to them

“So how long have you been working here?” she asked the guard on her right, the man remained silent staring straight ahead as they walked.

On reaching the gate the other guard offered Arthur his keys and motioned towards the car, Arthur took the keys and he and Kate got in the car and drove off.

“Well we didn’t get much out of that did we?” said Kate

“We know one thing we didn’t before!” said Arthur

“What?” asked Kate.

“We know the military’s involved!”

“That’s true, and we know they don’t want anyone finding out what there up to, which is exactly what I intend to do!”.

“What do you have in mind?” asked Arthur looking sideways at her.

“Well” she replied looking smug-

“Who’s most likely to have seen what those guys are up to?”.

“I don’t know,-God?” said Arthur wryly.

“Other than God” said Kate, Arthur thought for a moment.

“Oh” he said.”Of course, why didn’t I think of that!”.

“I know intelligence and looks Ive got it all!” said Kate smiling.

CHAPTER 6.

They pulled off the road and drove down the smaller drive for about half a mile until they came to a large house, it looked so out of place amongst its surroundings.

Arthur stopped the car and they got out, as they approached the door it opened

“Hello, what can I do for you?” said an elderly woman in an old faded flower print dress with a woollen shawl about her shoulders.

She had a friendly look about her, almost like everyone’s favourite granny all rolled into one Kate could almost smell the muffins baking in the oven.

She liked this lady instantly

"Hi, we've been out investigating the sites in the area and wondered if you knew anything about them?" she said

"Well then my dears, you'd better come in my names Mary, its so nice to get visitors, I hardly ever see anyone out here now days, what's your names then?" she said smiling.

"I'm Kate and this is Arthur".

"Do I know you?" said Mary looking at Arthur

"You might do I work in the camping store in town" said Arthur

"Oh yes, that's right I know your father, Albert isn't it?"

"That's him" replied Arthur grinning.

Mary led them through the hall into a large kitchen at the back of the house, it was wonderfully warm due to an old argar stove sat squat against the centre of the opposite wall.

“I’ll put some tea on, you two make yourselves comfy” said Mary indicating an old but very comfortable looking couch against the wall near the stove.

Arthur and Kate sank gratefully down into the cushions, Mary filled a tin kettle with water and placed it on the stove, she then sat herself down in the rocking chair across from them.

“Well what would you like to know?” asked Mary

“Its hard to know where to start really” said Kate

“Well, I always find the beginning the to be the best option”. said Mary with a smile.

Kate smiled back and began at the beginning.

Mary sat listening intently whilst Kate told her all that had happened up till this point only interrupting once to pour them tea in lovely little china cups and to offer them a piece of cake, which Kate accepted with a smile.

"Well now, sounds like the pair of you have had an extremely interesting time" said Mary when Kate had finished

"And now you'd like to know if I know what their up to out there, well I'm sorry to say that I don't, although the visitors have been around a lot more lately".

"The visitors?" prompted Arthur

"Yes dear, that's what we call them, you'd probably call them U.F.Os although Ive never cared for that term. I think its quite rude really visitors is a much more polite way to put it , don't you agree?, well they've always come around these parts although you wouldn't know that living in town.

Lately there's been many more visits than I can ever remember.

Of course John, that's my husband reckons they must be bored just sitting around up there, he thinks they've been watching us for some time now, just waiting around till we're ready for some kind of interstellar do-dar.

But that's my John for you. Still he may have a point, you never really know do you?"

"Well no" said Arthur looking flummoxed to hear an elderly lady speak in this way.

"Would you like to stop for some dinner my husband will be back soon and he'd like to hear what you have to say.

I'm sure he'd be happy to swap a few stories with you, and you never know your luck we might just get a visit tonight!".

Arthur and Kate were standing on the front porch drinking tea whilst Mary was in the kitchen preparing the dinner.

Kate had offered to help but Mary had shooed her out saying she likes to be left to her own device's when cooking.

"So what do you make of all that then?" asked Arthur

"I don't know really, why would this visits have increased lately?, and doe's it have any connection with what's going on at Highcliff holdings?" said Kate

"I'd be very surprised if it didn't, at the moment we've got more questions than answers and if we're going to get any answers we'll have to find a way into that complex, but that could be very dangerous with those gun totting guards about" said Arthur.

John showed up a little later he was also pleased to have the company of the two young people and delighted in telling them all the visits he'd seen over the years.

"There was this blue light that kind'a streaked across from the east and it met up with a green one that was kind'a jus hovering about in the west, but when they met the green one turned orange and dipped below the horizon then both of them went a light blue and shot off. You've never seen anything like it!.

But as to those people up at that complex- I don't know, it used to be a normal mining co-operation but about nine months ago they brought in those guards.

That's also when the visits increased they seem to be happening ever-other night now, if you two do find out what they up to do let me know wont you?".

“If there up to no good I reckon we should expose it, maybe tell the newspapers or something” said Arthur

“That would be a good idea” said Kate “But we’d better find out what their up to before we make any plans like that!”.

Mary came out and said the dinner was ready, they went through to the dinning room and sat down to an abundant spread of roast chicken three different vegetables and stuffing, all cooked in the traditional farmhouse manner, it was wonderful!.

Kate was enjoying herself immensely, as they ate they spoke on the events so far John was hanging off every word, he said

“You two should met my friend Mike his familie’s been here longer than anyone’s, he’s directly descended from the tribes people from these parts.

He's actually a bit of a shaman, a sure he'd be able to answer any questions you may have about your experiences, he's farms a few miles down the road.

If you like you can spend the night here and I'll take you to meet him tomorrow".

"That would be great Id love to know more about what we experienced, There's quite a bit I don't understand" said Arthur.

Kate was going to add something at this point but her mouth was crammed full of chicken and she missed the moment.

After dinner they all wrapped up warm sipping co-co, sat on the porch scanning the night sky for signs of life.

Unfortunately there wasn't any visits this time, after a couple of hours Mary showed them where the spare room was and her and John wished them a good night.

Kate and Arthur sat up a little longer watching the night sky and talking.

"I'm really looking forward to seeing that guy tomorrow I need to know what exactly was happening at that site we visited, you know the one I mean, the one that makes you angry.

Ive never felt anger to that extent before.

I didn't think I had it in me and now that I know I do I'm not sure I like the fact!" said Kate.

"Yeah, I know what you mean, its scary the way that place effects you.

What's been on my mind is the forth site, I told you before Iv never had quite so an intense experience at those sites until I went there with you but Ive always felt something, and that's what's been bothering me, the forth site usually has a strong vibe about it but when we were there it felt flat , you know hollow!" said Arthur.

"I think I understand what you mean, but what do you think it means?, don't forget those men were in there just before us as well" said Kate

"That's the thing I don't know what any of it means but it's definitely not a good omen, I hope we get some answers tomorrow".

At that they decided not to give it any more thought and went to bed.

The next day they got up early, or at least they thought they did.

John and Mary had been up for hours

"Enjoy your lay in!" said John to Arthur as he came into the kitchen John was sat at the table polishing off what looked like a huge breakfast of bacon and eggs.

"What lay in, its half past seven!" exclaimed Arthur standing in the doorway and looking at the large old clock on the wall of the kitchen.

“Exactly, me and Mary were up at five!” said John smiling at the rise he was getting,

“Five o’clock in the morning, what on earth for!” said Arthur.

“Cows don’t milk themselves you know!” said John.

“Oh” said Arthur, then after a moments thought.

“You haven’t got any cows!”

“John put him down!” said Mary

“I’m only playing with him” said John defensively.

“Well, not everybody has your sunny disposition in the morning” said Mary looking at Arthur and motioning to the table

"Take no notice of him and sit yourself down Arthur, bacon and eggs?".

"Yes please" said Arthur "see what a polite young man he is John you could learn a thing or two from him".

John didn't say a word he just scrunched his face up and mouthed her words moving his head from side to side Arthur laughed and Kate walked in

"Morning all, mm, that smells fantastic!" she said.

"Sit yourself down dear I'll rustle you up some, how you keep that lovely figure of yours I don't know, still its good to see a young girl like you eating well, don't see much of that these days it all seems to be slim ,slim, slim" said Mary.

“I could never be like that, I enjoy my food far to much and I enjoy your food even more!” said Kate settling herself down next to Arthur.

After they’d eaten and in Arthur case woke up, they jumped in the 4x4 and followed John and Mary down the road to the next farm.

The farm house was a little smaller than the Silverton’s (John and Mary) and not so well kept, they stepped up to the door and John called out.

Arthur noticed there were dream catchers and coloured streamers like those at the first site hanging from the rafters over the porch.

Mike came to the door he was a smallish man of obvious native American origin, seemed to be in he’s late sixties with a short greying beard and a deeply wrinkled face.

John introduced them and they went inside.

"So what can I do for you then?" asked Mike.

"We're trying to put together something of a mystery!" said Kate

"Do go on" said Mike intrigued and studying her as he spoke

"Yes go on dear" said Mary.

So Arthur and Kate went on to relate their experiences once again.

"So you'd like me to answer some questions for you, well firstly what you, Kate experienced at the statues was quite rare, in fact Ive never herd of anyone out side the tribe having such an experience.

Tell me have you been having any unusual dreams lately?" asked Mike when they'd finished.

"Well, now that you come to mention it I have, they've been very strange almost as if I wasn't myself, one in particular stands out.

I was in a burrow of some kind, you know like an animal and my mind was working very strangely indeed, it was like a sphere surrounding me and my consciousness was spinning around it picking up all sorts of information but at the same time connected to the center.

My body felt so strong and in tune with the environment, I must have been a dog or wolf, no it was a wolf I remember now".

"That's very strange,(Began Mike) There's a legend that's been with my people for a long time, it concerns those statues. It goes like this, apparently thousands of years ago, long before the coming of the white man or even that of the Spaniard some of our people.

Those chosen by the great spirit had the ability to shift their shape, to change into the animal that was their particular totem, but there was a rift among the chosen some of them began to forswear their people.

They counted themselves above the other members of their tribes, they forgot they were the trusted servants of their people and thought themselves masters!.

But not all the chosen felt this way, some remained true to the task the great spirit had given them and continued to protect their people but as is sometimes the way with these things the stronger in body were the weaker in spirit, these beings hunted down their brothers killing them and their lines so they were lost to the people for ever.

In time this angered the great spirit and moved it to take back the abilities which had been so freely given, until mankind had grown away from the ego enough to be trusted once again with this kind of existence".

"Wow" said Kate "What does it all have to do with me then?, why am I having these dreams"?".

"Well it may just be possible you had some link to these chosen in a past life!". said Mike

"Whoa!, past lives?, Id have never had thought that!, still it does make a funny kind of sense doesn't it?" said Kate

"I think so" said Arthur "Mike could you tell us something about the site that makes you angry?"

"Well all the sites in this area are connected by the same legend supposedly after the chosen split up the negative faction were based at the place of anger, I suppose the madness some how got into the ground itself or maybe that's where it sprung from in the first place!.

The first site you know the one, the burial ground but back before it was a burial ground, my people used it to bury their dead because of the obvious power of the place and they wanted it to remain sacred for the future generations.

You have to remember we're going back thousands of years here.

This was where the shamans used to do their work and the one with the statues is where the chosen were supposed to have met for their ceremonies, before the divide".

Arthur asked another question-

"You reminded us then about how long ago this all was.

If that's the case and your right about Kate being part of it all some how in a past life, which I personally think is quite likely going on our experiences over the last few days, how come its coming out now?".

"I would say that little mystery is for you to work out for yourselves!" said Mike

A little later they left Mikes with a standing invitation to return anytime they needed to talk and headed back to the main road where John stopped he's vehicle and got out as did Mary. Arthur and Kate followed suit.

“What are you two going to do next then?” John asked

“Where going to check out the forth site again to see if the energy’s picked up” said Kate

“Sounds good, tell you what when your finished up there you can come round and have dinner with us again if you like”.

“That would be great” said Arthur

“Aright see you two later then” said Mary.

They set off towards Highcliff holdings, the Silvertons turned off towards their farm whilst Arthur and Kate carried on .

CHAPTER 7.

They stopped a mile short of the complex parking the 4x4 off the road and headed on foot to the forth site.

On arrival they immediately noticed the difference of the place since their last visit, the place was buzzing with energy as they neared the cave they noticed everything becoming sharper and brighter.

They felt their minds open and rise as if from some fog they hadn't until this point realised was there.

"Wow" said Kate "This is incredible I feel stronger than I did at the last place's, the energy here is even more abundant.

At the last site's I was only getting glimpse's of this but now it feels constant, more stable. Even my hair feels as though it's standing on end!" she looked at Arthur, and could tell he was in the same state.

He was glowing, it was so obvious that here before her stood a soul wearing a body like you would clothes, she'd wondered how she could have missed the obviousness of it all before.

When she was made to go to church as a child the preacher had said this was so but until you actually see it for yourself you can't understand the implications of it.

Then a split second later the answer came to her, it was all based on perception and your energy level controls that perception and here her energy was going through the roof.

She looked around at her surroundings and could almost see but more so feel or sense the energy pulsing in the rocks and rock face's around her, everything was pulsing at a certain vibration that matched that of her own body.

In that second she knew it would be possible to raise the vibration of her body to that of the higher vibration that was emanating from deep in the centre of this place and then literally anything could be possible.

She felt Arthur agree with her and realised they were working as one mind and with that realisation came another, if everyone could let go of their ego's, their need for supremacy that animal instinct that had brought the human race this far and retain an (the term made her laugh inside) open mind then the entire human race could function like this, it felt like the logical step and so right nothing else would do, there was no more room for compromise, every other possibility had been explored, not to move in this direction would just be covering the same ground as before.

"Just think how wonderful it could be!" Arthur thought in her direction.

She instantly saw a thousand image's race through her minds eye, she could see lozenge shaped space craft and other star constellation's that she'd never seen but felt familiar some how.

It all ran so deep and came to her at such a speed she couldn't take it all in.

"That's why we all have to open our minds to each other first, to create a big enough mind to encompass all this knowledge but before anyone can do that we all need to work through our own personal puzzle's then all our puzzle's will knit together like individual pieces of a larger puzzle".

This thought came from Arthur.

Kate understood fully, she realised how important it was to work through the ego.

The controlling side of our natures to be able to link up with each other.

Kate suddenly felt it was time to go but she resisted, she wanted to see more, she wanted to know how she could help bring this about now, she didn't want to return to the mundane but that in itself was all part of her own puzzle.

Arthur also then felt it was time to leave but he like Kate wanted to stay in this space, it felt real, more real than anything he'd felt before, they both felt so complete.

Then the urge to leave came again, it was urgent that they left now!!.

Grudgingly they obeyed.

As they left the ravine their energy's began to fall almost instantly and they found they were returning to their normal state of mind, well almost normal they seemed to have taken a little of the energy with them, they felt as though their minds had been stretched it would take some getting used to but that it would be worthwhile.

As the ravine fell behind them they could hear the sound of voice's coming from up ahead it sounded like John and his friends.

"We'd better sneak around and see if we can see what their up to" said Arthur

They got close enough to see without being seen by walking round and climbing the slope that over looked the ravine, laying on their stomachs and peering over the edge gave them an excellent perspective over the scene below.

John arrived with what appeared to be the same men as before, (they were still wearing their decontamination suits) they started laying cables along the floor connecting three box's in a triangle formation, one of which held a dish antenna of some kind.

The other box's differed also, one looked like a transformer or CPU with a keyboard attached and small LCD screen whilst the other seemed like a power unit, it had prongs that one of the men had pushed directly into the ground and had a large orange light that was pulsing regularly on the top.

One of the technicians began tapping away at the keyboard

“That’s got it!” he said.

At that moment Kate and Arthur could hear the same almost inappreciable buzzing that they herd at the Highcliff complex on their first visit, they glanced at each other in acknowledgement and nodded.

“OK, you two stay here, I’m heading back to base, don’t set that lot off till I give you the signal!” said John, he indicated the walkie-talkie he held and set off in the direction of Highcliff Holdings.

“I hate that guy, he’s got no respect for what we’re trying to do out here, all he sees is dollar signs!” said the shorter of the two men.

"I know, but that's the kind of guy who always ends up heading the hands on stuff where this kind of work is concerned, that's life I suppose!" replied the other man.

"You mean someone who'll blindly follow orders as long as he gets what he wants out of the deal!".

"That's the one!" answered the other man pleasantly.

Kate and Arthur crawled away from the ledge.

"What do you make of that?" whispered Arthur" I'm not sure but that equipment looked like it was some kind of transmitter."

"Yeah, you don't think they trying to get in touch with U.F.O.s do you?

"Visitors, you mean!" corrected Kate.

“I don’t know, maybe but if that’s the case and judging by how secretive they’ve been I would say they’ve had some success”.

“Plus John and Mary both said the visits had increased lately” added Arthur.

“That’s true, we need to find out more though!” said Kate.

They crawled back to the ledge and looked down, both men were just sat down waiting, they didn’t speak.

There was a sound behind them, the crunch of a boot.

Arthur and Kate looked around to see a man dressed in the same uniform as the guards at the complex, he was pointing an automatic weapon at them.

“GET UP, SLOWLY!” he ordered.

“AND KEEP YOUR HANDS WHERE I CAN SEE THEM”.

Kate and Arthur got up slowly keeping they hands in the air.

"NOW TURN AROUND" he said.

They turned round facing the edge of the ravine.

The guard frisked them and handcuffed them together.

"NOW WALK" he said.

"Where?" asked Arthur uncertainly.

"I'LL TELL YOU WHEN WE GET THERE!, THAT WAY FOR NOW" he said indicating down the slope.

They walked down the slope and into the ravine.

The two technicians jumped to they feet as they approached.

“What are you two doing here?” asked the taller man, then he saw the guard walking behind them pointing his weapon.

“Oh, I see!” he said

“SIT DOWN!” said the guard.

“CALL THE BASE, TELL THEM IV CAUGHT THESE TWO SPYING, AND TO SEND OUT A VEHICLE” he said to the other two.

The vehicle arrived ten minutes later, the two technicians didn’t say a word to Arthur or Kate they wouldn’t even make eye contact.

John got out of the 4x4 that arrived, looking very pleased with himself.

“I knew you two were spies, now the supervisor will have to admit I was right!” he said.

The two other men looked away in disgust.

"You two stay here and wait, we'll deal with this!" he said to them "and you two can come with me" he said indicating the guard he'd brought with him and the one that had caught them.

"GET IN THE VEHICLE!" said the first guard.

Arthur and Kate rose shakily to they feet and got in the car, John slammed the doors shut behind them and got in the front, they drove cross country to the complex the gates were opened for them and they drove in.

Jack was waiting out side the admin building with his hands on his hips looking very stern and menacing.

"I think we're in trouble" said Arthur

"I think your right" agreed Kate.

They were taken to separate rooms in the building.

Arthur was sat in an upright chair facing a large mirror, the guard had cuffed his hands behind his back through the gaps of the chair, then he'd left the room and Arthur to his thoughts.

"This looks just like the interrogation rooms on T.V.!"

Thought Arthur bemused dispite his situation.

The door opened and Jack walked in looking calm, which only seemed to heighten Arthur's anxiety, he was closely followed by a beaming John.

"What were you two up to out there?" asked Jack.

"Before I say anything I want to know what you've done with Kate!" said Arthur

"Your girlfriends fine, for the moment!" sneered John, obviously enjoying the moment immensely.

Jack looked at John with obvious disgust.

"Leave the room, John" he said quietly.

John looked visibly hurt but done as he was told, Arthur couldn't help but smile but looked the other way. This wasn't the time for humour.

"Sorry about him, sometimes he worries me, but he has he's use's.

Kate's fine I just want to talk to you both separately, now do tell me what the hell your up to and why your taking such an interest in our work!".

Arthur thought about lying but didn't really see any point in it at this stage but he wasn't about to tell Jack everything.

“We were trying to find out what you were up to!” he said

“And whys that?” said Jack.

“We’ve been visiting the site’s, just for something to do really but since you guys have been doing whatever you’ve been doing the place’s just don’t feel the same and I for one want to know why!”.

Said Arthur, surprised at the strength in his voice.

Jack looked taken back but it didn’t last.

“What do you mean <u>feel the same?</u>” he said, staring into Arthur’s eyes as if daring him to back up what he had said.

“YOU KNOW EXACTLY WHAT I MEAN!” said Arthur, getting angry with this man, who did he think he was interrogating him like something out of a spy novel, this man’s a joke! He thought.

Something told Arthur this wasn't the way to deal with this situation, he closed his eye's and took a deep breath, letting it out slowly.

When he opened his eye's Jack was studying him closely.

"Finished?" he said.

"So you can feel the energy's can you?, to what extent?" he asked with a glint in he's eye.

This took Arthur totally by surprise, he wasn't sure what to say.

"What do you mean, to what extent?" he asked.

"Just that, I mean I now know your aware but now I want to know how aware you are?".

Arthur didn't know what to say, so he asked a question in return.

"How do you measure something like that?".

Jack laughed, "Is the right answer!" he said, then-

"Tell you what, you help me and I'll let you in on what we're doing, how's that sound?".

"What do you want from me?" Asked Arthur a little concerned

"And what are you going to do if I refuse?" he added.

"Well if you refuse I'll let you both go, you don't know anything that you can prove and I can always get more men and double security, you'll never get near us again and if you do get the media interested I can always relocate.

There's sites like these all over the world you know!.

As to what I want from you, not a lot really just a second opinion on a few minor issues,

-what do you say?".

Arthur was interested it meant they found out what they needed and got out of this mess, although Jack would probably only show them the bare minimum and improve his security anyway.

"Why not!" he said "But only if Kate agrees and you take me to her right now!".

"Atta boy!" replied Jack.

Jack took off Arthur's cuffs and led him out the room, past a shocked looking John who stormed off in the other direction.

"Don't let him bother you!" said Jack

"I don't" said Arthur sharply.

They continued on down the corridor, entering the first room on the left.

He gave Arthur the keys to Kate cuff's.

"I'll wait outside whilst you fill her in on current events shall I?" said Jack with a smirk.

Arthur gave him a dark look and entered the room.

Kate was sitting with her chin on her chest, hands cuffed behind her back in the same posture as was Arthur.

As he stepped into the room, Kate looked up, she looked scared but strong her jaw thrust forward in defiance.

"It's you, how did you?" she began.

Arthur interjected "Ive made a deal!" he said and began unlocking her cuff's whilst he filed her in on his and Jacks exchange.

“So what exactly doe’s he want us to do?” she asked when he’d finished.

“I’m not quite sure but I think we’ll find out soon enough!” Arthur replied.

They left the room and met Jack waiting outside for them.

CHAPTER 8.

"Well where now?" said Kate still looking defiant.

"Down stairs" said Jack, keeping his composure and led them further down the corridor and down some iron stairs on the right.

They went down two stories and found themselves outside a basement laboratory.

They went through the first door into an adjacent room to the main lab, where Jack asked them to don decontamination suits like those worn by the two technicians they'd seen previously.

"We need to keep the environment inside sterile for scientific purpose's" explained Jack with what sounded like genuine amusement.

"Oh" said Kate.

As they entered the lab they saw the two technicians working at a bench on the far side of the room.

The two men looked up surprised, they visibly relaxed when they saw who Arthur and Kate were with.

On the bench directly in front of them there was the same equipment they saw earlier at the forth site.

“What exactly does that stuff do?” asked Kate.

“You don’t miss a thing do you, why don’t I get our experts to show you” said Jack.

He waved over the two men and they walked over.

“These two have some questions for you, please answer them as best to your knowledge” said Jack.

The two men looked at Arthur and Kate expectantly.

“What exactly does this equipment do?” Asked Kate directing her question to the two men.

The shorter of the two answered her.

“Well, it’s all very complex but in laymen’s terms, it’s made up of three components as you can see.

The first component this box here (he indicated the box with the three prongs, and glanced at Jack who nodded reassuringly) pull’s the energy from the ground and stores it like a battery”.

“What kind of energy?” asked Kate playing dumb.

It’s not energy like we’ve ever seen before, it’s an atomic energy of sorts but we’re able to tap into it’s power with absolutely no risk of an explosion, we quite simply pull the energy directly from the layers of and between the Atoms instead of splitting the actual Atom itself.

Of course there is some loss in coercion of the atomic structure which a problem but we've found it rejuvenates after a limited period and it's still more viable than any other form of energy on the market.

From a scientific viewpoint it's entirely new."

"What do you mean when you say; from a scientific view point?" asked Kate.

"This sounds foolish but we think we've actually scientifically discovered what's known as Psychic or Spiritual energy.(Jack smiled at Arthur)

People have claimed in the past to have found a way to measure this energy but it's never really been conclusively proven!.

What's more we've also discovered a way to gather this energy and store it, which is a first and fascinating in itself.

But more than that we've learnt to manipulate the frequency's of the energy, like tuning a radio.

It really is a unique form of energy, so versatile and with so many far reaching possibilities.

The other box's you see here such as this one (he pointed to the box with a keyboard attached) is what we use to manipulate the frequencies of the energy's we store in the first box.

Whereas the third box here is the most exciting of the three, this one directs the energy, unfortunately it's all still very experimental at the moment and we've had a few mishap's along the way".

"What kind of mishaps?" asked Kate.

"Nothing too disastrous, quite amusing really we've had people forgetting to turn off the machine's(He glanced at the taller man who shrug his shoulders as if he'd heard this accusation one two many times.) and Iv come down the following day to find one of the pot plant specimens grown out to cover the door and had to break in!"

"Wow really that's very interesting" said Kate

"Yes" said the man, "like I said this energy is incredibly versatile, there's probably a purpose for it in commercial farming as well. One of the many reasons for carrying out this research.

Of course we're still reliable on the energy high points such as the site's in this area but hopefully in the near future we'll be able to literally suck the energy directly out of the air".

"That would really be something" said Arthur.

"Would you two like a demonstration?" said the other man.

"That would be good!" said Arthur.

The man switched on the second and third box.

“It’s still holding a charge from earlier” he explained.

The room at once began to hum with the same buzzing as earlier at the site.

“Watch this!” said the man.

He picked up the dish antenna and pointed it at a candle on the next bench and depressed a switch on the handle, the buzzing seemed to condense to a higher note and find a point of origin in the room , it was no longer coming from thin air but actually seemed to be from the dead wick of the candle which a split second later burst to life with a large spark and a loud crack.

The man turned off both box’s and turned expectantly to Arthur and Kate.

“Incredible!” said Arthur.

The man smiled with obvious pride.

“That’s not the extent of it, through different frequency’s we’ve found we can do all sorts, Iv even started a car at a distance of twelve feet and powered a radio from five feet away” he said.

The shorter man interjected.

“We haven’t yet found any limitations with this device, we’re still finding the right frequencies to do different things but Iv personally got high hopes for these device’s and there varying applications, at the moment we’re also experimenting with climate control.

As I said the applications seem to be limitless, we may well be close to solving the worlds energy problems, but we have to remember we’re still very much in the experimental stage and we have so much yet to learn about this form of energy, which is why we're keeping it all very hush, hush".

"Well I must admit I'm impressed!" Said Arthur.

"Me to!, but what you said earlier about the loss of coercion within the Atom, that worries me some, could it not cause problems if employed on a global scale!". Said Kate.

"You certainly have a valid point, as I said we are still in the experimental stage but this energy appears boundless and inextricably linked to that of living people and animals for that matter plant life also, it would seem this self perpetuating energy has been here all along. Just as, I'm ashamed to admit as a scientist, mystic's and folklore has always told us" said the taller technician

"How can you be so sure this energy is self perpetuating, what proof do you have?" Asked Kate.

"If we're to believe the mystic's, which after all the things Ive seen of late I'm quite prepared to do then this energy is self perpetuating by its very nature.

I think the fact we're finding any loss in coercion at all is something to do with the way we are extracting it, obviously we'll have to fine tune this procedure before we do it on any larger scale!"

"Your not accounting for the human element!" said Arthur suddenly.

Every body looked at him in surprise,

"How do you mean?" Asked the man.

"I'm not entirely sure, I think I mean the interaction between the human consciousness and the energy." said Arthur.

“Can you expand on that?” said Jack a subtle smile playing on his lips.

“Yes,-I think so” said Arthur.

“The energy needs the touch of a mind to guide and direct it, to ground it to a single purpose and to complete the circle to keep it self perpetuating”.

“What do you mean by completing the circle?” asked Jack.

“You see everything on this planet is so precisely balanced that to take this energy without the touch of the mind is to upset that balance, just as an unclear mind would, you need to create a new kind of computer that’ll incorporate the clarity of thought it takes to direct this energy with real focus.

You need a computer that is made in some way of this very energy itself!” Arthur concluded.

"That's pure science fiction!", spat the shorter man.

Jack span round on the man.

"If you weren't part of this work for the past year you'd say that demonstration you've just performed was a trick, but you know different.

Give our friend here his space and listen carefully! I think Arthur is about to make a very valid contribution.

Please continue Arthur, how do we incorporate this energy into our technology?".

"PLANT CELLS!,(Arthur's mind had been racing whilst Jack spoke.) you need to find a plant with a high enough vibration to hold the energy and if you can get the right plant it will hold the correct intention giving the very clarity of thought I mentioned, that element of life force within the machine bringing the two together and providing the balance necessary to complete the circle.

It's so clear to me know I can almost picture the energy moving through the cells, it'll work!".

"Plant cells, it certainly sounds feasible, it's going to take years of research to accomplish though, do you have any more information for us Arthur?" said the taller technician.

"Not much I'm afraid, Iv got a feeling of a place, Iv never been there so I can't see it clearly enough to describe but it's some where in south America, there's a tribe somewhere,- they have the information you need.

That's all I have!." He said.

Jack, Arthur and Kate left the lab.

The two technicians were involved in an intense debate over the information Arthur had just given them.

They climbed the stairs and went outside, evening was just settling in, the sky had a beautiful opaque texture to it.

“Well” said Jack “I think we all benefited from that little exchange, I take it I wont be seeing you two again now?”.

This sounded more like an instruction than a question.

“Well we wont be snooping into what your up to but you still might see us around this area, we’ve not finished investigating the sites yet” replied Arthur reproachfully.

“Plus we could still swap information from time to time, couldn’t we?” said Kate Remembering her last experience and the need for all people to work together, dispite the fact she personally didn’t like this man very much.

Jack studied her face for a moment.

“Sure, Why not, we should all work together shouldn’t we?” he said greasily.

Jack walked them to the exit of the complex and gave them their car key’s, the 4x4 was parked just inside the gate.

Arthur had a disturbing scene play through his minds eye, They get in the car, he turns the key and bang the vehicle explodes in a huge fire ball, Jack stands nearby smiling broadly.

“Don’t worry” said Jack reading the apprehension on Arthur’s face, “It’s not been touched, I promise”.

He seemed amused but sincere.

The guards opened the gate, Kate and Arthur drove out towards the Silvertons farm.

CHAPTER 9.

They arrived just in time for dinner, this pleased Kate immensely. Mike was also at the Sivertons place, as Kate and Arthur approached the house they saw the three of them sitting on the porch.

“We’ve been waiting for you, did you find out anything interesting?” called out John as they climbed the steps.

“Yeah, you wouldn’t believe the day we’ve had!” said Arthur.

“Well firstly lets sit down to dinner, you two look half starved” said Mary

“That’s sounds wonderful!” said Kate.

Mary smiled kindly and led them through to the dinning room where they sat down to a wonderful meal, during the course of which Arthur and Kate told everyone about their day.

They left nothing out.

“Well” said John “You two certainly don’t waste time when you set about a task do you?”

“We were lucky” said Kate.

“There’s no such thing as luck, in this life we make our own fortune!” said Mike who’d been very quiet up till now.

“So what do you think, could what their doing up there have anything to do with the visitors?” asked Arthur.

"I don't know really sounds possible though Ive always thought the visitors were waiting for some kind of event in human endeavour to make themselves known to us all!" said John.

"Could be, I mean it's not something Iv thought about before really, if they are, do you think they were waiting for us to discover this energy so we can be on equal terms. I mean everybody assumes U.F.Os must have a more technologically advanced society which they obviously do else how would they accomplish interstellar travel and just maybe it's based on this very energy!" said Kate.

"That would make a great deal of sense, you remember the technicians said they haven't yet found any real limitations for this energy I could all to easily imagine space craft being powered by this energy, it would be perfectly suited for the use!" Arthur replied.

"How's that?" asked John.

"Well it's clean there's no pollution its also fully renewable and seems as the scientists told us there's no limits as to what it can do!" Arthur answered.

They continued talking like this until the small hours, running over all the possibilities they could imagine and talking in flights of fancy letting their imaginations run wild, eventually they went to bed. Tired but pleased with the progress they'd made.

Arthur was shook awake it was a little before dawn, Kate was standing over him with her hands on his shoulders.

"Quickly get up!, their here!" she said, Arthur could hear a high pitched whine cutting through the night.

"What's that noise?" Arthur asked feeling bewildered.

"The Visitors!!" said Kate running out of the room.

Arthur leapt out of bed and followed her out, everybody was already out on the porch staring up at the night sky.

"Where?" Arthur asked Mike.

"There" said Mike pointing towards the north west.

Arthur looked where Mike indicated there was an orange light hovering over the horizon, it seemed to be moving ever so slightly from side to side almost wobbling.

It dipped below the horizon and disappeared from view.

Another craft came in from the west and headed towards where the other one disappeared, the first ship re-appeared and both craft flew directly towards the farm, they were going at in incredible rate as they came closer the whine also increased and seemed to be admitting an intermittent hum below the obvious sound of the whine.

They reached the farm house and the craft in front shot straight over the building whereas the second one stopped directly over the house.

It shone a violet light over the house, everyone ran off the porch and stared back at the spectacle.

The ship sat in mid air for a moment it was lozenge shaped with blue running lights around the circumference with an oval down lighter (the violet light) with the orange light which must have been the thrust at one end that must have been the rear of the craft then the violet light went out and the orange one turned light blue at which point the ship shot off after the other one at immeasurable speed.

"That was amazing!!" said Kate breathlessly.

They went back in the house, Mary put the tin kettle on the stove and everyone settled themselves down comfortably.

“That was incredible!” said Arthur, his face flushed and pink dispite the chill outside.

“Iv never seen anything like that before!” said Kate “Do you realise where the first ship was hovering?”.

It dawned on them all simultaneously.

“Highcliff holdings!” exclaimed Arthur.

“That’s right, I don’t think Jack shared all the information he had with us!” added Kate.

“Do you reckon they know why the visitors are here?” asked Mary whilst pouring the tea into five small pretty china cups.

“They definitely know more than their letting on!” said John.

"I wonder why they stopped here as well, do you think their aware of Kate and Arthur's recent experiences, that maybe their detecting the energy somehow" ventured Mike.

"That's spooky, but they might do! I mean who's to say what they do or don't know?" said Kate.

"Well I think we're about to get some more answers!" said Mary looking down the hall and through the glass panel in the front door, there was car-lights coming up the drive outside.

"What do you mean?" asked Kate looking at her from the couch.

"We've got guest's" said Mary nodding to the door.

Everyone jumped up and went to the door, John opened it and turned on the porch light.

They could make out the vehicles coming in the early morning light, they were 4x4's, the kind used by the staff at Highcliff Holdings and there were two of them.

The vehicles stopped in front of the house and Jack got out of one closely followed by two guards, the other vehicle held four more guards who stayed put- there was no sign of John.

"Hi there!" he called out sounding cheerful and friendly.

"What do you think your doing on my land at this hour?" yelled John.

"Sorry to bother you but we've had a theft at the complex and we're" began Jack stopping short as he caught sight of Arthur and Kate.

"I should have known!" he said aloud, "May I come in?" he asked John.

"Only if you tell those two monkeys to wait in their vehicles!" was Johns reply.

Jack spoke quietly to the men and they walked back to the vehicle, Jack in the mean time climbed the steps and John let him in, glaring at him all the while.

They all went through to the kitchen and once again sat down.

"Would you like some tea?" asked Mary.

"That would be lovely, thank you" replied Jack.

"What do you want?" asked John gruffly.

"This is Jack" interjected Arthur.

"Oh is that so!, we've been hearing a lot about you recently!" said John his tone still letting Jack know who's boss.

“I take it you don’t always get up this early!” said Jack expectantly.

“I really don’t see how’s that’s any business of yours!” answered John defensively.

“That’s enough now John, lets hear him out I’m sure he’s hasn’t come all this way just to exchange pleasantries” said Mary.

“Thank you my good woman, your quite right, I think Ill assume Arthur and Kate have filled you all in on what we’re doing up at the complex.

Which really wasn’t part of our deal now was it Arthur? but never the less lets get down to the task at hand.

You have obviously noticed our visitors tonight (a glance around the room at the face’s assembled told him this was correct) so Id like to know why they stopped over this house, how did you get their attention?” asked Jack surveying the room and settling his gaze on Arthur.

“We didn’t, I don’t know why they stopped here-they just did, why how have you been getting their attention?” said Arthur.

“Have you been using those machines?, did you stumble across the right frequency?” asked Kate.

“Your very perceptive! Kate we did happen to find a frequency that this beings have been finding interesting but so far all they seem to be doing is flying around the general area and we think- scanning us” answered Jack.

“The violet light!” exclaimed Arthur.

“So they scanned here too did they?” ventured Jack.

“They did, do you know what they’re looking for?” asked Mike.

“I don’t think Iv had the pleasure” said Jack looking at Mike.

"My names Mike I'm a friend of Kate and Arthur's I own the next farm down the road, this is John and Mary and as you may have realised; your on their farm" answered Mike

"Pleased to meet you all I'm sure" said Jack.

"So do you know what exactly their looking for?" repeated Mike.

"To be perfectly honest we've no idea!, all we know is a certain energy attracts them!" replied Jack.

"What type of energy?" asked Arthur.

"How do you mean?, I could tell you the frequency but it'll make as much sense to you as it doe's to me, it's only a number unless you know how the technology works.

But then again nothing would surprise me where you two are concerned!" said Jack giving them both a broad grin.

"No I mean was it the type that starts cars or lights candles?" asked Arthur.

"Do you know that's a very good question, I really don't know but I'll find out; excuse me!" with that he left the house and went out to one of the vehicles.

While he was gone the others spoke.

"I don't trust him!" said John.

"No neither do I, there's a lot he's not letting on. Have you noticed how guarded he is when he speaks, he's very clever that man, we'll have to keep a close eye on him!" Mike surmised.

Jack came back in the room and sat down.

"Iv just been speaking to my scientist friends, they said it's the same frequency that speeds up the growth of plants" he said.

"That's interesting, I cant think why that would attract the visitors though" said Kate.

Jack looked at her for a moment and stood up.

"Well sorry to bother you all but I really must be on my way, thanks again for the tea" he said to Mary "Bye then and don't be a stranger you two, remember we agreed to share our thoughts!".

"Will do, see you soon" said Kate trying to sound sincere.

Jack left the house, they heard the engine's start and the cars drive off.

"Yeah like you told us you were playing around with U.F.Os" said Kate sarcastically when she was sure he had left.

“Visitors! dear” corrected Mary with a smile

“I think there’s a connection in the frequency that’s been attracting the visitors and growing plants” offered Mike.

“How’s that?” asked Arthur.

“Well have you ever heard of spiritual healing?” asked Mike.

“That’s like faith healing isn’t it? the laying on of hands and such” Said Kate “up till now Ive always thought that was con men playing on peoples vulnerabilities but after the last few days I’m ready to believe almost anything now!”.

“What’s that got to do with U.F.Os?; Sorry Mary the visitors” asked Arthur.

Mary gave Arthur an “it’s ok” kind of smile.

“Well” said Mike” Basically it’s this, healing works by channelling the energy from the very universe itself, to enable someone’s body to heal at a faster rate than it would otherwise as long as the intention’s of the person doing the healing are correct.

Ive done a little myself in the past and when my mother, many moons ago now was teaching me how to do it I used to practise on plants.

I remember that the plants I worked on would out-grow the ones I didn’t and I realised through this that the energy I was channelling was in fact a very specific life force that regenerated each individual cell in the body.

My conclusion being that these Visitors are being attracted by this life force and not lets say by the frequency used to run a radio, which I believe shows a higher awareness working here!”.

“I see what you mean, these being’s are only interested when the higher vibrational energy is being employed, but I wonder what that actually implies?” said Arthur.

"That the use of that energy shows the visitors how far we as a race have come!" said Kate surprising herself.

"Ive another question" said John "If these visitors are being attracted by this; as you say Mike higher energy or life force they playing with at the complex then what made that ship last night stop here?"

"That's obvious!" said Mike, everyone looked at him expectantly.

"Our two young friends here ofcourse, they've both been having extraordinary experiences lately and I for one can see the change's its brought about in them and I dontthink I'm the only one.

Our friend Jack from the complex he sees it to, that's why he's tolerating you at all he thinks you'll be able to help him and he's probably right.

By what you told us of yesterdays events you've already helped him a great deal and I don't think that's a bad thing for the planet as a whole but we can all see he's intentions are unclear, probably financially motivated or maybe he has a need for power.

Whatever his motivation the work he's conducting will ultimately greatly benefit mankind so his selfishness will only slow down his own growth process and due to the good his ultimately doing it will balance out anyway.

But I feel the energie's Arthur and Kate have been working with will have in fact become integrated in their own personal energies to the extent that they attracted the attention of the visitors".

"Mike I'm interested in what you just said about Jack's growth process, what doe's that actually mean?" asked Kate.

"Your growth process is the process by which you learn to clear your imbalance's.

Imbalances are the dysfunctional aspects of your persona, you may not be aware you have them but everyone on this planet has these inbalance's in their make-up <u>at this time</u>.

Your growth process also works on a give and take basis, ie what you put in you get back, which as I'm sure your aware is reflected in many belief structures around the globe.

In Jacks case he's doing a lot of good but he's not doing from a giving space what he's doing he feels he's doing for himself thus slowing his growth, if he was working from a higher space he'd find he wouldn't need Kate or Arthur because he'd get most of his answers himself due to own his clarity of thought that would enable him to tune in".

"Thank you" said Kate" but you've just provided me with another two questions; what did you mean by tune in?"

"To be able to tune in is to pick up on the currents of information that are available to anyone that can hold a clear mind long enough to rise above their imbalances and see the bigger picture, I suppose like the tuning of the frequencies on that machine you and Jack were talking about earlier or like a radio turning out the static as it were to obtain a clear channel." answered Mike "What was the other question Kate?".

"Yes you also said that everyone on this planet at this time has these imbalances you mentioned but I couldn't help noticing the emphasis you placed on the latter part of that sentence, when you said <u>at this time ,</u> what did you mean?".

"Ah, well spotted Kate I did place an emphasis on that part of my sentence and that was for two reasons.

The first being what I said earlier about what you put in you get back and applying this same concept on a global scale by saying- at this time I'm also helping to manifest this by affirmation, which is like a conformation but in advance, in effect willing it so and thus helping the growth process of the human race as a whole and my own personal growth by the same rational-i.e. what you put in you get back, kind of acknowledging the way things are but also confirming that they will change.

This also leads on to my second reason for placing the emphasis, to help place the concept in the minds of those that I'm talking too and again helping to manifest the truth in this case that at some point in the near future children are going to be born with less and less of this imbalances as we as a whole race move forward".

"Wow" said Arthur "It's amazing that such a small action could have such a far reaching effect".

"That's precisely the point the smallest actions are so often the most important but we as people seem content to ignore this but this is due to the fast paced way of life we in the west especially have grown so used to that we just don't feel we have the time to think so in-depth on the smaller things, this is of course untrue but due to the fact we so often miss the higher truth.

This also carries on to the point that sometimes the best action of all is non-action, to allow the situation to flow naturally to the appropriate conclusion <u>at that time</u>!" added Mike.

Everyone sat quietly absorbing this information.

"So we've changed our personal energies to match these higher vibrations emanating from the sites in this area how come we've done this without even trying?" asked Arthur.

"In the case of you two I'm already fairly certain you have a close link to the chosen from the legend of my people, but this higher existence is open to everyone it's just that its more repressed in some than it is in others, this can usually be due to something as simple as a deeply ingrained imbalance that the person in question holds to be such a major part of their persona that their just not ready to let go of it!, although this usually stems from a deeper insecurity or trauma that the person in question just cant face.

At that time they can't deal with the root of a problem another good reason for people with the ability to heal at these levels to be encouraged but of course this should work in conjunction with other established forms of counselling and therapy's but in your case, you were already susceptible to the energy.

Which means you were both reasonably clear to begin with." answered Mike.

"It all seems to have such far reaching possibilities for us all as a people.

It's no wonder the visitors are taking such an interest in what's happening on this planet.-At this time!" added Arthur with a smile.

CHAPTER 10.

"Well" said Mary "Doe's anyone fancy some breakfast?".

The sun had risen fully and it was shaping up to be another beautiful day.

They had a large breakfast and chatted again, running over the previous nights events and deciding what to do today.

Mike spoke up "Id really like to visit the site of statues with you Kate and see if we can expand on your last experiences there!".

"That would be good, I think I'm developing somewhat of an addiction to the energies Id love to go back and feel that again" Kate replied.

"I think we should all go" said John "Id like to experience something myself!".

“I’ll pack us some food for the trip” said Mary.

They all got dressed and set out just before eleven, John and Mary took they own vehicle as did Mike, Arthur and Kate followed in Arthur’s 4x4.

They took the longer route to avoid any contact with anyone from the complex back to the main highway and drove through Vantage then taking the side road to Lake Stillgood where they drove around the lake and started out on foot towards the third site.

They reached the site by mid afternoon and split up looking around at the statues at their own pace Kate thought the energy was alluding her every time she thought she felt the it she’d make a mental leap towards it but it would seem to immediately slip through her metaphorical fingers.

Mike called everyone over to where he was stood, he was standing in front of a statue that resembled a man/dog of some kind, the lower half was man shaped but the upper area was that of a canine it was made out of a blue stone that was speckled with black marks.

“This is the one I think” he said.

“What do you mean?” said Kate.

“Do you remember on our first meeting, you told me about your dream?” asked Mike.

“The one where I was a wolf” said Kate looking at the statue.

“That’s the one” said Mike “I want to try to see if we can tune in to that dream whilst in this place!”.

“That may be a little difficult I’m having trouble connecting with the energy” said Kate looking concerned.

“What’s the problem?” asked Mike

“I seem to be getting a glimpse of the energy but every time I try to hold it seems to flitter away”

“I think your trying to hard, you need to relax to allow the energy to move in its own way.

By trying to hold the energy immediately on sensing it your actually trying wrap it around yourself to capture it as it were and control it.

The energy wont respond to that kind of approach, you need to clear your mind and hold a genuine feeling of love in your heart, it’s not as hard as it sounds (he added seeing the look on Kate’s face) its very easy actually all you have to do is release the need to control the energy which your unconsciously doing by trying to reinvent the feeling you experienced last time.

That's impossible this is a different time and there's also other people here that will influence the energy as you perceive it, just let go and you'll balance again and your perception with you.

Also try not to get frustrated it may take a while to let go to the extent you need to, this is directly related to your energy level at the moment so just try to relax, it may help to sit down.

Plus if your having to much difficulty I can always help!" said Mike.

Kate sat crossed legged where she stood.

"What should the rest of us do?" asked Arthur.

"You can join us if you like it can only help" answered Mike.

They all sat down in a rough circle, Mike began to chant.

The sounds he was making seemed to rise and fall in octave but at the same time they could hear a single continuous note in the midst of the sound, Arthur closed his eyes and found himself focusing on that single note, as he did he felt himself contract to a single point at the top of his head.

Nothing else seemed to exist, he was aware of where he was and of those sat around him but it had all drifted further from his perception somehow, all he could sense of his surroundings was the rhythmic note of Mike's chant.

He remembered what Mike had said about letting the energy move in its own way and decided to let himself drift.

As soon as he did so his minds eye filled with circular geometric shapes moving in unison, these fell away as quickly as they came and Arthur felt as though he was being propelled forward at an incredible speed until suddenly he stops, before him lays a vast expanse of space dotted with unknown stars.

He felt a presence.

It was Kate, he couldn't see her but he knew she was there, so were the other's. They had linked together Arthur could feel the links between them like an elastic cord the link didn't hinder their movements instead it would support them.

"Where are we?" Arthur thought out to his friends.

The answer came in conceptual form- it was negative, they didn't know!.

"What are we doing here?" he sent next.

Again the answer was negative, he saw movement they weren't alone!.

He couldn't see who it was but whoever it was they felt warm and welcoming.

Arthur reached out to them with his mind, his friends supported this action and that somehow proved it was correct.

He remembered the feeling of one mind he and Kate had experienced before and came to the conclusion that this was precisely what he and the others were functioning as and in so doing were a stronger channel to the higher truths.

They were meant to touch in on the other being, at that Arthur realised it was another cell just like his the one he was part of with the others.

As they linked in both cells were instantly bombarded with an overwhelming amount of information.

Arthur couldn't focus on any of it, he couldn't hold a single thought it was all moving to fast .

He felt Mikes touch and remembered briefly what he had said again about letting the energy move in it's own way.

Arthur let go, it was the most difficult thing he had ever done!.

He felt he was losing himself in the process, the more information they were absorbing the more distant he felt from himself, he was getting worried.

He felt a presence outside of either cell.

It touched his heart dispelling the fear, replacing it with a feeling of warmth and was gone.

There were more cells floating around the space they began pulling together, propelled by some kind of magnetic force and touched in on them quite suddenly they had all linked in a star of David formation, like sky divers but there was no sign of their bodies they were each nothing more than points of light.

They began to spin faster and faster blurring into one.

Arthur's consciousness span out of his own cell reaching the limits of the formation, then out beyond that linking once again to other formations that were in themselves part of a yet larger formation until each star was just a point of light making up the still larger matrix- this was it we are all truly one!.

He felt he knew all there was to know, it was all in his grasp all he had to do was reach out and take it, it was all there.

But he felt there was no need to do this it was all in the right place but the temptation was almost overwhelming.

At this the image began to shrink back to the one collective then back down to the one cell and finally back to himself yet he could still feel the tenuous bonds linking him to the higher reality.

Arthur opened his eyes and looked at the others, they all looked amazing they were quite literally glowing, their skin looked like silk and their eyes were so clear the whites appeared blue.

“Wow!” said Kate “What was that all about?”.

"Ive no idea!" said Mike.

"Kate, do you remember the experience we had at the forth site before we were caught by John and his friends from the complex?" asked Arthur.

"Yes-I see what your getting at. The puzzles!" said Kate.

"The puzzles?" asked Mary.

"Yes we discovered everyone has to work through they own particular puzzle.

Just as Mike was saying earlier about imbalances.

We all have a puzzle within us to work out and by so doing we find that our individual completed puzzle is essentially only part of a larger puzzle!"

"That certainly corresponds to the experience we've just had!" said John.

"And" said Mike "It's confirmed again by the fact I had no idea what that just was but I gave you the information to put it together by sharing the completed aspects of my own puzzle.

You see it all ties in!"

"Yes but where's it all going to lead us?" asked Mary.

"That's obviously the next step" said Arthur.

They heard someone approaching the clearing.

It was Jack and the two technicians.

"Well well well" he said "and what a nice surprise to see you lot so soon!".

"What do you want?" asked John.

"Nothing; I was at the complex and my two friends here informed me the sensors were picking up on some rather impressive energy, so we thought we'd come have a look-see.

Tell me, what have you been doing out here, we didn't realise our sensors were that sensitive.

The energy you've been playing with must have been really something to effect them all the way back at the complex!"

"Well I'm sure we don't know what your talking about!, we've just come out here to enjoy the day but you've put pay to that.

I think we'll be off now" said John.

With that he got up to go, the others followed suit.

"Now there's really no need to be like that.

We're all working towards the same thing here we should pool our resources and work together shouldn't we Kate?" Said Jack.

"Well we're not doing it for our own gain!" replied Kate.

Jacks demeanour changed instantly.

"DON'T GIVE ME THAT!.

YOUR DOING THIS FOR YOURSELVE'S JUST AS I AM AND THE FACT YOU WONT SHARE ONLY PROVES THAT!" he shouted at them not even trying to hide his anger.

"That's true!" said Mike "but at least in our case it's not for money!".

They walked away towards the lake leaving Jack silently fuming.

The two scientists looked bewildered.

On reaching the lake Mary unpacked the lunch and they sat down to enjoy the food and view.

The lake looked beautiful, the sun was once again dancing on the surface of the water giving it that limitless sparkle.

“Well that was unexpected” said Mike after a while.

“Jack hasn’t shared all he knows with us including that sensor he mentioned!” said Arthur.

Kate sat a little apart from the others studying the view before her and listening to what they were saying.

“I wonder what other device’s they have?” said John.

“That’s a very good question and quite a scary one in many ways” said Mary.

“I know what you mean, you could get quite paranoid if you thought to much about that!” said Arthur.

“I want to go back to the site” said Kate suddenly.

“Why?” asked Arthur.

"We still didn't get the answers we came for did we?" she said.

Mike looked up, "I agree Kate perhaps the two of us can go back and see what we can find out about your dream".

"I'd like that" said Kate" Id like to find out what those dreams meant".

They left the others at the lake and set off towards the site. (thankfully Jack and his friends had left.)

They found the same statue as before and sat down.

"Right where do we start?" asked Kate.

"I think we should start by going through the sequence of events in your dream" said Mike.

"Well the first dream I had I was being chased by an animal of some kind" whilst she spoke she was looking at the statue before her, studying every contour of its from and the texture of the stone.

"By what you said before" she continued "I beginning to think that was one of the other faction of the chosen".

"So you believe you were one of the chosen then?" said Mike.

"I don't really know but it would certainly fit don't you think?" replied Kate.

"Sounds like it but there is the possibility you were just another victim, a member of the tribe" said Mike.

"But what about the second dream the one where I was a wolf, hiding in that burrow" she again looked at the statue before her.

“That would certainly fit but why do you think you’d be shown this now in this life?” asked Mike.

“That’s just it, I don’t know could it just be that returning to this place had invoked these memories!” said Kate.

“That could be it but Ive always found that nothing just happens there’s always a reason even if we don’t see it ourselves at the time” said Mike.

“Then what do you suppose the reason is?” asked Kate.

“Well it could just all be a part of your own growth process I mean that as we wake up to this existence we are pulling all our higher aspects together and manifesting them at this time in the now as opposed to just knowing them intellectually and continuing to live as we did before this realisation, which is a mistake I feel a lot of people make.

Its very easy to listen to someone sharing a higher truth but to disregard it instantly by saying - well I know that already, the thing being it's easy to know something but living it in your every day reality is an entirely different matter" said Mike.

"That makes a lot of sense but Id still like to know the details!" replied Kate.

"Wouldn't we all!" laughed Mike "But seriously to know everything about all our past existence's would most likely have a detrimental effect on our lives now!".

"How's that?" asked Kate.

"Well" said Mike "lets say that to learn to deal with a particular block or imbalance say for instance self worth, we've all met people that don't value themselves.

You can guess the problems that could arise from this, the obvious being that the person in question wouldn't place any value on others or it could go the other way where they'd believe everyone to be better than themselves which is of course illusion because as you know no ones better than anyone else.

But these things do happen and it doe's have a very far reaching effect on someone's mental stability, so this person obviously needs to balance this out to move forward.

Lets say that in a past life this person was in an advantageous position in society that led them to believe that they were better than those around them and they held this thought to be true throughout this previous life.

Well back in the present this person has on a higher level realised the opportunities lost to them in that life due to this inbalance.

Coming to that realisation that they now must work on these negative patterns but in this scenario they have gone to far in the other direction and are still unbalanced.

They need to bring it to a correct point of balance.

If this person was to see in full this past life they may come to a reasonable balance but it would be more likely, due to human nature they would key in to the ego and relive the last existence because it is instantly gratifying due to the fact that in a social context every one likes someone who's confidant and those with a superiority complex can to the untrained eye appear socially adept in this way but again this is illusion because these people are generally trying to hide the fact their quite insecure which in fact this person was in the first place being of a low self worth and thus vulnerable to astral influences in the social context".

"That does make a lot of sense in a round-a-bout kind of way" said Kate" but you've brought up another question, the term Astral influences- what doe's that mean exactly".

"Ah, now you've opened a can of worms but Ill try to simplify it as much as I can.

The Astral is a term used amongst people operating on the higher levels of reality.

The Astral is the lowest of the psychic levels.

Its where all the ego games are played out, the fight for supremacy and one up man ship that we've all been guilty of at one point or another.

It is on this level that psychic's do battle to prove that they are better than one another which as Ive said before is pure illusion.

The only reason it carries any weight at all is due to the fact that many people buy into it and perceive it to matter and in so doing they create a mass illusion i.e.; mob-consciousness or to put it another way; sheep.

Although this level doe's have its use's, in helping people work through their lower aspects it generally cause's more problems than it's worth and hinders the growth of the human race as a whole because it has us all chasing illusion and reacting to these influences and thus not following our divine purposes which is ofcourse to come to balance and wholeness in the now".

“That’s all very interesting I think I know what you mean by reacting to the Astral influences there’s been a few occasions in my life when Ive found myself acting out of character to impress someone or just to get along with people its just the same as peer pressure really its just a matter of finding the strength to stand in your own centre” replied Kate.

“That’s just it and to be comfortable with your self just the way you are, to remember there is no real higher or lower we’re all just treading our own paths in our own unique way without judgement including that we place on ourselves.

Which is again unnecessary and only serves to hinder growth.

Basically we need to be good to ourselves and in so doing find the strength to be good to others” said Mike.

“Well I didn’t get the answers I thought I needed but I’m glad we had this chat, Ive learnt a lot.

Thank you Mike” said Kate.

“Your very welcome Kate.

There is one more thing; you and Arthur have come along way in a very short time, its going to take a lot of getting used to and I don't think its going to stop here either but I do advise you and Arthur to think very carefully about your next move and what exactly motivates your choice's".

"Thank you Mike I'll definitely take that onboard, I think I understand what you mean by what exactly motivates our choices- doesn't the motivation directly effect the outcome somehow?"

"That's right Kate but I wont tell you exactly how it works, I'll leave that one for you to figure out for yourself!.

Well we'd better get back to the others they'll be wondering where we've got too!" said Mike.

They arrived back at the lake, everyone was waiting to go.

"How it go?" asked Arthur.

“Very informative. I tell you about it later. What are we going to do now?” said Kate.

“I’m going to head for home” said Mike.

“Yeah we’d better do the same, its getting on now. Do you two want to come back to the farm?” said John.

“I think I’d like to get back to town, my parents will probably be getting a little worried by now!” said Arthur.

“And you Kate?” asked Mary.

“I think I’ll do the same, Ive got a lot of thinking to do?” replied Kate.

“OK then dear’s, don’t be strangers will you?” said Mary.

"Definitely not!" said Kate.

They all hugged and got into their respective vehicles and set off back towards Vantage.

Kate was very quiet on the drive back.

On reaching town Arthur turned off towards his parents place hooting a good-bye to the others, they hooted in reply and drove on.

"Could you drop me at the inn?" asked Kate "I'd like some time to mulch over everything that's happened".

"Sure" said Arthur thinking she looked tired "I'll nip over and see you tomorrow night".

"That'll be great!" said Kate.

Arthur stopped outside Bob's, they hugged Kate kissing him lightly, said "See you soon babe!" and got out picking her bag of the floor she smiled at Arthur and was gone.

CHAPTER 11.

Arthur woke early the next morning.

On getting home the previous night he'd gave his parents a brief summary of his and Kate's recent experiences, missing out most of the more sensational stuff thinking they'd think him mad.

They were both very happy Arthur had enjoyed himself so much but now as far as they were concerned it was time for him to get back to reality.

Arthur's dad told him he was needed in the shop the next day and he expected him to be up bright and breezy and ready to work.

Arthur felt his parents were being a little unfair, their tone was very degrading and they didn't really seem that pleased about how well he and Kate were getting on.

“Oh well” he thought “I suppose they mean well, probably a little worried about me!.

Getting up was a chore the following morning Arthur really had to struggle just to get out of bed, he couldn’t quite figure out why this was, he just felt so tired and weak.

He also had a strange shaky feeling almost as if he was disjointed somehow- kind of sitting outside himself, his mind wasn’t working right either he couldn’t put his finger on why it just felt as if it were spiralling out of the norm.

He thought it might have something to do with the change in energy since he was back in town but immediately dispelled this thought thinking it was foolish and illogical, he decided to just get on with his day so he got dressed and went down stairs to breakfast.

The rest of the day continued like this, it didn’t help that his father seemed to be purposely trying to wind him up.

He wouldn't stop, every five seconds he seemed to be on Arthur's back getting him to run around back and forth to the store room fetching this and that.

On days like this Arthur usually would just relax into it and it wouldn't seem so bad but today it was really getting to him.

When he thought of all the fantastic things that had happened recently it all just seemed so pointless and small but at the same time part of himself was telling him at the back of his mind he had to blend with these conflicting emotions but dispite that he still couldn't shift the feeling of unease that seemed to be dogging him.

He resigned himself to his fate and tried to get on with his work.

Kate's day was quite different she got up feeling great all the stuff that had happened recently was simply incredible the experiences they'd had plus the insights that had followed whilst talking to Mike, it was so fantastic and now she was feeling totally exuberant.

She started her day with a rather large breakfast of fried sausage with poached egg and toast toped off with heavy lashings of butter.

Kate had never enjoyed a meal so much in her life,(unbelivable as that may seem!) she didn't even flinch when Bob the owner of the aptly named "Bobs hole" came over with her coffee and the usual lewd remark.

"So, ya like the mountains round these parts do ya?.

Bet our Arthur showed you all the site's, Eh lill miss!" he had said giving the obvious connotations to his little speech and an ugly little grin.

Kate didn't bite, she just said "Thank you!, yes!" and gave him her sweetest smile.

Bob looked affronted and a little disappointed, he walked back over to the bar and turned up the sport commentary on his radio.

Kate smiled to herself and turned her attention to her note book and began writing the last few days events, as she wrote she began to take on board all that had transpired once again and seeing it all from entirely new angles, her mind was buzzing.

Reliving her experiences whilst she wrote she didn't notice the man enter the bar order a beer and sit across the room from her, he was studying her face and movements with an interested look on his face.

"May I join you?".

Kate looked up, he seemed to be in his late thirties with dark hair and an open friendly face.

"Certainly" she said in a non-chalant manner but was a little annoyed at the interruption.

“Thank you, my names Scot Timberton I’m a sales executive from Telberg I’m doing a little business up at the mall here in town, What’s your name?”.

“I’m Kate” said Kate extending her hand, he took it and smiled expectantly, Kate continued.”I’m a writer, Ive been doing some research in this area trying to put together some ideas for a book” for some reason Kate felt she didn’t want to tell this man anymore than that, in fact all she wanted to do now was stand up and walk away.

“Any luck?” asked Scott.

Something about his manner routed her to the spot, she felt her very will draining into this man, her mind began to warp the warm constructive feeling she’d felt whilst writing was quite suddenly gone and replaced with a feeling of extreme discomfort making her want to leave but for some reason it felt impossible to leave this man.

Like to do so would be rude and to be rude to this man was so very wrong.

Also she knew he was doing it on purpose but every time she tried to hold that thought to break his hold she'd suddenly feel that to do so would make something horrible happen, some kind of disaster would befall her.

"Eh, mmm" -she couldn't believe how weak she sounded, it made her feel disgusted with her self, who the hell was this man!.

"A little" she said instantly finding a new 'strength' in herself to tell this man all that had happened recently and all she felt.

The man sat quietly waiting, Kate felt compelled to speak.

-Sometimes, help can come from the most unexpected places.

"Dear-o-dear, what's going on here then!?" said Bob leering at Kate, suddenly standing over them.

Kate could have kissed him.

“Nothing!” she said finding her voice “Could you send a coffee up to my room please Bob?, its been lovely talking to you Jack,(she lied) oh sorry Scott (she said in all honesty), bye then”.

She hurried away.

“See you again Kate!” Scott called smugly after her.

It made her skin crawl, she felt him laugh to himself at this.

Up stairs she paced the room trying to shake the dirty feeling he had congaed to her, he’d managed to touch deep inside her, right to her heart and violate her.

She felt jumpy and scared, why would he do that?.

He’s life must be a living hell, Kate was tuning in to his energy and analysing it, the fear was gone she was surprised to find she was feeling pity towards him.

He was a slave to his own weaknesses and he thought himself a master, he was actually so insecure he needed to constantly reassure himself by manipulating people and proving he's worth.

Kate wanted to laugh but knew in part that was due to the residue anger she felt towards him for what he'd just tried to do and that to do so would be giving in to her own lower emotions and would sink her to the same level thus opening her to his influences once again.

There was a knock at the door, it was Bob with her coffee, she opened the door.

Bob looked very pale and shaky also quite furtive, his eye's kept darting about the room and he did'nt make eye contact even once.

"Thank you Bob" said Kate taking the coffee, he looked like he wanted to say something but didn't, she closed the door.

“He’s had a go at Bob!” thought Kate·“What a bastard!, praying on people like that, bloody parasite!”, the anger rising once again, she took a deep breath and let it go.

Getting that off her chest she soon calmed down and settled down to write in her note book, a few moments later she was once again in the same space as earlier, relaxed and comfortable.

Arthur’s torment finally came to an end, the working day was over. He left the shop telling his father he was off to meet Kate and he might be late, he headed down to Bobs feeling that same simple joy he’d felt that night when he’d first met Kate. The joy of having a beer after a bad day although this time was a million times better because he knew he was going to see Kate as well.

He entered the bar and glancing around couldn’t see Kate anywhere so he went up to her room and knocked on the door.

A couple of moments later she answered looking as beautiful as ever in blue jeans and a red top with her hair flowing over her shoulders and down her back.

"Hi, Ive just woken up" she said "I must've fallen asleep.

Come in, Ive just got to shower and I'll be right with you!".

Arthur followed her into the room and sat on the bed whilst she went through to the bathroom.

"How was your day then?" she called from the shower.

"Totally crap!, yours?" he replied.

"Not to bad, I got some work done, have a look if you like my notebook's on the bed" Kate had decided not to mention the incident earlier with Scott, she didn't want to worry Arthur.

Arthur began looking through the book he noticed he's own name came up time and time again this made him feel good, as he read on through the parts about the sites he sort of felt the energies once again and again it dawned on him how much and how incredible all that had happened was.

They'd been really lucky to do what they'd done but it had all felt so far away whilst Arthur had been at work it was so hard to hold in that environment, but he was sure with practice he would get better at it.

Arthur wanted to ask Kate a question, he wanted to know what was going to happen next.

What was their next move?

They went down to the bar and ordered a couple of drinks and something to eat, the bar was full with the usual crowd at this time of day.

They took their drinks and sat at the corner table surveying the room, Arthur asked Kate.

“I don’t really know!” said Kate “Mike did tell me we’d have to think very carefully about our next move but I don’t know why”.

“Sounds ominous” said Arthur.

“It doe’s doesn’t it?” said Kate.

“Well what do you suppose our options are then?” asked Arthur.

“I don’t know perhaps we could return to a site and see what we feel” ventured Kate “or maybe we could check out Highcliff holdings again?, but I don’t think we’ll be very welcome after Jacks last performance at the second site!”

“I agree, I think our best bet at this point would be to just sit tight for the time being” offered Arthur.

"You've probably got a good point but I still feel as though I want to get involved again" said Kate.

"I know what you mean, I'm finding it so frustrating getting back into the normal more mundane aspects of life!" said Arthur.

"I think it's important to balance with the mundane as well as with the new reality we're experiencing, the mundane provides the root as it were you know the foundation on which the rest is built and without it the new reality would become kind of top heavy and collapse in on itself leaving the individual in an extremely unbalanced emotional state and society as a whole in complete turmoil, so it is very important that this balance is achieved!" said Kate.

"I quite agree although it doesn't really make it any easier doe's it?" said Arthur.

"No it certainly don't" said Kate with a smile "but it is definitely necessary".

Jane Bobs wife brought over they food “How’s it going you two?” she asked.

“Good” said Arthur.

“Glad to hear it Arthur, you seem really happy I’m pleased you’ve finally met someone, you two make a nice couple!” said Jane with total sincerity.

Arthur blushed and withdrew into himself.

“Thank you” said Kate thinking it was a shame she couldn’t say the same about her and Bob.

“What doe’s she see in that oaf Bob?, I mean she seems lovely and he’s such a pig!” said Kate to Arthur after Jane walked back to the bar.

"I don't know, perhaps he was different when they were younger or maybe she didn't see him for what he is, you know what they say love is blind!" replied Arthur.

"I suppose" said Kate doubtfully.

They settled down to enjoy their food speaking periodically and laughing together.

"Do you want to spend the night?" Kate asked after they'd finished.

"I'd love to" said Arthur" I'll just call home to let them know".

"OK. then I'll meet you upstairs" said Kate.

Arthur made the call and went up to Kate's room, she'd left the door open and he walked right in.

The lights were off and Kate was in bed.

Arthur closed the door, undressed and slipped in next to her.

They made love and fell into a deep sleep.

Arthur was dreaming-

The world was spinning before his eyes, it was out of control, everyone was running around chasing shadows nothing seemed real anymore it was all translucent.

The very substance of the planet itself was being pulled apart someone was sucking the life force directly out of it.

People were screaming trying to escape the tirade but there was no-where to run, he heard the planet and everybody on it scream from the very centre of their souls a scream of the purest agony then nothing...

He woke with a start, Kate was sound asleep next to him her rhythmic breathing keeping score with the night.

Arthur lay there quietly staring at the shadowed ceiling and playing the dream over and over again in his minds eye, "Could it mean anything?, and if so what?" he thought.

Eventually he fell back into a deep dreamless sleep.

Morning came, the suns rays playing, gently illuminating the wall next to the bed a warm rich golden glow permeating the otherwise sterile room.

Arthur woke to the sound of the shower, he got up walked into the bathroom slipping into the shower behind Kate, making her start at the contact.

"Can I do your back?" Arthur asked.

"Only if you kiss it first!" replied Kate her eye's alight.

They again made love confirming their coupling, they felt completely at ease with each other and had developed that symmetry of movement that people sometimes do when they feel they have found that someone special.

Their lives had joined in symbiotic union but not of the dependant variety more a supporting role helping each other and guiding each other but not directing or controlling one another.

Kate felt she'd finally found that unique relationship she'd always looked for with Arthur and she only hoped it would last and not degrade, but she was aware this was going to take a conscious effort on both sides.

As they were getting dressed they discussed this and both decided they were going to make the effort because it just felt too good to loose.

They headed down to the bar.

The bar was empty due to the time of day and the fact this was a Saturday and everyone was taking advantage of the fact to have a lay-in.

They had breakfast and decided to visit the Silvertons, along the way, before they left town Arthur decided it would be a nice idea to pick up a treat.

They stopped at the grocers and bought a nice bottle of wine and some good chocolates, with that they headed out of town towards the Silvertons farm.

Taking the side road off the main highway they came up behind a motorcade of two 4x4's, the kind used at Highcliff Holdings, one in front of and one behind a large military looking truck, the truck had a rather large object on the flat bed that was covered in a green tarpaulin strapped in place by thick thongs made of a durable flexible plastic with metal fasteners one of which had come loose and the area of tarpaulin it was meant to be holding was flapping around in the breeze.

"I wonder what's under that then?" said Arthur looking past the 4x4 in front at the loose piece of tarpaulin.

Kate followed his gaze, "Yes, I'm quite interested myself!" she said.

At that moment almost as if on command a gust of wind lifted the edge of the tarpaulin high over the lump, revealing what appeared to be drain-pipes held together in a block formation.

Arthur looked on puzzled, his brow creasing as he did so.

The answer came to them both simultaneously, picturing news reports in their mind's eye.

"That's a rocket launcher!!" said Kate shocked.

"Yeah, the ground to air type, Ive seen them on T.V!" replied Arthur "What on earth do they want with one of those?".

Kate already knew the answer to that,"Their going to try to shoot down a visitor!" she said.

The car swerved dangerously "No, they cant be that stupid!" said Arthur, his countenance instantly changing to belay that yes he thought they probably could be that stupid, Jack would do anything if he thought it would advance himself in any way.

"We'd better get over to the Silvertons" he said.

They turned off onto the drive to the farm and pulled up out side the house and got out.

"Hi there you two!" called out John from the porch, "Mary guess who's here!" he called into the house.

Mary came out on to the porch “Oh hello dears” said Mary “Do come in wont you”, they climbed the steps. “What’s wrong?” said Mary taking in the look on their face’s.

“You wont believe what we’ve have just seen!” said Kate.

“Come in and tell us all about it then my dear” said Mary placing an arm around Kate’s back and leading her into the kitchen, the two men followed, John looking expectantly at Arthur.

Kate and Mary sat on the couch, Arthur pulled up a chair from the table and John put the kettle on and did likewise.

Kate reiterated what they had seen on the way over.

Mary had gone white whilst John had gone scarlet with rage.

“The dumb bloody assholes!, what do they think their doing, when I get my hands on that Jack fella’ I’m going to rip him in half!” said John.

“Language John!” said Mary, some colour returning to her face. “That’s not going to help any one, what are we going to do?, doe’s any one have any ideas?”.

“I reckon I’ll give Mike a call and get him over, the more minds the better on this one!, I think” said John calming down somewhat, he went out to the hall to make the call.

Mary poured the tea and Arthur opened the chocolates, “They might ease the tension!” he said taking in Kate’s look, she gave him a weak smile and took a chocolate.

She had to admit it did make her feel a lot better.

John entered the room “There’s no answer!” he said looking concerned.

Arthur offered him a chocolate and a half smile, John returned the smile and ate a chocolate.

There was a knock on the door, John jumped up and answered it.

The others heard a guffaw of surprise.

John re-entered the room, behind him walked Mike.

“So what’s up then?” he said looking serious, Arthur offered a chocolate.

Mike laughed at himself and took one.

Kate told him what they’d seen.

“Well we’ll have to do something about that then wont we!” he said taking another chocolate.

“Yes, but what?” asked Arthur.

“I don’t know!, I’ll have to meditate on it.I’ll be back in an hour” he took another chocolate, left the house and walked off towards the fields.

“Well, I’ll put something light to eat together, you make yourselves comfortable I think we’re in for a long night!” said Mary.

Mike was back in just over an hour, he entered the kitchen and sat down.

The air around him seem to crackle with energy, he stood out from he’s surroundings.

“Ive got a plan!” he said, everyone looked at him expectantly.

“First we’ve got to build your energies, we’re going to need to be at our best for this!”.

Mary passed out the sandwiches she’d made.

“Don’t fill up on those!” warned Mike as they began to eat, “eat just enough to quell any hunger you may be feeling” at this he noticed the empty box of chocolates and couldn’t help laughing.

Arthur looked up guiltily. “So what’s the plan?” he asked.

“Well after we’ve eaten I’m going to take you all aside one by one and channel some energy into each of you, after Ive done that you have to sit quietly being very careful not to expel any of the energy I’m going to give you.

If you do this right which I think you will you find your awareness will rise, you must I cant stress this enough!, you must remain in your own centre with this energy and allow your perceptions to rise.

Once we’re all operating on this level we’re going to link up and try to divert the visitors with our combined energies, I’m guessing that the people up at the complex will be using those machines you told us about to attract the visitors, hopefully we can out do they energies and bring the visitors to us instead and maybe even warn them somehow” said Mike.

“Sounds plausible” said Kate “After all we did attract them before and that time we wasn’t even trying but I don’t think we should do it here, we don’t want Jack to know that we’re the one’s spoiling his little plan”.

“I agree” said Arthur” Also we don’t want to bring them to John and Mary’s doorstep, if we can help it”.

“Where then?” said John.

“My place” said Mike “there’s another site on my land and no-one knows it’s there, we can use that, also it would be easier to raise your vibrations there”

“You’ve never told me about that!” said John looking alittle hurt.

“There was never any real cause to John, until now!” replied Mike with obvious concern.

“Sound good to me, but aren’t you worried about them tracking us there?” asked Arthur.

“It’s hard enough to get there on foot and impossible to do it in a vehicle- they’ll never be able to get there in time” said Mike “It’s the obvious choice”.

A little later they set off, it was just approaching late afternoon.

CHAPTER 12.

They arrived at Mikes farm.

"Wait here, I wont be a moment" said Mike as they got out of their respective vehicles.

He ran inside the house and came out with a couple of torch's and an armful of out-door candles.

"This way!" he said indicating a dirt track leading due east.

They followed the lane for about a mile and then turned off through a field, walking around the perimeter of the next field they came across a strand of pine trees which they entered Mike still leading the way Arthur had taken some of the candles for him.

They walked a little way in amongst the trees until they came to a small ravine with a stream running through the centre.

They cautiously climbed down to the bottom, it was just moving on to dusk.

As they reached the bottom Kate noticed there were the same kind of dream poles that were at the first site her and Arthur had visited plus there were standing stones dotted around in a rough circle, these were nothing like the stone statues they'd seen previously these were just plain granite but there was something in the layout that gave Kate that same familiar feeling she'd experienced before.

Mike began placing the candles around the perimeter of the circle, Arthur was helping.

"Kate stand in the centre of the circle will you" said Mike "and let me know what you feel".

"OK." said Kate, she entered the circle and was immediately struck by the intensity of the energy, it was whipping around her at an incredible speed, she felt completely lost. Her mind was spinning she didn't know what to think.

"Well" said Mike "What do you feel?"

"Lost" said Kate "I can't hold a single thought!".

"Like I told you before" began Mike "don't try to hold anything, sit yourself down and let it all go you'll feel a little strange at first but as long as you don't try to hold on to any thing you will stabilise.

Try it, sit down and let go!".

"I'll try!" said Kate, she sat down and tried not to concentrate, it was the most difficult thing she'd ever been asked to do.

The abstract thoughts were increasing, she was disgusted with some of them her repulsion to the worst of her thoughts only seemed to increase their prevalence and make them stronger she tried to push them away but again they came back stronger so out of desperation she sat with them and was amazed to find them start to lift and dissipate.

As this happened Kate could feel her energy level increase but not only by the amount but also the quality of her energy had improved, she mentally reached out to this feeling,- grateful for the cessation of the previous thought patterns and as she done this her energy plummeted.

"Don't hold it not whilst your building it, just let go and sit in yourself, it'll come of its own accord" said Mike watching her intently.

She done as he said and immediately her energy began to rise again this time it felt stronger and more secure, she understood what Mike meant about sitting in herself she did just that and could feel self control return and with it that absolute clarity of thought she'd experienced before, after the abstract thoughts of a moment ago this was complete bliss.

"Well done!" said Mike, he and Arthur had lighted the candles and Mary and John were both watching her smiling.

"Now Kate" continued Mike "Come out of the circle but once you do you'll have to hold the energy, now you must do what you couldn't do earlier, hold the energy and that feeling of love you must try to do this no matter what your environment"

Kate stood still "I don't understand" she said "why must I now hold the energy when a moment ago that was the very thing I mustn't do!".

"Because" said Mike "When building your energy in a place like this you have to let the energy enter and rely on your subconscious to align the energy correctly, it does this by first dumping your lower expressions then allowing the energy to enter and align correctly. So its very important you let go of the ego and need to be in control and let the process complete itself, but once the process is complete it takes a conscious effort to hold that vibration and not drop back to your usual functional level, its like a muscle the more you tense or train it the more it'll grow you'll find this is true throughout your growth process at least until you reach a point in your personal evolution where you'll need to make less effort to hold your energy".

"But then there's always other stuff to keep you busy so in truth it never really gets any easier" he added with a small laugh.

"I understand" said Kate and she stepped out of the circle, making the effort to hold her vibration.

She seemed to manage it, Mike smiled at her "Well done" he said again.

"Thank you" replied Kate "but shouldn't we be getting started?".

"We already have, Arthur will you go and sit in the circle, Kate go and sit somewhere out of the way and try to sit in your own space and don't key in to anything as your perception widens, remember you need to keep your energy".

Arthur went and sat in the circle and Mike talked him through the same process, it was now dark.

“I’m glad we decided to come here to do this, it’s a lot easier this way than my channelling the energy into you all myself” said Mike as Arthur came out of the circle and found somewhere quiet to sit alone.

Mike again repeated the process with Mary and John.

After Mike stepped in the circle himself and everyone had had the chance to sit for a while. Mike asked them to join him in the circle.

They sat down facing each other and burst out laughing, their minds had already connected and were working as one.

“Right” thought Mike “Ready!”.

“Yes” the others thought back in unison.

With pure conceptual communication they knew what they had to do.

As one they tuned into the life force and spread it around them and up, like a beacon to light up the sky, although only to the inner eye.

It was the most wonderful feeling, the purest kind of love totally unconditional this was the substance of the Universe the very life blood of all things.

It pulsed through them, around them and connected with the beings.

They heard a high pitched whine and there was a new star in the sky…

Back at the complex Jack was fuming all the work they'd put in and now finally the powers that be had given him the hardware he needed to prove just what this technology could do, he was going to get one of those ships or at least part of one but still enough physical evidence to prove once and for all to those bum's in Washington that this project wasn't a waste of money and man power.

But now something had gone wrong, they'd been running the machine's for over an hour now and just when the radar picked up a ship entering the area it had gone else where.

This couldn't happen now not with the official here, he'd come down with the hardware.

Jack had no idea they were sending someone along to observe, it had to happen tonight, he could feel the smugness emanating from this man in the grey suit he was so confidant it was all crap and Jack knew if he didn't provide results tonight they were going to close down the project as just another failure and he just couldn't let that happen. They were just so close. Plus John the snide was being no help what so ever, sucking up to this man when ever the opportunity arose, it made Jack sick but what felt worse was the fact he was actually starting to miss the weasel sucking up to him- this made him shiver with self disgust.

"I bet those two kids have some part to play in all this!" he thought.

"Where's it gone?" he asked the man at the radar screen.

"It's disappeared sir!" said the man "about 12 miles south of here"

"What's gone wrong?" he asked the two technicians, -they didn't want any part of this but didn't feel as though they had a choice.

"We don't know, the machines working perfectly!" said the taller man, secretly pleased at this course of events.

"We've had ghost reports on radar before and found nothing!" said the man from Washington calmly.

"These are not ghosts!" said Jack through gritted teeth.

The man from Washington just gave Jack a disdainful look over his half moon bifocal spectacles.

At Mikes the ship hovered above them illuminating the area with its soft violet light.

Kate and Arthur began sending mental image's of the rocket launcher and the complex, whilst the others kept up the flow of life force.

Kate and Arthur felt a receptive mind "Their receiving us!" they sent to the others.

At that moment the light changed to a bright green, Kate vanished closely followed by the ship.

"Oh my god!" spluttered Arthur "They've taken her!, why would they take her we were trying to help them!".

"I don't know!" said Mike.

Their energy had plummeted, all they could feel now was fear.

“We must raise our energy!” said Mike.

“SOD YOUR ENERGY MIKE!” shouted Arthur suddenly getting angry “WHERE’S THAT GOT US, KATE’S JUST BEEN ABDUCTED BY BLOODY ALIENS”, tears were streaming down his face.

“Arthur I know your upset, none of us saw that coming but I honestly don’t think their going to hurt her do you?” said Mike, trying to sound calmer than he felt.

“I don’t know if their going to hurt her or not do I?” said Arthur starting to calm down a little “What can we do?”

“If we raise our energy again we may be able to re-establish contact!” said Mike.

"Lets do it!" said Arthur breathlessly, beginning to regain control.

Kate found herself in a soft chair of some kind, it felt like jelly but more cohesive and stable.

She was surrounded by a pink glow that obscured any detail except three purple orb's about six inch's in diameter that were floating about four foot in front of her, they were moving in a horizontal figure of eight formation following each other around the circuit.

Surprisingly she felt no fear instead she felt warm and loved, she knew instinctively she was amongst friends how ever far removed those friends were!.

"Why did you take me?" she asked out loud.

"We chose you because we thought you were the most susceptible to what we had to show your kind!, and we thank you for the warning us about the intentions of those troubled ones of your kind, we thought the energies they were exhibiting were too advanced for them".

This came in conceptual form immediately raising Kate's vibration to match, she'd not realised it had fallen since being taken on board the ship.

"What do you want to show me?" Kate asked.

The space around her exploded into a million stars then nothing a pure blackness that seemed to last for an age but in fact only lasted a couple of seconds then was replaced with the image of a planet very much like Earth but Kate knew it wasn't Earth, the land masses were different shapes and there was obviously no pollution in the atmosphere.

"Of course there wouldn't be!" Kate thought ironically.

She felt the beings share the joke.

"So you have a sense of humour then?" she sent to them.

"You'll know all you'll need to know about us soon enough!" was the reply "first we wish to show you our home".

Kates awareness entered the atmosphere and zoomed in on one of the continents, as they flew over the land mass a city came into view, it was beautiful, made up of tall streamline towers and gossamer like bridges spanning rivers of the most clearest blue and stretching impossibly between the buildings at unimaginable heights, the towers were the most delicate silver that caught the light of the sun and reflected it in a thousand rainbows over the surrounding metropolis, the sun was very much like our own only it looked a little bigger and warmer.

"What a wonderful place to live!" thought Kate.

"The reason we wish to show this to you is to tell you this is still a possibility on your planet, it's not yet to late for your kind to develop this society, a society built on Love and compassion or to put it another way Heaven on Earth, this was the plan we had in mind when we populated your planet just as it was on ours but we left you too long and you got lost just as we did, but now you are finding yourselves once again releasing who you truly are O sibling of the stars!"

Kate was dumb struck there was so much to take in. "What do you mean you populated our planet?" she asked.

"No little sister we are not that which you call god(they sent reading her underlying thoughts), we know this is hard for you but you are not alone we have contacted many like you who are waking up, you are the fore bears of your kind and you will help change the way your people think but not with words or instruction only with your presence will you accomplish your tasks and bring in the transformational energies that will ignite your peoples memory of who they are!"

"Why did you create us?" asked Kate.

"You still miss-understand us sister we did not create you.

We are your kin, we once travelled the stars together, there were many such tribes at that point we were the students of the cosmos, children of the stars, living light conscious but we felt we'd learnt all we could from our elevated position and there was more to be learnt at the lower levels of existence so we allowed ourselves to drop into the denser reality that is the flesh state.

In so doing we found such things as emotion and pain but most dangerous of all we discovered the ego that which makes one adopt the lowest energies and hold them like your own, things we knew not in our previous existence and like you we forgot our true purpose and began to relish this life of the ego and went to far, this will not happen to you.

Like you we to were aided in our return just as we now aide you helping to provide the energies needed to guide you home but there will be a thing done with you that has never been done in all the universe before now.

You will bring the flesh with you on your journey back to the light and incorporated it in your lives to walk once again this higher path but you shall go above that which went before now you will be truly whole in this combined existence of loving light and flesh, one feeding the other we welcome you our kin back to the fold you are now the true teachers, many of us are now being born to you to help bring in this wonderful reality but we have another motivation.

We too wish to experience this higher existence".

"It's all so much to take in, by what your saying you never made it to this reality- you died?" asked Kate her heart suddenly filling with grief.

"This is true little one we did not complete our turn just as many others did not, you and your Earth are the only ones left of this particular expression of life but because you managed to out live all the others you now are our only hope and so we are all helping you to complete that which you are so close to completing".

"So we're alone in the Universe?" asked Kate.

"No you are not alone their are many aware beings on other planets that like you are in the flesh but yours is the only one from our tribe and the first in the cosmos to make this transition, life explores every possibility little one this is true from the single celled creature to a galaxy our tribe was exploring this possibility but out of the many yours is the successor!.

"I think I'm beginning understand" said Kate "I'm not sure of the ramifications in my reality, but I'm willing to find out!"

"That's the way little sister never tire of the urge to explore, just as your people once explored the surface of your world you must now explore the inner surface of your world!"

"Thank you I will!" said Kate.

"Know that we Love you and will always stand next to you in your explorations to guide and aide you in your growth process, most sacred of beings we must now return you to your friends and loved ones".

CHAPTER 13

It took Arthur and the others a full hour to regain their energies enough to send out the life force needed to attract the visitors, as they joined in mind and sent the energy up the ship appeared directly above them once again glowing bright green then light blue and was gone leaving Kate behind.

“Oh. thank God!” said Arthur tears forming in his eyes.

“Not quite!” Kate replied “Iv got so much to tell you all”.

“I bet” said Mike “Let’s go back to the house shall we?”

“Sounds good” said John eyeing Kate suspiciously.

They reached the farm house and entered through the back door straight into the kitchen, Mike fed the banked fire in the grate, turned on an electric kettle and got out a bottle of brandy from the cupboard.

"Now your talking!" said John nodding at the bottle

Mike poured everyone a stiff drink and settled himself down.

"Well Kate?" he prompted.

"You know I know what just happened but the more I think about it the crazier it sounds" said Kate.

"We know it's happened" said Arthur holding her hand "We saw you get abducted!".

"No I wasn't abducted they just wanted to show me something, but that's the maddening thing, it was so unreal if it didn't happen to me I wouldn't believe it!" said Kate.

“Don’t worry dear we’ll believe you” said Mary showing concern.

“I hope so!” she said and went on to share what she had learnt.

“Wow!” was all Arthur said.

The others were quiet for the longest time.

“That’s certainly a lot to bear in mind” said Mike but it would make sense, I mean life doe’s kind of mirror itself and its true that life as we know it doe’s explore every available possibility to find the most effective way to survive in a given environment, you know-that’s natural selection”.

“But that’s a hell of a leap in thought to what Kate just said” said John.

“Not really its just on a larger scale and lets not forget we saw Kate taken” said Arthur.

“Still, all that stuff about living an existence comprising of both the body and the energy in that context is certainly possible in theory, I mean it’s not like it hasn’t been said before.

In fact some ancient cultures are believed to have done just that and in a lot of cases ascension of this sort has been linked to crude models of what would appear to be space craft and space men, it’s not a widely accepted theory in scientific circles but its definitely present and has been for some time” said Mike.

“I’m willing to let it in and take it all on-board but I’m not quite ready to integrate such a concept into my everyday reality as yet” said John surprising everyone with his sudden eloquence.

“Well it’s been a long day shall we turn in then?” asked Mike “Your all welcome to stay there’s a spare room out back and the sofa in the lounge turns into a bed”.

"We'll take the sofa then" said Arthur.

There was an authoritative knock at the door, making everyone jump, they looked at each other around but no-one offered an explanation.

Mike went to the door followed by Arthur and John.

It was Jack from the complex and he was alone!.

"Hi there!" he said "May I come in?

"What are you doing here?" asked Mike keeping Jack on the doorstep, Mary and Kate joined them at the door.

"Ive just come to let you know, you've won!" he said looking as sneaky as ever.

"What do you mean?" asked Arthur.

"Well I know you did something to distract the U.F.O from the complex because it disappeared from radar near here and I remembered you(he indicated Mike) told me your farm was out this way well basically due to tonight's outcome Ive lost my funding and Ive just come over to congratulate you on costing the human race all the advances we could have made in this area of science and I hope your all very proud of yourselves in keeping human evolution at a standstill".

Kate couldn't help laughing.

"Well I'm pleased you find it so funny Kate!" said Jack angrily and with that his turned on his heel and walked away into the drive where he span around.

"I'm not stopping this research you'll see I'm gonna be famous, I might be leaving this area but as I told you before there's lots of these sites around the world!" he said.

"Your forgetting one thing!" said Mike.

"What's that then?" asked Jack arrogantly staring at then fixedly.

"There's lots of people like us too!"

Mike replied, they all laughed and went back in the house leaving Jack standing in the cold.

ADVANTAGE -PART 2

CHAPTER 1

It's been three years since Kate and Arthur's adventures in and around the town of Vantage.

After that fateful night at their friend Mike's house the 'Visitors' stopped coming to that particular part of the world and Kate wanted to continue her journeys around the United states, Arthur decided this was what he'd been waiting for and continued with Kate.

Over the course of the last few years they'd shared a lot, their relationship had gone through some difficult times that they'd both done their utmost to work through.

Through this process they'd discovered the differing aspects of their personalities that had clashed and had resolved to work on the conflicts, some they had managed to balance and some they hadn't.

They'd learnt that you cant have everything and that some conflicts were actually good for their every day lives and their growth as people- they continued to work.

Now they were preparing for their biggest journey yet, Kate had with Arthur's help wrote the transcript of their previous adventures in Vantage and the eventual out-come.

They'd originally tried to relate their work as an account of their actual experiences but had found no one willing to publish it until they changed it to fiction, then there was no stopping it.

The book was a raging success it had stayed in the best sellers for an unbelievable twelve weeks.

The money resulting from this had given them the opportunity to widen their horizons, with that in mind they began to prepare for this journey.

They were going to Europe, their trip would start in Britain and progress to the continent, that was the extent of their plans, following their combined intuition they'd decided to leave most of the trip open to chance.

They arrived at the Airport late, flustered and irritable the cab ride through New York had been a night-mare, the traffic was horrendous.

The city was yet to recover from the travesty that was September 11th 2001 although this was some nine months later (June 2002) the issue of the taliban in Afghanistan was still far from fully resolved and there was definitely an aura of miss-trust palpable in the city that seemed to have an underlying effect on all that went on.

No one really spoke of the terrifying event that had transpired but it was certainly present in their minds.

Kate and Arthur couldn't wait to put the place behind them.

The Airport was worse still, there were security men every where and all the staff seemed to be more than a little jumpy, which was of course understandable given the recent events.

They just made their flight and were rushed through the boarding routine.

Finally they were settled on the plane awaiting take off, the plane taxed and took off shaking and rattling as it did so, Arthur and Kate held hands this was a first for both of them and neither were enjoying the experience.

Eventually they were in the air and the ride smoothed out, Kate ordered a large brandy and Arthur a beer.

They discussed the trip ahead,

"So we're landing at Gatwick and staying at one of the local hotel's then?" confirmed Arthur.

"Yeah I reckon that'll be the best bet for now!" replied Kate "At least that way we can get our bearings before we move on".

"I tell you one thing, I don't fancy going in to London- after New York Ive had enough of city life for the time being" said Arthur grimacing.

"Yeah I know what you mean, it was a bit trying wasn't it?" said Kate.

“A bit!, my energy’s all over the place!” replied Arthur.

“I know” said Kate “I can feel it!”.

“What, and yours isn’t?” said Arthur accusingly.

“Well a little!” Kate conceded.

The hostess brought over their drinks and asked what they wanted for their meal, they ordered and she left.

After they’d eaten Arthur fell asleep and Kate watched the in flight movie, it was one of her favourites.

The plane arrived at Gatwick a little after mid-night and they found a room in one of the surrounding hotels.

That night they tried to decide as to where to go next, they were both to tired to reach a mutual choice so the only decision they made that night was to go to bed.

They woke early due to the jet-lag and after a shared bath went down to breakfast,

Kate thought the food was fantastic, "there's subtle differences in the flavour" she said whilst munching toast referring to the British food.

"That's probably due to the lesser amount of additives, they don't go for them here like we do in the states" answered Arthur.

The waitress brought over their cooked breakfast's of fried bacon, sausages and scrambled egg's, plus more toast.

"That's more like it!" said Kate "Thank you" she said to the waitress.

"Your welcome" said the waitress smiling.

The waitress left them to it.

"Where are we going next then?" asked Arthur pouring over travel magazines of the British Isles.

"I like the look of Cornwall" said Kate.

"It doe's look pretty doesn't it?" said Arthur.

"Yes plus I'm kinda interested in the stories of witchcraft and sorcery that permeate the area!" said Kate, her eyes lighting up with mischief.

"You'll suite it, you look like an elf yourself when you pull a face like that" said Arthur.

Kate gave an impish laugh.

After breakfast they went upstairs to pack.

“We can rent a car from the Airport” said Arthur “and drive ourselves down”.

“Good idea!” said Kate “We could check out Glastonbury on our way down” she added gesturing with a road map.

“Sounds good” said Arthur feeling excited about this trip for the first time in ages.

They set off a little before lunch, Arthur was driving and finding it very hard to relax whilst (as he saw it) driving on the wrong side of the highway or, this was going to take some getting used to- the motor way.

Reaching Glastonbury during the mid afternoon, they’d been very lucky with the traffic, they drove into the main part of town and eventually found somewhere to park getting out Arthur was immediately struck by the diversity of people in such a small place.

Everyone seemed so relaxed it was contagious, Kate and Arthur gently slipped into the groove and wondered around the shops.

Kate bought a large rose quartz rock crystal and Arthur bought a bo-raun, a type of Irish drum made from a thin strip of wood bent and fixed into a circle with cross supports in the centre and a skin stretched across the circumference which is beaten with a small rounded piece of wood in a circular motion that the shop assistant had promised Arthur he'd get the hang of eventually.

After that they decided to stop for something to eat before going on to Cornwall,

they found a nice cafe called The Rainbow and sat down outside enjoying of last of the days warmth whilst watching the people go by, the waiter came over, he was wearing an unusual waist coat covered in little mirrors and brightly coloured embroidery with wonderful coloured stripy trousers and a load shirt, he took to Kate instantly and began pouring on the charm.

Kate was really enjoying herself, she got hit on quite a lot, especially since she'd been with Arthur but she generally paid little or no attention to it, this man on the other hand had her captivated he's smile was so open plus his demeanour gentle with an underlying strength that she found gave off an irresistible feeling of knowledge and promise.

Arthur was beginning to feel uncomfortable, Kate didn't usually behave like this.

The man was completely ignoring the fact Arthur was there he found this completely contemptuous, it made him feel small and un-wanted also a little hurt, it was almost as if he were invading this mans space as opposed to the other way round.

He decided he was going take action, this man wasn't going to get away with treating him this way.

As he made this choice he noticed the mans demeanour subtly change, he didn't seem so confidant or self assured in fact he seemed less radiant.

Arthur knew he would need to act now if he was going to act at all but there seemed to be no real point anymore because Kate also seemed less enthralled the spell so to speak had broken.

The man turned his attention to his work, took their order and walked away.

“That was strange” said Kate as the man left.

“I know, you were completely hooked into his energy for a while there!” Arthur replied a little curtly.

“It was funny” said Kate reading Arthur’s tone “I mean he had me captivated I forgot you were there, I’m sure that wasn’t entirely false, he’s energy I mean but he was being completely incorrect in his actions.

The way he used his energy to cut you out and pull me in, he’s obviously still got a lot to learn dispite he’s obvious talent, he needs to work more on he’s intentions and to truly look at what it is that motivates him in certain situations”.

“I agree” said Arthur “but still he’s just shown us something we didn’t know, so I suppose we can thank him in many ways”.

The waiter came back with their order, he’s manner was decidedly different; he seemed withdrawn and he’s energy had noticeably dropped, although he was polite and still quite nice.

“What do you make of that?” asked Kate.

“I think he knows he was in the wrong and feels a little bad about it” Arthur replied.

“I agree but I don’t think he’ll have to much compunction about doing it again when that particular button is pushed next time” said Kate.

“Yeah, well some people never truly learn do they?” said Arthur.

"No, I would guess in that case it'll be some time before he manages to break the cycle, still never mind that's his journey not ours!" answered Kate.

"Quite right, besides all our journey involves at this moment as far as I can see is to make the most of this wonderful food in front of us before it gets too cold!" said Arthur smiling.

The meal was really good, they had a selection of grilled fresh vegetables, cheese's and bread with a couple of organic coffee's whilst watching the people go about their evenings.

"This towns amazing everything seems so clear and obvious, especially after the hustle and bustle of New York" said Arthur between mouthfuls.

"I know" said Kate" look at that couple over there", she indicated a young couple holding hands walking down the opposite side of the street, the girl was looking about her continuously as if she were trying to see everything at once.

She would occasionally make eye contact with another man and then suddenly look away, she didn't seem to realise that she was causing them to look at her and when they did she took on a pained exasperated look like she was always bothered by such things and wished they would stop.

The young man on the other hand was trying his utmost to appear strong as if these things didn't worry him and he could handle it, it was obviously taking all he had to keep this up.

"What a way to live!" said Arthur" Imagine spending all your time projecting such an image, the opportunities lost and the lack of quality of life must be awful, it cant help but have a detrimental effect on your state of mind.

I mean to have that illusion shattered would pretty much crush him and it's such a fragile illusion to uphold, doesn't he know that there's always someone bigger around the next corner!".

Arthur's words were prophetic the couple crossed the road and almost walked straight into another older couple obviously living a similar lifestyle, the older man instantly taking offence at the younger energy and throwing his own at him.

The younger man buckled as they passed, losing his stride and rhythm in his walk.

But was supported by his partner, she putting her arm across his mid drift and laughing at some relived private joke.

The man regained his composer and they walked on, him once again projecting the same "strength".

"Wow" said Kate "I wonder if they even know what just happened".

"Probably at some higher point in their awareness but a doubt if it registered consciously, that's Ego for you I suppose!" replied Arthur.

“Yeah, Ego will always come up and bite you on the bum!” said Kate “and sometimes like that with those two you don’t even realise it!”.

“Yeah but that’s why we have each other to spot it when we don’t ourselves, you know to be supportive and not dependent like our two friends there!” said Arthur.

“Yeah, we are very lucky to have found each other I think sometimes I forget that!” said Kate by way of an apology.

“I think its good to remember in that case that it’s all in the right place at the right time, you know sometimes you have to forget something’s to learn others” said Arthur also by way of an apology.

“And to talk openly without fear of judgement is also very important” added Kate.

“I agree” replied Arthur.

They finished their meal feeling closer than before and called for the check, the same waiter came over obviously forgetting his last experience and tried to once again captivate Kate, he had no chance his energy couldn't find entry, he took Arthur's card and walked off obviously miffed.

after leaving the cafe Arthur and Kate booked into a Hotel and settled in for the evening.

The next day they headed on towards Cornwall, as Kate was driving (she adapted to the British roads easier than Arthur) Arthur was looking at the maps of the county.

"There's a place called Tintagle here, looks like it might be interesting" he said.

"Oh yeah" said Kate "What's there then?".

"It's supposed to be the same area that King Arthur lived in back in the dark ages" said Arthur.

"Sounds good but wasn't Arthur meant to have lived in Glastonbury?" asked Kate.

"I know but I reckon that's true for a lot of places in Britain, besides Ive got a good feeling about the place!" said Arthur.

"OK but just because you've got the same name I hope you wont be getting any fancy ideas above your station!" teased Kate.

"How could that be possible!" joked Arthur.

"Quite easily actually!" responded Kate "What's there though?".

"Wells there's a place called St Nectans Glen that looks good!" said Arthur holding a leaflet he'd picked up at the Cafe. "It's a waterfall and shrine plus there's also a monks cell that's still intact!".

"Another site?, this sounds familiar!" said Kate.

"It doe's doesn't it, I hope the energy's good, maybe we'll get some new material for another book?" said Arthur.

"Possibly but you never know we might have had only one book in us, but then again with everything we seem to be learning I very much doubt it" said Kate.

"Well there's always more to learn" said Arthur "You know the Zen saying don't you?"

"Which one?" asked Kate.

"The wise man admits he knows nothing!" quoted Arthur.

"Oh that one- its quite apt for us all I think" said Kate with a knowing look "But if we're talking Zen one of my favourites has to be- No conditions are permanent;

No conditions are reliable;

Nothing is self."

"Well like all Zen" said Arthur "There's a thousand different connotations that can be drawn from that, each one taking you a different route to the same truth- all is one!"

"Like -We are one being yet separate like the stars!" responded Kate "And there are many paths to the top of the same mountain".

"Yeah at the end of the day we're all cut from the same cloth, a good way to look at things if your trying to work on your Ego!" said Arthur.

"Confirmation once again!" said Kate "Everyone's puzzle is just a piece of the lager puzzle!".

"I remember!" said Arthur.

They settled down to a thoughtful silence and headed on down to Cornwall, neither expecting what was to come…

CHAPTER 2.

They reached Cornwall by early evening and found a Hotel in Boscastle a town a few miles from Tintagel, the receptionist told them that St Nectans glen was between the two towns and would be hard to find without knowing where to look.

He gave them the directions they needed and checked them in for two nights.

After moving their things into the room Kate and Arthur decided to have a look around the town.

Most places were beginning to wind down for the evening so they found a nice looking restaurant and enjoyed a good meal before returning to the Hotel.

The next morning they had an early breakfast and set off towards Tintagel, it was an overcast day the sky threatening to open at any second and pour down, the weather report had promised scattered showers throughout so they both brought macs.

The receptionist was right it was difficult finding the glen, after asking a few walkers for directions they parked in a lay-by and crossed the road following a tiny hand written sign down an equally tiny lane towards the glen.

"It's almost as though whoever runs this place doesn't want too many visitors!" exclaimed Arthur as they walked.

"Yeah I think your right but even so it's very well advertised in the local press's, maybe they think that only people who really want to visit the place will bother enough to find it" speculated Kate.

"Yeah that would be an effective form of crowd control!" replied Arthur.

The lane turned into a well walked track and led them through a woodland alongside a gurgling stream which helped give the place a very tranquil, calming quality.

Arthur and Kate settled into an almost trance like pace.

“I feel like a pilgrim or something” said Arthur after a while.

“Yeah, I can almost imagine wearing a cloak and hood and bearing a cross” said Kate.

“Yeah I see it too, a line of pilgrims the leader carrying a cross whilst the others are bearing incense and food for the monk who lived here” added Arthur.

“You mean the guardian!, -this is a very special place!” said Kate.

Their perceptions began to rise as they spoke, the surrounding trees took on an ancient feel and the air was sparkling with a thousand points of light, Kate and Arthur stopped to enjoy the spectacle, as they did so Kate began to see colours floating about an inch above the flowers and leaves.

“Can you see that?” she asked Arthur.

“See what?” he replied.

“The colours on the foliage and flowers” said Kate.

Arthur looked at the surrounding foliage allowing his eyes to relax, as he did so the colours began to appear.

“Wow!” he said “That’s amazing!, it looks so delicate almost as if its painted in water colour directly on the air.-What was that?” he added looking startled.

“What?” asked Kate.

"I don't know, I just saw something move, it looked like a hole in the air but seemed lighter somehow" he said.

"Where?" asked Kate.

"Over there by that tree" said Arthur pointing.

Kate looked where Arthur indicated and sure enough there was a disturbance in the air, kind of like small a tear in an unseen fabric.

As she looked on it move back about a hundred yards in a split second to stop by another tree.

"Wow it moved!" she said.

"I wonder what it is?" said Arthur.

As he said this both him and Kate felt their eyes being drawn to the left and as they looked back they saw that what ever it had been was gone!.

“That was strange” said Kate.

They walked on puzzled.

A few moments later they came across some steps carved directly in to the bed rock and a crude wooden hand rail, the steps were obviously ancient where as the hand rail looked very recent, they climbed the steps and followed an adjoining path along the top of the ledge looking down at the thick trees growing below.

On reaching the end of the ledge they came across a wooden gate and more recent looking steps, they followed these until to their surprise they came to a garden and Tea shop with tables and chairs set out underneath large umbrellas that was run by a friendly retired couple that owned the property, Arthur asked where the waterfall was and was told to follow an adjoining path down the rock face.

As they did so the sound of the waterfall could be heard as a loud gushing, after a moment they found themselves on a precipice over looking the waterfall.

It was amazing the water was moving at such a pace as to look white, it hit an outcrop, which over the passage of time had been worn into a bowl and cascaded over into another bowl where it swirled around like a huge washing machine then poured through a hole in that bowl and into a small lake that ran out into the stream they'd passed earlier walking through the woodland.

"The energy's wonderful here!, it's so clear and strong, I wish could live here!" said Kate semi-shouting over the noise of the fall.

"I know, I feel so much negativity draining from me, a lot of my narrower preconceptions seem to be lifting- I never knew I had so many!" said Arthur also raising his voice.

They sat for a while quietly absorbing the energy being given and letting their minds rest whilst they cleared their heads of the most prominent imbalances they were carrying at that time, finding themselves drifting into a more relaxing centred space.

After a while they felt it was time to move, this took some doing; they found they were having difficulty establishing more conventional mind-set.

This was soon helped along by the intervention of a young family coming around the corner of the precipice to admire the view.

Arthur and Kate didn't want to interfere with the family's enjoyment of the scene so saying a few polite words of greeting left the ledge and headed back up the steps towards the Tea shop.

They sat down at a table over looking trees below still feeling a little out of sorts, the weather had change slightly for the better, the sun was beginning to peak through the clouds sending a few shafts a light down where they sat.

A couple of the other tables were occupied, an elderly couple sat at one and at the other were two women in their late forty's, everyone seem preoccupied in their own conversations.

The man Arthur had spoke to earlier came over to take their order, they asked for a pot of tea and some cake and tried to acclimatise themselves to their surroundings.

A moment later the man brought over their order and left them to it, as they began to eat they started to feel better, Arthur noticed one of the women on the other table was staring at him, it began to make him feel very uncomfortable, Kate asked what was wrong.

"Those two" said Arthur slightly inclining his head towards the two women. "They keep staring at us!".

Kate looked and the other woman quickly glanced away, Kate looked back in Arthur's direction and could feel the woman's gaze on her once again, she too was starting to feel uncomfortable.

"What are they doing don't they know how intrusive their behaviour is?" said Kate angrily.

"I don't think they care!" said Arthur, he felt them laughing at his and Kate's reaction.

This made him feel angry, "How dare they, who do they think they are!" he thought.

If it was in Arthur's power at that point he would have struck the pair of them down, the sky once again became overcast.

"Your probably right, what the hell is their problem?" said Kate now starting to fume.

The two women seemed to have picked up on their change of mood, but instead of backing off they began to goad them on with their energy.

"Their bloody enjoying this!" said Arthur under his breath to Kate.

"I know, how nasty can you get!" said Kate.

The two women loved this it played right into their hands, Kate suddenly felt weak and very young- she felt like a victim and this appalled her instantly but she felt powerless to change it, the two women seemed to grow in stature and knowledge.

Kate could feel them sapping the energy out of her and Arthur to increase themselves.

She looked at Arthur to see if he saw it too but he's energy was too depleted, he looked pale, tired and weak.

She had to stop this-but how, as she thought this a glimmer of an idea came but before she could grasp it it vanished.

She mentally groped for the answer but it still eluded her, she stopped trying, she could feel the women watching her and with that came a thought,

"They were trying to see what she was doing, by groping after the illusive thought she'd moved her energy away from them and they wanted to know how she'd done it and how they could pull her back in!" with this came another realisation "They didn't know everything!, they were pretending to be knowledgeable, oh they knew how to pull from others but that was pretty much the extent of their knowledge -the rest was illusion!!".

Kate jumped, the women were leaving; they looked worried but were obviously trying not to look that way, Kate wanted to laugh no she wanted to roar with laughter but something instinctively told her that if she did she would lower herself to their level and that was one thing she would never do!.

Once the two women left Arthur very quickly recovered himself.

"What just happened?" he asked.

Kate explained.

“Well I’m glad you were together enough to see what they were up to, once they pulled me in I lost it completely!” exclaimed Arthur.

“It wasn’t due to my being more together it was, I would say luckily but I don’t believe in luck so I’d say we were just taught a valuable lesson, one I wont forget in a hurry!” said Kate.

“No, me neither!” exclaimed Arthur” although from another perspective they couldn’t have pulled me in if there was no reflection on that level, so I have to admit I have an element of them in me!”.

“That’s true!” said Kate without judgement.

The sun once again broke through the clouds sending bright shafts of light among the tables, they sat enjoying the warmth, listening to the birds singing in the nearby trees and drinking their tea.

"Have you two seen the shrine yet?" asked the man that had served them as he picked up the crockery off the recently vacated table.

"No" said Arthur "Where is it?".

"Right there" said the man pointing at the wooden door next to the kitchen area.

"And what's the building above?" asked Kate.

"That's our house" said the man "It's built over the original monks cell!".

"Wow" said Kate "The energy must be amazing!".

"That's what people tell me" the man replied "I don't know about that but since we moved here we've never had a days illness!, why don't you two check out the cell before you go?".

“Is that the shrine?” asked Arthur.

“Yes, it’s the actual place the monk slept, have a look” said the man.

“We will” said Arthur.

They got up and went through the door.

Inside there was a statue of Buddha in one corner that people had left small coins in front of and along the wall was a large water basin fed by a series of bowls coming from the ceiling, creating a wonderful tranquil gurgling as the water overflowed the bowls.

There was also a bench along a wall that Kate and Arthur sat on, they closed their eyes and let their minds drift with the sounds of the water.

Kate felt herself lift, she had the feeling her body had expanded and her inner self with it, in her minds eye she saw a calm lake;

bubbles slowly rising from the depths and popping gently on the surface.

She likened this to the negativity she knew she like everyone carried and let go.

With each bubble bursting on the surface she felt lighter, her heart felt hot in her chest, the heat spread through her tousle settling in her stomach and down her limbs, reaching the tips of her fingers and toes the energy sparked and settled to a warm glow- she felt totally at home.

Arthur relaxed against the old stone wall of the cell, closing his eyes he could feel a heart beat pulsing through the rock into the pit of his back and up his spine, spiralling across his shoulders and down his arms settling into his hands.

His hands resting on his knees began to grow hot.

This heat spread down his shines back along his thighs to his stomach and then back down his legs to his feet, making them feel like hot pieces of lead.

He felt strong, centred and at peace with himself and the world around him, at this point all was right with the world and life was a golden experience.

Arthur felt privileged to be alive.

After a while they came back to themselves and without comment left the shrine, Arthur taking a few coins from his pocket placed them in front of the Buddha and stepped out into the mid-day sun, which had now once again broke through the cloud cover and looked as though it was going to stay that way.

They thanked the man they'd spoke to earlier and walked back along the ledge towards the woodland still feeling warm and comfortable, laughing together they half slipped/half walked down the ancient steps back into the woodland.

Walking back through the woodland Arthur found he couldn't shift the feeling he was being watched.

"There's something in this wood!" he said after a while.

"You mean that strange lightness we saw earlier?" asked Kate.

"Yeah, maybe, I'm not sure, but I definitely feel like I'm being watched!" replied Arthur.

"I know what you mean" said Kate "Remember these woods are very old, there's likely to be some unusual energies here".

"Yeah that's probably it" said Arthur uncertainly.

They walked on for a while in relative silence until they came to the lane leading them back to the car.

They drove on towards Tintagle and spent the remainder of the day walking about the town taking in the shops and sights, it was a nice little town full of curiosities and images of King Arthur and wizards.

They also visited the ruins of a castle that was said to have been the home of Arthur himself "Just like Glastonbury!" said Arthur as they walked.

They left Tintagle and headed back out to Boscastle, it was getting on to early evening and they were beginning to feel quite hungry.

As they neared the turn off to St Nectans Glen Kate noticed a sign in the next lay-by promising good sea food and a nice atmosphere, she pointed this out to Arthur and they decided to stop for dinner.

They parked in the lay-by and took the adjoining path down to the restaurant, the building was beautiful, it was an old mill house with a water wheel attached and wild flowers growing out of the wall Kate thought it was very scenic.

As they approached they saw two older men coming up the path towards them.

"Good evening" said one of the men.

"Good evening" replied Arthur.

"Off to see the labyrinth?" asked the other man.

"Labyrinth?" said Kate.

"Yes you walk passed the restaurant and follow the public footpath through those trees" said the first man pointing passed the restaurant.

"Thank you" said Arthur "We'll check it out".

"You do that!" said the first man with a twinkle in his eye, with that they walked on.

"Bye, and thanks!" said Kate.

“Your welcome” said the first man over is shoulder.

“We should go and look while its still light” said Arthur.

“Yeah” replied Kate.

They walked passed the restaurant and followed the path taking them through the trees and over a small hill, as they crested the hill they saw a ruin, there were old mill stones laying around and a few people wandering around in the greyish light of dusk, they looked like phantoms in the dying light.

“I don’t see a labyrinth” said Arthur.

“We’ll ask one of those people” suggested Kate.

The two of them walked down the slope into the ruin.

“Excuse me” said Arthur to a woman walking back the way they had come.

“Yes” said the woman, Kate noticed how bright the woman’s eyes were, her skin seemed to glow with vitality and her hair looked like velvet surrounding her with an aura of warmth and clarity.

“What can I do for you?” she asked.

“Do you know where the labyrinth is?” asked Arthur.

“Through there on the wall to your right” said the woman indicating what looked like it was once a room in the ruin.

“Oh” said Kate “On the wall?”

“Yes its a carving” said the woman “Have you not seen one before?” she asked.

"No" Kate replied "I thought it would be a maze, you know like with hedges".

"Oh no" laughed the woman, "Come on I'll tell you about it".

She led them through to the area she'd indicated before.

"My names Victoria, what's yours?" asked the woman.

"I'm Kate" said Kate.

"And I'm Arthur" said Arthur.

"Are you American?" asked Victoria.

"Yes I'm from North Dakota" said Arthur "And Kate's from Kentucky".

“I’m from London originally, but Ive been living down here for a few years now!” said Victoria “Here we are”

Arthur looked at the wall, there before him were two concentric circles carved into the bedrock and below them was a small sign that read-.

ARTHURIAN LABYRINTHS

Dated C14.

“Their really older than that” said Victoria following Arthur’s line of sight.

“What do they mean?” asked Kate.

“They represent life, there’s a larger one in the south of France at the Cathedral in Chartres that you can actually walk around, that would give you the total experience-as you walk the Labyrinth you go through the stages of life and touch on the energies of your chakra’s bringing you an overview of your life it's really metaphorical but Ive heard its an experience that's well worth doing.

With these two smaller Labyrinths you have to place your hands on each and focus on the energy and you should have a similar experience, although these two each represent the male and female aspects of life they also help to bring balance of the two".

Arthur kneeled before the labyrinths and put his hands on each, closing his eyes he felt a surge of energy spark across his palms and race up through his arms meeting like a clap of thunder in his heart then running down through the small of his back and out of the base of his spine feeling like a lead weight anchoring him to the floor.

His mind went blank, phasing out he fell deep inside himself tumbling through the inner dimensions and differing aspects of his own make-up, seeing for the first time a complete over-view of himself.

Almost as if he's mental makeup was a map strewn before him on a table, he could see he's lower aspects at the south pole of the map and above that precariously balanced he's other more mediocre levels, where he spent most of his waking life then above that the higher more dynamic aspects where the knowledge of all was contained, pulsing with an energy so intense to stare at it too long hurt his inner eye, the amount of information was overwhelming and at that point he knew it would take him years to integrate this knowledge but as he came to this realisation he felt the quietist voice in the back of his mind telling him that this was up to him, he could integrate this knowledge as quickly or as slowly as he chose depending on how open and clear he could keep his awareness to watch for the signals shown to him in he's everyday life.

If he could remain clear enough it would be possible to integrate this knowledge without even trying because he already held all the keys,

What you wish to be you already are!!.

This was too much, instinctively Arthur's brain shut down and he opened his eyes.

He looked up at Kate, she looked stunned.

“What” he asked, he’s voice seemed a little more husky than usual.

“You were glowing- you looked beautiful!” responded Kate.

“Don’t I always” joked Arthur beginning to feel a little self conscious.

“No you really did seem to glow, Ive never seen anything like that before!” said Victoria.

Arthur gave Kate a help-me kind of look.

“Budge over then” said Kate recognising the look.

Arthur stepped back and Kate took his place.

She kept her eyes open and drifted into a comfortable space inside herself, she felt nothing of what Arthur had felt but an overflowing of warmth and peace.

After a few moments she stood reverently feeling very respectful of this place and the energies contained here and turned to face Victoria and Arthur.

"That was wonderful" she said "I feel really warm and settled in my self".

She looked at Arthur and could see he was still a little ill at ease with his own experience and was about to say something when Victoria spoke up.

"Have you been down to the cove yet?" she asked.

"What cove?" asked Arthur taking the opportunity for distraction.

"Just down there" said Victoria indicating a path leading on through the undergrowth.

She led the way, once they passed through the undergrowth they crossed a small wooden bridge over a stream that Kate assumed went on to the cove to meet the sea and followed the path along the side of a ridge until they saw the cove.

It was a beautiful sight the hills either side of the small cove dropped away sharply revealing jet black stone moving down in a step like formation until it met the white foaming waters that crashed amongst them giving the scene an impressive contrast of black on white.

The day was fast moving to it's end adding to the majesty of the scene a wonderfully colourful sunset that only served to highlight the contrast and mystery of the place, the air was alive with the sparkling essence of life yet it had a restful quality, you could sense the area changing from day to night like the change of the seasons.

CHAPTER 3

As it began to grow dark Kate and Arthur wished Victoria a good night and headed back to the restaurant to enjoy a quiet romantic meal, they spoke over the days events eventually bringing up the strange lightness they'd seen at the wood on their way to the waterfall.

"I wonder what it was?" said Arthur.

"I don't know but I'd like to find out!" said Kate.

"How can we do that?" asked Arthur.

"I suppose we'll have to ask about, you know find out if anyone's seen anything like that before" Kate replied.

"That guy running the cafe, he'd be a good bet.

After all he doe's live there!" suggested Arthur.

"That's a very good idea and he seemed quite open minded, I reckon he wont be too thrown by the whole thing" said Kate contemplatively toying with her wine glass.

They finished their meal and drove back to Boscastle, they were quite tired by this point and decided to settle for the evening with an early night.

The next day they headed back out along the road to Tintagle stopping once again at the lay-by leading to St Nectans Glen.

Walking through the woods back to waterfall they were constantly scanning the vegetation around them for signs of the lightness they'd seen before but there were none.

"You don't suppose we imagined the whole thing do you?" said Arthur realising instantly how stupid that sounded.

"No but it does seem very unreal now doesn't it?" replied Kate.

They walked on reaching the cafe a little later.

"Back again!" said the man looking up from a table he was clearing.

"Er-yes!" said Arthur "We'd like to ask you some questions if we may?".

"You can ask all you like but I may not be able to answer all of them!" said the man smiling.

"It's about the woods" interjected Kate.

"Oh, yeah what about them?" said the man taking a tray of used crockery out to the small kitchenette and returning with an expectant look "Would you like some tea?" he asked.

"Yes please" said Arthur sitting down, Kate joined him.

The man came back shortly carrying a tray laden with crockery and took a seat at the table “Shall I be mum?” he asked.

“Sounds good” said Arthur.

The man poured the tea “What do you want to know?” he asked.

“It sounds weird” said Arthur.

“Go on” prompted the man.

“When we were walking up here yesterday” continued Arthur “We saw something in the trees, it appeared to be a small lightness in the air and I got the unmistakable feeling we were being watched”.

“What do you mean by a ‘lightness in the air’ “ asked the man.

“It’s hard to say almost like a rip in the air itself, there was definitely something within the rip but what it was I couldn’t tell you” answered Arthur.

“You mean like a doorway?” asked the man.

“Yes I suppose but more personal than that- it had a consciousness!” said Arthur.

“How can you be sure?” asked the man.

“The feeling of being watched it was to intense, it must have come from a sentient being” said Arthur.

The man smiled “Looks like you’ve answered half your question”.

“Yes, your right it was a being!, I suppose I had that part of the answer all along” said Arthur.

“Yes” said the man “but can you tell me what kind of being it was?”.

“Not yet” said Arthur “How about you Kate have you got any ideas on that?”.

Kate had been sitting quietly listening to the exchange “I don’t really know, if I think back it felt kind of childlike yet very old, I know that doesn’t make much sense but that’s what I felt”.

“And what do you think that have could meant?” asked the man.

“I’m not sure” said Kate.

“Well I’m not sure myself but I am sure the answer will become apparent in time if you keep at it” said the man “Besides there’s lots of things in these woods it could be any number of things!”

They finished their tea and thanked the man.

After which they paid him for the tea and began to walk back through the wood, Arthur suggested visiting the waterfall again but somehow it didn't seem appropriate so they just settled into a relaxing walk through the woods and reached their car feeling calm and at ease.

"Well what are we going to do next then?" asked Arthur "We're due to leave the Hotel today, do you want to stay longer or shall we go on else where?".

"I quite fancy going somewhere else, do you have any ideas?" responded Kate.

"Lets go have some lunch and decide on a full stomach" suggested Arthur.

"Sounds good" said Kate.

They drove into Tintagel and found a nice cafe affording them a good view of the Castle ruins.

After which they drove back to Boscastle and checked out of the Hotel.

Kate wanted to have a last look around the town so an hour later they were back on the road heading deeper into Cornwall, Arthur was at the wheel determined to get the hang of the British roads but still finding it difficult.

By the evening they reached St Austell and found a Bed and breakfast on the outskirts of the town, being it was now Friday they decided to go out and check out the local night life.

There were a lot of younger people moving about the town getting very drunk and having a good time, Arthur and Kate found it all very disconcerting.

Everything and everyone was moving at warp factor five, friendships were made and lost in the blink of an eye and no one seemed to be standing in there own centres, they were all keyed completely into co-dependency's and engage in what Kate referred to as the battle of the Ego's, to which Arthur added was like the war of the worlds but not quite as impressive.

Kate laughed and they decided to retire early thinking they must be getting old prematurely.

It was strange but Arthur couldn't shake the felling of loss this gave him, he'd never really been the type to stay out partying all night especially growing up in a small town like Vantage.

Oh he'd occasionally been up to Telberg with a few friends when he was a bit younger but had never really felt part of that scene and was never bothered by the fact until now which just made his present feelings all the more unsettling.

He tried to relate this to Kate when they reached the B+B but she couldn't grasp what he was saying, she seemed totally unaffected by the experience which Arthur put down to the greater emotional stability that most women seemed to posses.

Kate went to bed but Arthur sat up thinking, he didn't like this feeling but knew he had to explore it if he truly wished to grow.

He sat up for hours twisting the feeling of loss in every direction possible, holding every abstract thought that entered his mind against the emotion looking for a conclusion that fitted so he could release the pattern but unfortunately this night it wasn't forthcoming.

He decided to go to bed when he began losing his train of thought entirely.

The next morning he woke to an empty bed, he mentally appraised himself, the feeling had ebbed but not left him entirely, he could feel the residue sitting in his gut.

He did a few yoga stretches to clear the residue but reminded himself this was a reflection of something he carried (since childhood) and needed to be worked on.

He headed to the on-suite to relieve himself, his mind felt clear he noted mentally to himself (since childhood).

"There it was again" he thought.

"What was that?"

(since childhood) it whispered in the back of his mind.

"Don't let it back in" thought Arthur "Ive just cleared it there's no need to step back in".

But this isn't always the case.

Pushing the thought back into the recesses he felt better again but at the same time he couldn't shift the feeling something was being shown, that he was being given an opportunity.

He stood still, naked in front of the WC, letting out a long breath he took hold of himself.

He caught himself steeling for a shock and forced his mind and body to relax, his hands by his side he allowed his control to recede.

An image jumped to mind.

The sea drawing back from the shore just after a small wave had broken and just before another came..

The image dissipated as quickly as it came only to be followed by another..

Himself as a child standing before a group of friends sharing his sweets out between them.

Arthur remembered this, he was about seven.

He smiled to himself, he really wanted to make sure he shared the sweets fairly, it really mattered to him, he remembers how meticulously he had counted them..

He's friends take the sweets and they set about forming the teams for a game of football, Arthur, the child knows he's in good favour and expects to be chosen first.

He's not, but it's OK that boys a better player, he would have chose him too.

He'll be next..

He's not.

He's not.

He's not.

The sweets?.

He's not…

"Oh all right we'll have Arthur!" say's the boy.

Arthur cringed at the memory.

He's the last…

Arthur, the man opens his eye's "I played really well that game!" he said aloud to the empty bathroom.

"I felt so rejected, we were only children they didn't have to pick me because I shared my sweets that wasn't why I shared them they were my friends, what's this got to do with anything?" again he spoke aloud.

The feeling of loss returned, stronger than before, like a punch in the stomach..

Arthur reeled but stood firm holding the image but it was gone.

Instead he's faced with thoughts, his adult mind returning…

"Why did I feel so much rejection, I hadn't really expected any return, I knew I was the worst player, I was never really big enough to compete with the other kids, although I could outrun most of them but kids football's more about tackles and huddles we took it so seriously, nothing compromised our games.

AH, I did expect a compromise and was disappointed, I took it to much to heart, have I really held that all this time? and if so what had

I expected last night Of course the shifting loyalties we saw last night they reminded me of the shifting loyalties we had when I was a child, God I really carried that!"

Arthur began to feel better he now understood the feeling and now he would recognise it when or if it came up again.

"Or if?" he thought.

"Oh yeah I remember at the Labyrinths I felt it was entirely up to me how fast I moved this doesn't have to come up again as long as I can remain vigilant!".

"No not necessarily" he added "if it doe's come up again I just have to bless the knowledge being given and let go, not let it take hold and in time, it'll fade entirely".

He smiled to himself whilst he dressed and washed then headed down to join Kate for Breakfast.

CHAPTER 4

After checking out of the B+B Kate and Arthur drove deeper into Cornwall eventually reaching a small town on the north coast just as dusk was setting in.

They drove around the town going from hotel to hotel only to find them all full (it was as one of the owners had told them, the height of the holiday season and this particular area was one of the most popular!, he also suggested they head a little out of town to the camping grounds and that they may have more chance finding a caravan).

Following this suggestion Kate and Arthur began checking the camping sites, only to find that once again they were full.

At the last, most out of the way place they came to, which was also full the owner suggested they try a farm down an opposing lane at which the farmer had a caravan that he let out from time to time.

They followed the given directions taking them almost three miles down the lane and eventually came to the farm.

It was now getting quite late and they were relived to see a light on in what appeared to be the kitchen.

"I hope he can let us the caravan" said Arthur getting out "I really don't fancy sleeping in the car!"

"No me neither" said Kate also getting out and looking decidedly bleary eyed.

They approached the door, which opened to reveal a shabby but healthy looking man in his late fifties with a rosy unshaven face, sparkling blue eyes and a rather large belly highlighted by his stance.

"Wha' can I'r do fur yor the'n!" he asked with a smile in thick Cornish tones.

“The man at the camping site said you may be able to let us a caravan, we’ve been all over the place and had no luck at all” said Arthur trying not to laugh.

“Yeah, sorry it’s so late but we are kinda stuck!” added Kate.

“Don’ yor worry bout tha’, me an’ t’ miss’is is up most ta nigh’ any-ways,

yoos be Americans then!” answered the man.

It took Arthur a few moments to get the gist of what the man was saying, “Yes, we’re jus travelling round taking in the sites”, Arthur did a mental double take, and yes he was picking up on the hyphens of the mans speech.

“Well yor pick’ a bootiful place ta do thaat, and yor in lock t’ vans impty righ’ now”.

Kate was beginning to go scarlet, she didn't want to be rude but this man was a walking stereo-type, "Oh well" she consoled herself "stereo-types must have some basis in fact I suppose".

"Tha's great!" said Arthur (he'd done it again!) "may we rent it for a couple of days?".

"Ye, itbe fifeteeen ponds anight!, I'r git t' missis t' git yor sum frosh shits!" he disappeared back in to the house.

"What an incredible accent!" said Arthur after he was gone.

"Yeah and you sound as though you'll fit root in!" said Kate laughing.

The door opened and she snorted through her nose as she stifled herself giving her a sharp pain down the back of her throat and making her eye's water.

A large woman with warm eyes stepped out and smiled benignly at them.

"Well then you two will need these" she said in a softer Cornish peel, passing them each a pile of bedding, "this way!" she added striding across the yard, gauging by the easy grace of her step she was obviously very fit dispite her size.

She led them through a gate at the far end of the yard and across a field, it was now dark and Kate was being very careful where she stepped, at last they reached the end of the field and headed out across the next one.

Arthur could just make out the out-line of the caravan at the other end of the field as they approached, it looked very small.

"It's pretty out the way but I'r reckon you'll appreciate that come the morning" said the woman over her shoulder.

"I'll appreciate a good nights sleep!" said Kate.

"You'll git that here!, it's really quiet cos we're so far from the roads" she replied.

They reached the caravan the woman opened the door and stepping over the threshold turned on the light, Kate and Arthur followed her in.

"Well what do you think?" asked the woman.

Arthur and Kate surveyed the interior, it was very small and the caravan was obviously very old but it held a kind of oldie-world charm that gave the place a warm cosy feel.

"It's lovely!" exclaimed Kate.

"Yeah, cosy!" agreed Arthur.

“Well I’ll wish you both a good night then” said the woman “By the way I’m Ann and my husband’s name’s Michael, if There’s anything you need don’t be afraid to ask!”.

She gave them the keys and closing the door behind her left them alone.

The caravan was split into two parts, the first held the sitting area that also contained a pullout double bed, the other was the small kitchen area with a small double ringed gas hob and a kettle plus a door leading to a tiny WC and the newer addition of a shower unit.

Arthur left Kate to sort out the bed and headed back across the field’s to get a few essentials from the car.

Kate just finished setting up the bed when Arthur returned carrying a large holdall and a smaller bag.

He left the holdall in the kitchen area and emptied the other on the bed, inside were a bottle of wine and a few sandwiches they’d picked up earlier.

Neither of them could face the wine so Arthur placed it on the side and opened the sandwiches, they got into bed and began to eat but before they finished they were both sound asleep.

Arthur found himself sat by the bank of a river, gazing at the ripples and eddies forming around the stones.

He imagined himself one of the stones, the currents and swirls of the water he likened to the form of his thoughts, mirroring the surface of the stone and extending into the water.

"I wonder" he thought "How if at all do the ripples of the mind affect the flow of the river?, do they influence it's shape?, it's structure?, where it lead's? and doe's it matter? everything's in the right place after all.

If I remove the stone will there be another a little down stream of the same shape?, and after that?".

He sits quietly with his thoughts, once again admiring the majestic flow of the river, doe's the fish in it's watery world and translucent sky ponder the world beyond this boundary?, does the insect apon the surface ponder the death lurking below, and what by the intervention of man does the fish feel when the supposed pray becomes the master dragging him beyond his boundaries pulling the panicked creature into a alien world where even the atmosphere is death?....

Kate slept on..

She finds herself floating in warm liquid, movement is a joy without the weight of gravity she moves like quick-silver, her thought goes before her and without the tiniest effort her body follows.

She now understands how constrictive the world she knows truly is.

Above she sense's sustenance flittering along on legs of pins, she races towards her goal before she made the decision to act and close's her mouth over her meal.

The meal turns sour, it bites back hooking through her tissue it wrenches her from her world into a place where the mass of her body pulls like a stone, yet she expends her energy thrashing against her "pray", gasping for breath but that which comes doesn't sustain instead it burns like liquid lead ...

Gasping for breath she wakes to a strange environment, searching the darkened room for a familiar sight she sees Arthur in slumber and relaxes, letting out a breath she settles into herself and thinks on her strange dream.

What could it mean?, does it have to have meaning or could it just be an obscure unrelated occurrence?.

Her mind switching away from these questions Kate falls back into a deep slumber.

They wake late feeling refreshed and comfortable, after making love they head out through the fields holding hands and enjoying the mid-day sun on their backs, making their way to the car they wave cheerfully to Michael and Ann as they cross the yard and drive into town.

On reaching the town they first stop at the stores to buy supplies then spend the afternoon wandering around the town taking in the scenic buildings and small curiosity shops indulging in the supposed fantasy of pixies, fairies and goblins looking at the models and colourful pictures, they find a picture of the waterfall at St Nectans glen and buy it on the spot.

After what seemed no time at all the day was drawing to a close and they drove back out to the farm and decided to cook themselves a meal on the small gas stove and spend a quiet evening together.

Whilst Arthur cooked the meal Kate put away the bed and set out the table, in the centre she placed two yellow candles and the bottle of wine.

Arthur brought over the food whilst Kate dimmed the lights and lighted the candles Arthur poured the wine and they sat down to enjoy their meal.

They'd had such a wonderful day and found this the perfect way to end it.

After they finished eating Arthur cleared away the dish's and opened another bottle of wine, Kate brought over a bowl of crisp whilst Arthur put away the table and set out the bed.

They snuggled down together and put on some music, Arthur felt great he'd never felt so relaxed and settled, his mind was totally clear and at first this sort of worried him but he decided to let go and felt Kate do the same also he was sure the wine was beginning to take affect, he could see slight hue's of colour at the peripherals of his vision, he mentioned this to Kate but she seemed distracted, she was staring at one of the candles.

"What is it?" he asked.

"Cant you see that?" she said.

"What?" asked Arthur looking at the candle, "Oh Wow!" he exclaimed.

"I know isn't it beautiful!" answered Kate.

"Beautiful?" prompted Arthur.

"Yes, it's the most beautiful thing Ive ever seen" said Kate.

"What do you see?" asked Arthur.

"There around the flame, it's like a rainbow etched on the air and those threads streaming off the flame, they look like cob-webs, see how they reach out to everything like cords or power-lines.

And the flame looks so distinctive, so bright and intense, why what do you see?" said Kate.

Arthur had been staring intently at the flame whilst Kate had spoken, he had a strange far off look to him like he was actually looking beyond the flame at something in the middle distance.

“People!” said Arthur, but as he spoke the image before him change slightly revealing more detail, “Us” he added.

To Arthur’s vision the colours surrounding the flame had melded together to form a sort of screen about two inch’s in diameter and about an inch from the flame it self, the thought that he was seeing things crossed Arthur’s mind and the image wavered, he quickly purged the thought and the image sharpened.

“Us?” prompted Kate sitting up.

“Yeah” (Arthur spoke whilst still staring at the image) “we’re at a church of some kind, no it’s bigger than a church, maybe, yes it’s a cathedral, it’s huge.

We’re going in, I can see the altar and a large golden cross at the far end of the hall but we’re walking passed that and going through a door with steps leading down a narrow passage, There’s a large open space below with small windows set high in the walls, oh wow!”.

“What?” asked Kate listening intently.

“On the floor is the Labyrinth!, it’s set into the floor with black marble on a white background, and people are walking around it following the lines”.

The image wavered and disappeared.

“That must be the labyrinth that Victoria was telling us about at the cove, didn’t she say it was at Chartres cathedral in France?” said Kate as Arthur turned to face her.

“Yes” said Arthur “I remember”.

“Well it looks like we know where we’re going next!” said Kate smiling.

Arthur was staring at the floor whilst Kate spoke.

“What is it?” she said.

“I don’t know, it’s weird, there’s a strong light blue line going straight across the floor of the caravan, it looks like a stream” said Arthur.

“There’s another one there!” said Kate pointing towards the kitchen area.

Arthur stood up “Follow me” he said to Kate.

They left the caravan walked about a hundred yards away and turned back towards the van.

“Wow” said Kate.

“Oh” was all Arthur could manage.

Before them spread across the field was a whole network of light-streams, some of them connected to make larger streams and what could only be described as rivers, others criss-crossed in front of them, each appeared to be made of particles of light that gave them the appearance of flowing water.

“I know what these are!” said Kate “Ive read about them, they’re Ley-lines!”.

“Oh wow” said Arthur “Ive read about those too, they’re the energy pathways of the Earth, like veins and arteries they pump the life-force of the planet like ours do blood!”.

Kate was staring at a nearby tree, “Can you see that?” she said indicating the tree to Arthur.

As Arthur looked he could see light being drawn up the trunk in quick pulses and spreading through the branches, sparking at the very tip of each releasing a mild hue of colour in to the air just above, as Arthur focused on the hue he noticed it spread around the tree to form what appeared to be an aura of colour, it was beautiful!, but as he admired this he saw there was a depression in the aura on the right hand side of the tree.

The light here was literally compressed and was moving very sluggishly as opposed to the free flowing movement elsewhere on the tree.

Arthur walked closer to get a better look at the depression, as he neared it he saw the area on the trees foliage at this point was brown and dying, there was some kind of fungus attacking the tree, Kate was next to him peering over his shoulder.

"Oh, wow!" she said.

They stood outside admiring the spectacular display of colour before them for another half-hour until it got too cold, then regretfully they returned to the caravan and retired for the night feeling very tired and content, they were asleep as soon as their heads touched the pillow.

CHAPTER 5

The next day Kate and Arthur paid Michael and Ann for their time in the caravan and after phoning the car rental company to make sure they could hand the vehicle back at one of their other office's they headed back up the country to Bristol and boarded a plane for France.

They arrived at the main airport as close as possible to Chartres but still found they had quite a distance to travel to the Cathedral so decided to check into a hotel for the night and set out in the morning.

The next day they set off by train to Chartres.

On arrival at the town they decided to leave their luggage at the station and walked the remaining distance to the Cathedral, as soon as they left the station they could see the spires in the distance looming over the town.

"At least we wont have to ask for directions" said Arthur "My French isn't up to much!".

"Mine neither!" replied Kate.

Walking through the town gave them the opportunity to take in the sights and smells of the place, it was very different from Britain the people seemed a lot less concerned about the way others saw them which could have been miss-taken for arrogance but didn't (on the whole) have quite that quality.

There were a few people that were unmistakably arrogant but they conceded you get that anywhere.

With that stereo-type dispelled Kate thought of another the French definitely seemed to have an air of sophistication and a natural grace that both Arthur and Kate agreed was very appealing.

As they approached the Cathedral square they were both taken back by the beauty of the structure.

The stone, which was obviously cleaned regularly was cut with such precision that it was hard to believe the building was built hundreds of years ago and the stain-glass windows were exquisite.

The cathedral was square in shape with a spire at each corner and each spire held a golden cross.

Running down both sides of the building were many elongated arched windows, each holding a saint in stain glass.

But the most impressive window was set above the arched main doors, it looked like a flower and was at least twenty feet in diameter made up of twelve segments each split into two parts giving the image a more flower-like appearance.

"Doe's it look like the image you saw?" asked Kate.

"Yes exactly" said Arthur "Lets go in" he added after a moment.

Kate and Arthur approached the building reverently, feeling almost intimidated by the sheer size and strength of the structure.

They entered feeling very small and isolated, after passing through the entrance the feeling fell away replaced by an overwhelming feeling of serenity and peacefulness.

“Imagine” said Arthur “All those years of prayer and positive thinking saturating this place with all that good feeling, I don’t know why I never thought about that before”.

“Did you ever go to church much when you were growing up?” asked Kate.

“No” replied Arthur “Ive never thought of myself as a religious person and thankfully my parents never forced me into anything like that!”.

“Maybe that’s why you’ve never realised the energy contained in places like this is usually very positive” said Kate.

“You mean due to my preconceptions regarding religion” said Arthur contemplatively “You could have a point!” he added.

“I wonder if the feelings like this in the holy places of other religions” said Arthur after a moment.

“Have you forgotten the sacred Indian grounds you took me to in America?” asked Kate “The same grounds your father used to take you to when you were a child, and not to mention the sacred places we’ve visited on this trip?”.

“You may be right those places were places of worship too and I suppose the thought-forms of those people must have affected the energy there also, but the energy was very different from this,

People must be subconsciously drawn to the energy that suits them best -thus inspiring faith!” said Arthur enigmatically.

“Could be” said Kate with a coy smile.

They walked the length of the church taking in the artistry, history and energy of this structure, each going their own way to have a close look at what took their particular interest when Kate noticed a sign.

"Pssst" she called trying not to bother the people praying at the pews, Arthur walked over to where she stood.

"What?" he asked, Kate just pointed, Arthur followed her finger and there in front of where they stood was a sign indicating a small door.

<u>LABYRINTH</u>

"Shall we?" asked Kate.

They walked down the passage, Arthur was a little thrown at how much this looked like what he saw, he knew just what to expect when they reached the bottom.

The passage opened up into a large hall set just below ground level with small windows set high in the walls which must have been at pavement level to the world outside.

On the floor before them was the Labyrinth just as Arthur had seen it, laid in black marble against white, also there were candles spread out around the circumference which hadn't been there in the image Arthur had seen.

There was another difference as well, there were no other people around.

"Well" said Kate "Now what?".

"I suppose we walk it!" answered Arthur.

"How do mean walk it?" asked Kate.

"We follow the markings around the labyrinth in a clock-wise direction" Arthur replied.

"How do you know that?" asked Kate.

Arthur just smiled and approached the labyrinth, he's face had taken on a very serene expression and he's movements were slow and deliberate.

Kate hung back to watch, Arthur began walking the labyrinth.

As Kate looked on Arthur's energy expanded, he seemed to grow in stature

and Kate could just make out a bluish glow emanating around him in a perfect sphere with flecks of gold swarming within it like fireflies or the embers above a camp fire.

Arthur stepped into the labyrinth, he could feel he's energy buzzing around him but knew instinctively that was not where he's focus needed to be at this time, he turned his attention within and immediately felt he's solar plexus begin to hum and pulse with light, it felt strong yet not focused somehow like it needed to be honed in in some way.

He began to walk along the markings, as he reached the first turn he's attention moved sharply away from he's solar-plexus and straight to he's groin where it again pulsed, causing him some dis-comfort at first but quickly becoming a warm and satisfying glow anchoring his feet to the ground.

On reaching the second turn he's energy shifted once again moving he's awareness to he's sphincter muscle, between his anus and scrotum which again began to pulse but this time the pulse was rapid and very hot causing him to stop and catch his breath, the sensation became a little less intense and Arthur moved on feeling very grounded and secure.

The next turn was the best yet, Arthur's chest seemed to burst open in a corona of dazzling light and colour giving him a feeling of absolute joy and love filling he's whole body with a liquid heat that ebbed and flowed with the beat of his heart.

Arthur stopped and closed he's eyes to fully appreciate the sensation before moving on to the next turn, at this the top of his head started to throb radiating down the sides of his face and finishing at the point where the back of his head met his neck, this was an unusual feeling and Arthur wasn't sure if he liked it all that much.

He's pace quickened towards the next turn in the labyrinth.

“Ow” he thought as a bolt of searing heat hit him between the eyes then ebbed away leaving a strange coolness where the heat had been, the last turn before the centre brought on a coughing spasm as a tickle suddenly erupted in his throat, after a moment it stopped leaving he’s throat feeling raw. With only the centre of the labyrinth left to go.

He stepped into it and the room swam out of focus, before him stood the most beautiful woman he’d ever seen, she was dressed in a white gown of indiscriminate cloth that shimmered in the inner glow this being radiated.

She smiled at him and was gone.

The room returned and he glanced up at Kate.

“How are you?” she asked as Arthur took the straight-lined exit from the labyrinth.

“Good” he mumbled.

As he approached Kate thought his skin looked as if it had swollen, he had taken on an air of an overstuffed cushion, he was emanating a golden light that seemed to come directly from the pours of his skin, although he was obviously a bit thrown by the experience.

Kate took his hand and led him wordlessly to a pew next to the wall, they sat down and Arthur rested his head in his hands.

After a moment he spoke.

"That was amazing!, I'm not sure if I can believe what just happened!" he said.

"How did it feel?" Kate asked.

"As I walked around I got a different sensation in a different part of my body at every turn of the labyrinth, it was quite weird but at the same time really nice!" he said returning to more his own self.

"What kind of sensation?" asked Kate.

“It’s hard to describe, you’ll have to try it for yourself!” answered Arthur.

“I will” said Kate.

“But the strangest bit was right at the end there” continued Arthur “As I entered the centre I saw, and this is going to sound incredible, I saw a woman!”

“A woman!” asked Kate incredulously.

“Yes, she was beautiful, she was wearing a white gown and she smiled at me” he’s face had taken on a look of awe.

“What then?” asked Kate.

“What, oh” Arthur was obviously miles away, “reliving the experience” thought Kate, “She just disappeared” he added.

“Are you going to try it?” he asked.

“Yes” said Kate getting up.

“I’ll wait for you upstairs in the main hall, I’m feeling a little weirded out” said Arthur also standing.

“OK, see you in a bit then!” said Kate moving with some apprehension towards the labyrinth.

Arthur left her to it and headed up the stairs back to the main body of the church.

As he entered the hall he felt the urge to light a candle for himself and Kate, he approached the stand and put a few coins in the box, taking a candle for each of them got the strangest impression that he should think on the rest of the journey ahead of them as he lit the candles.

"Kind of like a blessing" he thought following he's intuition and suppressing the religious connotations of this act.

"Did you enjoy the labyrinth?" asked a voice over he's shoulder.

Arthur turned to find a priest standing behind him, "Yes it was great" he answered.

"It's been here for hundreds of years you know!" said the priest in uncertain English.

"Really!" said Arthur "Do you know why it's here?" he asked.

"Not really" said the priest "I know it's got some thing to do with Saint James though!".

"Saint James" said Arthur "I don't think Ive ever heard of him!".

"Really" said the priest "Your not Catholic then?".

"Oh no" said Arthur "I just admire these buildings and I'm always interested in the history of place's like this!" he prompted.

"Well" said the priest smiling "Saint James was Christ's cousin he was concerned with the faith in Spain more than anywhere else, he helped fight the moors but was killed in battle and after laying in state here was carried across the Pyrenees then across the northern province's of Spain to the Cathedral in Santiago de Compostella where he's body was entombed and is still there today, as is the route they took, it's actually become quite a big thing for pilgrims to walk even now!".

"That all sounds very interesting" said Arthur "and you say people still walk it today?"

"Yes, and you don't even have to become Catholic, lots of people do it just for a cheap way to see the country-side, plus there's lots of cheap places to stay and eat along the way if your a perigino!" said the priest smiling.

"What's a perigrino?" asked Arthur.

"That's Spanish for pilgrim, but even if your not Catholic and you are walking the trail your still called a perigrino and treated with much respect!" said the priest.

"Do you know where I can find out more about this trail?" asked Arthur.

"Well" said the priest "It starts right here!, if you ask at the tourist office across the square when you leave I'm sure they'll have all the information you'll need".

"Thank you" said Arthur.

“Your very welcome” said the priest, with that he made he’s exit off towards what looked like the confessional box.

Arthur went and sat down at one of the pews to absorb this new information.

Kate entered the hall a little later and spotted Arthur sat at the pew, as she approached he stood to meet her.

“How you feeling? he asked.

“Great, totally invigorated I feel like a million dollars” she said enthusiastically.

“Good” said Arthur “Did you see the white lady?”.

“No but I did feel those strange sensations you mentioned, kinda hitting me in different place’s as I walked round and when I got to the centre I felt a strong sense of peace and serenity but no white lady, that one must have just been for you” replied Kate.

"Well I'm glad your feeling good as Ive got an idea as to where to go next!" said Arthur.

"Oh really!, where?" asked Kate.

Arthur related his conversation with the priest to her.

"Sounds like a good experience but I don't know if I fancy walking the whole distance; can we just walk it for a bit?" asked Kate.

"I don't see why not!" replied Arthur.

They left the Cathedral and found the tourist office picking up all the needed literature for the journey ahead on what they found out was called the Camino de Santiago, which translated meant "way to Santiago".

After which they caught a taxi to pick up their luggage and found a good hotel to spend the night.

Kate insisted on a last night of luxury before heading out into the sticks, with the help of the hotel's staff they arranged to send most of their luggage on to the hotel's Santiago branch leaving them with no more than a small rucksack each to carry.

With all the arrangements made they settled down to a good nights rest.

CHAPTER 6

The next day they left the hotel early, with to their surprise the heartfelt blessings of the hotel staff headed out to pick up the trail.

They found the way very well marked as they headed out of Charte's by following the yellow hand painted arrows that littered the place and had previously gone unnoticed.

They soon found themselves outside the town, faced with a broad expanse of fields either side of them and the mountains of the Pyrenees looming ahead in the distance.

"Now I'm worried!" said Kate.

"It doe's look quite far off!" conceded Arthur.

They walked on until lunch stopping at a small Cafe/bar by the side of the trail, they would have liked to have talked to the various people coming and going who were obviously walking the trail but due to the language barriers they found this impossible and gave up after a few tries.

"I'm going to have to learn a new language at some point" said Arthur looking over at Kate who'd taken a small note-pad out of her bag and begun writing.

"You haven't done that in years" he said gesturing to the pad.

"I know" said Kate "But Ive just kinda got the urge again, I mean so much has happened on this trip already, I don't want to forget any of it!".

After lunch they once again began what was fast becoming the laborious of walking.

The mountains in the distance seemed to be getting no closer.

Where as their energy levels seemed to be depleting at an astonishing rate, they plodded on.

As it was getting dark they saw the lights of a village ahead and thought it would be a good time to stop for rest, they entered the village and followed the yellow arrows through the close-knit streets ending at a small two storey building the, sign in French that Kate guessed was the name of the place but in fact turned out to be a reference to pilgrims walking the trail.

They checked in and slept a tired dreamless sleep on a set of bunk-beds in a crowded dormitory.

The following morning they woke feeling stiff and full of aches.

“Can we go home?” asked Arthur “I’m beginning to think this wasn’t such a bright idea”.

“Don’t be a wuss, it’ll get easier as we go!” answered Kate.

They got dressed with Arthur grumbling all the way and went down to eat, the only thing on offer was biscuits and sweet tea.

"Now we can go home!" joked Kate eyeing the meagre spread.

"It'll get easier as we go!" mimicked Arthur laughing.

They set off, the mountains seemed to have moved closer during the course of the night.

"We'll be there by lunch" said Arthur pointing.

"Wonderful!" said Kate sarcastically.

The weather had turned out good, there was a cool breeze blowing towards them from the hills and the sky was a clear pristine blue.

They reached the lower slopes of the Pyrenees by lunch as expected and stopped at another of the Cafe/bars that seemed to litter the trail for a bite.

Kate was ravenous she had two sandwiches and two slices of the most dangerous looking chocolate cake she'd ever seen, followed by a large coffee.

Arthur had a lighter lunch of only two sandwiches and a coffee also buying some sweet biscuits for later, after an hour they set off into the Pyrenees.

This was the most difficult bit yet, there was no cafe/bars and they saw no people right until dusk when they began to get a little worried.

"It's getting dark, do you think we could have come off the path somewhere along the way?" asked Arthur.

"I suppose it's possible, but Ive not seen another path all day so I don't

think so" she replied "Best to just keep moving, I reckon!".

"Yeah your probably right" said Arthur.

They continued on as the sky darkened above them.

Unfortunately they had managed to wander off the trail and were actually four miles in the wrong direction.

It was getting on to mid-night when Kate and Arthur began to get really worried, until they saw a building in the distance and headed towards it hoping it was the youth hostel they desperately needed.

Which on reaching the building they found it wasn't.

It turned out to be an abandoned old hut and they decided it was better than walking about in the wilderness all night so settled down to an uncomfortable night.

They entered the hut, it was old smelly and dusty with an old wooden table set in the middle of the one room they pulled out and lit some candles that luckily Kate had packed on the off chance and got out their sleeping bags.

As they did so they noticed there was writing on one of the walls, Kate moved closer bringing a candle with her to have a closer look.

Arthur followed her over, the first piece of script appeared to be a verse-

The warrior stands alone.

The unwanted king.

Turns to those he loves,

open.

Revealing all he holds to be true,

bearing his soul,

willing to share all.

None will listen.

"What do you make of that?" asked Arthur.

"Ive no idea!" said Kate "There's another over there" she said pointing further along the wall.

They walked closer to the next verse.

I sleep, my children have grown distant.

Locked behind the barriers of their own creation, their consciousness caged.

They no longer hear me, they no longer know who they are and thus I sleep,

I wait and I call, my call grows in strength.

Pushing through the walls around their minds.

Aiding the release from their souls confinement.

Hoping they will question that which they've been taught to hold true.

"Who could have wrote this?" said Arthur.

"I don't know but they wanted to make a point, what that is, I don't know!" answered Kate.

They settled down for the night feeling very tired but glad to have found a place to sleep.

Once again they shared a dream..

They were standing on top of a large hill or mountain over-looking a lush green valley, before them floating in mid-air stood a woman, Arthur had seen her before she was the woman he'd seen at the Labyrinth, again her beauty took his breath away.

She couldn't have been human, no human looked like this-she was pure light, almost angelic excepting the wings.

She speaks..

"Sibling of the light, we are the children of our own souls creation, you are all, you are the father the mother and the child, within you as within all are all the keys and foundations necessary for all your kinds growth at this time".

"How?" asked Kate "How can we use this?" the question was asked in thought before Kate even recognised she was asking.

The woman, the white lady smiled and spoke.

"Life is in many ways a flowing river, one thing always leads to the next.

There is always a higher truth behind the first, that always contradicts the original truth but never fully discounts it.

Trust in this first truth and allow your mind to be flexible but always strive to stand in your own truth, that you are a seeker and are able to let go of the restrictions of self and the attachments of the ego".

"I understand" said Arthur not sure in his own mind he spoke the truth.

"You speak from the heart little one.

Now I leave you with this blessing.."

"Be whole most sacred warrior,
most humble seeker,
gather your strength,
trust your perceptions,

set your sights and reach for the stars!

ohm shanti, blessed be my love".

They wake, the song birds whistling above and the early morning light cutting swaths across the room shinning through the boarded windows of the hut.

Arthur looked over at Kate.

“Did you dream?” he asked.

“Yes” said Kate “It was really strange there was this woman and you were there to!”.

“I was there!” exclaimed Arthur “She blessed us!”

“That’s right!” said Kate “Was it the same woman you saw in the Labyrinth?”.

"Yes it was" answered Arthur, "That was the white lady!".

"Really!" said Kate "your right she is beautiful!".

"In more ways than one" replied Arthur.

"Yeah!" added Kate dreamily.

They left the hut and walking back in the direction they had come soon found the trail once again.

After an hours walk they reached a cafe/bar set amongst the glorious back drop of the Pyrenees and stopped for a bite.

After eating they set off again along the trail enjoying the blissful serenity of the place, Kate felt her energy lift and open up until she really felt as if she were part of these surroundings.

Just a glance at Arthur confirmed this was also the case for him, they held hands as they walked with not a word spoken between them just an underlying understanding of the love they shared with each other and the very planet itself.

They passed a solitary grave by the side of the trail and stopped to read the epitaph.

REST IN PEACE

Here lies Frederick Ohssen

Left this life on this spot doing

what he loved, struck down by his heart.

Circa-1934-1988

Buen' Camino!

"Oh wow" said Arthur "There's a fair warning not to over-exert your self!"

"Yeah, he must have really enjoyed walking!" said Kate, then remembering what she had in her bag "Shall we light a candle for him?".

"That sounds like a good idea!" said Arthur.

Kate took her bag off her back and felt the familiar ache between her shoulder blades that had begun to develop over the last few miles.

"Ow" she said.

"What's up? "asked Arthur.

"My backs a little stiff, it's nothing really!" answered Kate.

"You wanna be careful, you only get one back" said Arthur "Do you want me to take some off your stuff?" he asked.

"No, I'll be aright" she replied.

She took a candle from her bag and melting the base a little fixed it to the small ledge at the base of the headstone.

She lit the candle and stood back.

"It kinda feels as though we should say something!" she said.

"I know what you mean but what?" replied Arthur.

"I cant really think of anything!" said Kate.

"Never mind, you know what they say-Actions speak louder than words!, I'm sure he heard us!" said Arthur.

"Yeah, your probably right!" answered Kate, she picked up her bag and put it on, "Oh wow" she said.

"What?" asked Arthur.

“Your gonna think I’m making this up, but my bag actually feels lighter and its not pulling at my shoulders like it did before!” said Kate excitedly.

“That’s because you’ve got the chest strap twisted over the shoulder strap!” said Arthur laughing.

“Yes but it feels more secure and comfortable” said Kate.

“Maybe our old hiker friend here gave you a hint!” said Arthur.

“Could be!” said Kate, she took off her bag, tightened the chest strap and as an after-thought tightened the shoulder ones as well, as she did so she was sure she could hear the sound of distant laughing.

“Can you hear that?” asked Arthur.

“Laughter?” asked Kate, the laughter stopped and Kate had the feeling someone was standing beside her, she didn’t want to look because something told her this would break the sensation.

“Like” she thought “logic would step in and she’d block the feeling out!”.

“He’s standing next to me!” she said tentatively to Arthur.

Arthur’s face had taken on a serious expression “I know” he replied, they both felt it was time to walk on and without a word they did.

“Can you hear me!”

“Yes” said Kate.

“Yes” said Arthur.

“Thanks for the candle, you got my attention”

"Your welcome, you've got ours!" said Kate.

"Thought I might!" (There was strong sense of humour behind the words).

"Frederick?" asked Kate.

"Yes that's right" said Frederick. "*I'd like to share something with you by a way of thanks but first I'd like to tell you a bit about myself and who I was in life.*

I used to walk all over the world, Ive been to most place's and walked any trail I could find.

Hiking was truly my passion as was poetry, in fact for me the two went hand in hand, I'd compose my verse's whilst walking.

I hated being around other people, they just annoyed me and never took me seriously which was my downfall really, I never took anyone else seriously either. I should have stopped hiking when I first felt a twinge in my heart, that was five years before I eventually died, but I couldn't settle, I'd never learned to feel comfortable around people or Society in general for that matter.

I wish I had now, but what's done is done I suppose, still I want to share something with you, that is of course if you want it?, you may not find it any good, I know I'm rambling on, but there isn't that many people who can hear me, so very closed in they are!, but then who am I to judge I was far worse than them in life!.

I still walk with them for a while from time to time, just listening to what they think, it's quite interesting sometimes.but enough of me this is what I want to share-

It's just a little poem of mine".

"Keep your eye's open to the world around you,
see what you've always seen but never fully understood,
Try to understand and,
in time- you'll see!".

We are one!,

the time is now,

let go of the reasonable doubt

and trust in what you feel,

take a step within to embrace your light

and be free!".

"well what do you think, does that help you at all?".

"Yes" said Kate "it doe's clarify a few things!".

"I am glad, it's nice to know I can still be of help from time to time!.

I'm going to leave you now, so before I go is there anything else I can do for you?".

Arthur thought for a moment, "Just one thing; a question?".

"What?".

"There's an old shack a few miles back along the trail, we had to spend last night there!".

"Did you dream?"

"Yes actually!" replied Arthur.

"Did you see her?"

"You mean the white lady?" asked Arthur.

"Who else?, did she talk to you?"

"Yes, she kinda blessed us!" said Kate.

"You are very lucky, you've been given a wonderful gift!".

"Yes, I think so" said Arthur. "but I wanted to ask about the verse's on the wall".

"There still there!, how wonderful!, did you like them?, I spent the night there before I died, she came to me too but mine was a blessing of a different sort!".

"You did write them then?" said Arthur.

"Oh yes, that was my passing gift to the world, not much I know but something never the less!, well all the best- I hope you find what ever you wish for!.

Buen' Camino!"

And he was gone.

Kate and Arthur spent the rest of the day walking and discussing the unusual incident, they both decided that dispite the beings obvious good humour there was definitely an under-current of sadness to his tone.

They spent the next two days walking the Pyrenees until on the afternoon of the second day they finally left the mountains behind them following the trail across a broad open meadow to the gratefully received cafe/bar on the far side.

CHAPTER 7

After they had left the Pyrenees the land took on a dusty, almost dessert like appearance.

The trail wound it's way through empty fields lined with the debris of the last harvest, only serving to add to the feeling of isolation.

Kate and Arthur pushed on. Viewing this part of the trail as an arduous and uncomfortable task.

They fell into a plodding silence, both eyeing the distant horizon with trepidation and longing.

Days passed but the unforgiving landscape didn't, staying at the near empty hostels the other hikers seemed to be in a similar state of apathy.

No one really spoke they were just caught in the routine of arriving at dusk eating, sleeping and leaving early in the morning.

Walking in a semiconscious daze the few people there were had taken on the appearance of automatons, grey and lifeless.

For Kate and Arthur the events of the recent past had drifted into obscurity and became little more than a half remembered dream, neither of them were quite sure anymore of what was reality and what was not.

Late one afternoon Kate was sure she could see some kind of localised low lying cloud on the horizon but as she was going to mention this to Arthur the thing disappeared and she thought she must have imagined it.

A few hours later they were in the area Kate surmised the thing had been, She glanced around searching for any sign of it, and got one.

About half a mile ahead was what could only be described as a mini tornado, it was about ten feet tall and five feet wide plus it was coming towards them along the trail, fast.

It seemed no time at all between seeing the thing and it's arrival, suddenly it was apon them.

They stood still as it passed over, whipping around them and pulling at their clothes. Kate got the impression it was searching, kind of like an x-ray it seemed to go right through them and was gone.

They turned and watched it move steadily on back the way they had come.

"What on earth was that?" said Arthur.

"A dust devil!" said Kate recognition dawning, she'd heard of them growing up in Kentucky but until now had never actually seen one.

"That was strange!" said Arthur.

"I know" said Kate "It felt like it was alive somehow!".

"How do you mean?" asked Arthur.

"I'm not sure, like there was a consciousness of sorts but scattered in some way!" she replied.

They walked on, the next day passed with much of the same slow paced boredom as had gone before.

By the afternoon of the following day the land took on an altogether different appearance, quite suddenly as if turning a page it was green and glorious.

The sky was the clearest blue, the summer sunshine creating a lattice-work of shadow through the trees along the path and the air had an element of sweetness to it that satisfied the body, mind and soul giving them both a very definite spring to their steps and lifting the stale feeling of the past few days.

They messed about childishly whilst they walked, a mood that seemed contagious to those they passed on the trail.

Bringing a hint of amusement with the usual greeting of Buen' Camino, the day went by quickly leading them to a small village where they would spend the night. On arrival at the hostel Kate, carefully putting together a few words of Spanish asked the attendant if there was a good place to eat in the village, the happily weathered looking man in his sixties directed them to the village's only cafe and showed them their bunks.

After a quick shower Kate and Arthur headed down to the cafe.

The cafe itself was tiny but clean and warm, filled with the heady aroma of many spices and various food stuffs. Kate and Arthur thought they'd died and gone to heaven.

They took a corner table and awaited the waitress, Kate took out her note pad and began sporadically jotting down and shooting quick glances about the room. Arthur looked over her shoulder and feeling her discomfort resettled himself back into his own space.

Kate surveyed the room, there were lot's of tables crammed in to the small area filled with what appeared to be mostly locals, Kate recognised a few faces from the trail and received a nod of acknowledgement whenever she made eye contact.

Her gaze eventually settled on a guy who seemed to be in thirties with long shoulder length dark hair and strong Romaine features, he glanced her way as she looked and smiled briefly before returning to he's conversation.

He was talking to an older man sat with his back towards her.

Kate surmised the conversation was good due to the focus both men seemed to be attributing.

Kate closed her note book and look up as the waitress arrived to take their order, they ordered some pan fried fish and boiled potatoes plus a bottle of wine and settled in to a light conversation.

Their meal arrived and they set about it, as they ate they became immersed in the feel of the place and began to really feel at home, Kate had not noticed how tense she was until it began to lift.

Pretty soon their meal was finished and they were both completely relaxed, sipping their wine and talking about nothing in particular.

The man Kate had noticed earlier approached their table.

“May I join you?” he asked, his accent was a mix of French and something else.

“Sure” replied Arthur, intrigued by the mans appearance, he had the most gentle eyes Arthur had ever seen. He warmed to him instantly.

“Are you walking the trail?” asked the man as he sat.

“Yes, you?” replied Kate.

“No, I’m just passing through. I’m on may way to a fiesta in Solaria”.

“Solaria?” prompted Kate.

“Yes, it’s a small town about five kilometres from here, I’m going to meet some friends and camp for a few days”.

“What kind of fiesta?” asked Arthur.

“Oh the usual kind of thing, celebrating the life of a local saint though I can’t remember which one, still there generally quite good.

It’s mostly just about people getting together and enjoying the moment, you know?”.

“Yeah, I know what you mean” said Kate “It’s like every moment is a religious, or more to the point spiritual moment”.

“That’s very astute, sorry what was your name’s, I’m Carl”.

“I’m Kate and this is Arthur” replied Kate.

“It’s good to meet you” said Carl.

“And you” said Arthur.

"Yeah, every moment is a spiritual moment. In fact I like to see life as one huge meditation" added Carl.

"How do you mean?" asked Kate.

"Well" said Carl "life as I'm sure you know is the greatest teacher and life itself is a being, or maybe God if you prefer. The important bit to remember is that we're and I do mean all of us are a part of this being and we hold all the keys, every possible conclusion is already in our make up.

Like the most wonderful thought you've ever had and the most lowest thought, feeling or emotion are all part of your make up, you as a human being have the capabilities to be both, for want of better terms, the God and the Devil. It's just a matter of where you chose to place your focus, remember- where you place your focus is exactly where you'll learn or to put it another way- what goes around comes around.

But we can never forget that because of this universal law our choice's make us who we are".

"You mean like taking responsibility for who we are?" asked Kate.

"Yes exactly" replied Carl "As part of life itself you are your greatest teacher, if you can remain balanced enough to keep your objectivity.

Although there is pitfall here as with most insights there's always a preceding lesson, life never stops!, and whilst integrating this knowledge there is always the danger of letting the ego take control and never stopping to listen to what others can teach you and by the very nature of objectiveness, the key word here being "object" it alludes to the third person and try as we might for whatever reason sometimes we can't attain the necessary level of objectivity we may need for the given situation".

"That doe's make sense" said Kate "But going back to what you said about being part of life, I don't think I misunderstand you if a say that by that you mean we also have to understand the lessons of cause and effect".

"Ah, taking responsibility" said Carl.

"Yes, that's right" said Kate.

"Well, I'm sure you know one of the basic law's of physics, in that every action has a equal and opposite reaction and I'm sure you've also noticed that this, especially where people are concerned isn't always the case!" responded Carl.

"Yeah, why is that?, some people seem to get away with murder and some people get caught doing the smallest thing wrong" asked Arthur.

"That's a huge can of worms!" said Carl laughing "And to be honest I'm sure I've only got half the answer to that one, maybe not even half!.

This is how I look at it and it comes down to the sub-conscious if someone is completely sure they'll get away with something they probably will unless of course there's a form of divine intervention be it by someone of a higher consciousness or a higher being" at this Carl paused and look at Kate and Arthur, they both gave a nod and he continued "but of course on the flip-side the person concerned may be thinking their going to get caught or maybe even want to get caught. In which case the action itself was probably a cry for help or attention seeking both of which need to be acknowledged and worked through between the people involved.

But I digress if the person is sub-consciously thinking their going to get caught then that person is willing themselves to get caught, their actually sending the signal to the cosmos, to life that this is the outcome they desire.

It's the same as someone whose always failing in business but outwardly appears to be doing all they can to succeed, again in most case's this would be due to that subliminal signal. This problem can be solved if the person concerned is willing to open if you will-Pandora's box and can mostly be attributed to a lack of self worth of other emotional or mental disorder, both of which seem to be promoted in most western cultures amongst the majority of people.

But again I digress I'd like to return to the Pandora's box analogy, just to say that a lot of people are afraid to open the box for obvious reasons but if this is the case the thing to remember is it only gets better".

"How do you mean?" asked Arthur.

"Well, once you open your "box" you will find a lot leaps out like a Jack in the box but after this initial wave of turbulence if you keep at it, it will begin to clear and as it doe's your consciousness will grow as a direct result and this will be reflected in your life, of course like most things this is an ongoing process but you can stop at which ever point you wish but most people once they perceive these higher truths find they wish to continue, after all that is what life is about!".

"Although not entirely" added Kate "That's not all life is about, it should be a celebration a joyous experience and I do feel this is important to remember for the sake of balance".

"Yes, that's right" said Arthur "balance is the key to growth, although once a growth process has begun it can sometimes be very unbalancing but that is down to choice, it's up to each individual to what extent they indulge in the process but we have to remember we are human and so are emotional and are certainly not perfect,- well not yet!".

"I'm glad you said that" said Carl "it reminds me of the fact that we are in control of our lives but they are things quite beyond our scope as humans, although the only limits we have are those we place or allow others to place on ourselves. So as far as I can see, in the future as a race we will have no limits at all!".

"Sounds good!" said Kate smiling.

"Which raises another point" said Carl "Continuing from the point I made earlier that we are all part of life and one being could also stretch to the point that service to others is service to one's self and that a selfless act is also a self fulfilling act and vice versa!".

"It's amazing how much can be drawn from one truth!" said Arthur.

"Also life" said Carl "Is much like this very conversation, which only serves to prove yet another point-as above so below or yet again every action has an equal and opposite reaction!".

"It's all double answers!" said Kate looking bemused "Carl, what do you mean when you say-life is like this conversation?".

"Well life like our present conversation explores every possible pattern in a seemingly unguided or random motion, let's not forget that in essence life is motion but once again like you say Kate we have another double answer in the idea that the deepest possible meditation is complete stillness, not so much holding a thought as holding no thought.

But once again I've gone off on another tangent, yes life moves in apparent randomness, but I personally don't believe anything is truly random just exploring every possible expression of life, at this level of being.

Remember we're one impossibly complex being, a some of parts forever contracting and expanding and most importantly growing!".

"Yes, I see how you've made the correlation between life and our conversation" said Kate "But I think I may have garnered something a little more practical for me, at this time, from our conversation".

"Go on" said Carl.

"Well it's just something that's kept occurring to me through this conversation" said Kate "I think and feel free to interrupt if you disagree" she paused Arthur and Carl were listening intently, neither seemed about to interrupt.

“Well” Kate continued “If we contain the whole universe and as you say, which I’m inclined to agree are all an integral part of it then surly to have complete control over oneself, which I feel could only be achieved with a perfect sense of balance would in affect mean you’d have complete control over the universe!”.

“But” interrupted Arthur “you’d be in balance with the universe so there wouldn’t be any control as such because there’d be no ego separation, just a quiet resignation to let what will be, be!”.

“Yes, the ego is generally not as big as the universe!” said Carl laughing “In fact we place so much of ourselves in ego’s that some people are still caught in the Pandora’s box scenario we spoke about earlier”.

The night had drifted on, they hadn’t noticed the cafe was empty until the waitress very politely asked them to leave, Kate and Arthur bid Carl good night and with smiles around parted company.

Kate and Arthur spoke whilst they walked back to their lodgings.

"That was great" said Arthur "he really made a lot of sense!".

"Yes" said Kate "He had some interesting ideas".

"What do you mean?" asked Arthur.

"It's just that I'm beginning to see that the entire universe is open to interpretation, and the great thing is, no one's wrong!, Carl was right when he said we're all part of the cosmos but by that rational it's up to each of us just how we see ourselves!" said Kate looking very pleased with herself.

"Yeah" said Arthur "I see what you mean!".

CHAPTER 8

The next day, feeling refreshed Kate and Arthur set off once again along the trail. The surrounding countryside remained green and pleasant, as did their mood.

By midday they'd reached a wooded grove and stopped to rest and enjoy the space, Kate really felt liberated, her energy seemed immense and open.

She looked at Arthur through the corner of her eye and could just make out the swirling energy fields around his body, he looked back, she saw the recognition in his eye's and knew he was in the same space.

They smiled at each other and began to share their thoughts, Kate could feel the exchanges in their fields and knew they were helping each other de-code.

“De-code” she thought “interesting, but that’s just it!, we have everything within us we’ll ever need we’re just helping each other remember!”.

Kate felt a presence behind her and remembered Frederick, the soul they’d met before.

But this was different, it felt what could only be described as woody!, she could almost taste bark! and she could positively feel the life force of the greenery, this was an entity!.

She looked at Arthur.

“Can you feel that?” she asked.

“Feel it. I can almost see it!” he replied.

Arthur could make out a hazy almond shaped disturbance a couple of meters over Kate’s left shoulder.

It spoke.

-Sort of.

Kate could feel it's thought's trickling into her mind much the same way as with Frederick but this time it had a musical quality to it, it seemed to tickle ever so slightly creating an unusual but very pleasant sensation in her head and through her body, the thoughts themselves were more like gentle nudge's easing her mind along the line of her own thoughts, the concept this being wished to communicate became clear-

The mind is but a tool, do not allow it to be all that you are.

See it and use it for what it is.

An instrument not a control.

You have many varied source's of power, if unchecked they too will rule you.

You must keep the mind clear and it will by it's own true nature play it's role in the dance that is truly your life.

And a joyous dance it is...

The presence left, Kate and Arthur looked at each other dumb-struck.

"No matter how many times that happens it always surprises me!" said Arthur.

"Yeah, it doe's but for it to continue we have to accept it as the norm and move with it!" replied Kate.

"I wonder where this is leading us?" said Arthur.

"I think we covered that last night" answered Kate.

"Yeah, I suppose but it's so hard to accept that sometimes but I know that's due to my own programming and insecurities, I will work through it!" said Arthur with an air of determination.

"I think we may have already made that decision" replied Kate.

“How do you mean?” asked Arthur.

“Well” said Kate “I think we made that choice before we even left America, maybe even before we were born!”.

“How do you know that?” asked Arthur.

“It just seems as though although we have free will all what’s happened over the last few years has been leading us to this point and if I think back beyond to my childhood it all fits the same criteria.

I think we chose to come to earth from where ever to do just this!”.

“What?” asked Arthur.

“Evolve!” said Kate.

“Evolve” repeated Arthur “How?, in what context?”.

"Well as far as I can see we as a race don't need to evolve any more in the physical, it now seems the focus of our evolution is in the esoteric-the spiritual, we need to remember who we are and what we're capable of.

I mean to say look at us we're moving at an incredible rate and yet I think we both know we haven't even touched the tip of the ice berg, as people we are complete, we have all we'll ever need we just have to de-programme ourselves and to forget the limits we've placed.

The only reason we have limits at all is because we've put them there, and forgotten we've done so!, that's the only reason why these limits appear to hold true is because through the same power each and everyone of us processes makes them true!".

"I understand" said Arthur "but why have we blocked ourselves like this?".

"The only possible reason I can think of, admittedly there may be others, is control, if only a select number of people know this truth then their have all the power, again we're back facing the ego!.

That's the only dimension of a person that wants to control another and lets not forget- it's the smallest part!.

Remember balance is the key to growth, the more we can remain detached from the ego or self the faster we can evolve and realise our true selves as part of the whole, and like Carl said 'service to others is service to yourself we are one!'.

The more we can help others to evolve the quicker we ourselves will evolve".

Kate's energy had shot through the roof whilst she spoke, as she was speaking her awareness was becoming multidimensional she saw everything she said from a hundred different angles at once. Her minds eye was full of a kaleidoscope of colours and geometric forms plus all the while she was fully present with what she was saying and yet everything she was seeing and feeling on every other level was being absorbed and catalogued in her mind, the feeling was incredible and she felt unbelievable, she looked at her hands and could see spirals of light cascading off the tips of her fingers and a deep warm throbbing emanating from her palms, she truly felt golden.

Arthur was rapt whilst Kate spoke he could feel her energy surrounding him and being absorbed into the structure of his own body and energy fields strengthening his resolve as it went, he caught impressions of her thoughts, dancing like a light rain on a pond, rippling to the shore of her consciousness from a thousand points at once.

Arthur's thoughts pulled gently back to what Kate was saying, his mind resounded with her words, boosting his own awareness aiding him to see the truth of what Kate was saying but not overpowering his own, allowing him to reach his own conclusions, his own interpretations of the same truth to the degree he was ready for, at this time.

It was working just as Kate had said!.

They sat for a while, enjoying the feeling of oneness and secure in their connection to the universe, after a time their energies settled leaving them feeling very comfortable with themselves and each other, they set off once again along the trail.

After stopping for lunch at yet another trail-side cafe, Kate and Arthur found themselves approaching a small village.

As they closed on the village they passed a faded sign announcing the name of the place (Solaria).

“Isn’t that where Carl said he was going?” said Arthur.

“Yes, I think it was” replied Kate “He didn’t mention we’d be passing here, I wonder why”.

“Perhaps he didn’t know” suggested Arthur.

“Maybe” said Kate “We might see the fiesta he mentioned”.

“That would be good” said Arthur “You never know we may see Carl again too”.

“Might do, the village doesn’t look that big!” said Kate.

They walked into what looked like the main square, which was decorated in colourful banners of red and yellow and pictures of Christ and another saintly figure neither Kate nor Arthur could name.

The town also comprised an ancient looking church and of course a cafe/bar, into which Kate and Arthur entered and after ordering a couple of fruit juices asked the bar tender about lodgings and when the fiesta would start.

Thankfully the man behind the bar spoke English and was able to tell them the fiesta would start that very evening and if they didn't fancy staying at the Hostel he could let them a room upstairs.

They gratefully accepted the room and thanking the man headed up the winding back stairs to their appointed room.

On entering the room Kate dumped her back pack and thankfully sank into the double bed, Arthur did like wise and they were soon both sound asleep.

They awoke to the sounds of laughter down in the bar, Arthur glanced at the wall clock and noticed it was 8:15 p.m.

“Time for dinner?” he suggested.

“Sounds good” replied Kate “let me have a shower first though” she added rising from the bed and pulling off her T-shirt.

“Can I join you?” said Arthur, a gleam in his eye.

“Sure” replied Kate turning with a smile.

Some time later Kate approached the bar and asked the barman if they served food, the man showed them through to a back room come restaurant and indicating a table left them to it, seconds later a young girl apparently the barman’s daughter judging by they startling resemblance came over and gave them each a menu, they ordered and asked the girl when the fiesta began. Her English wasn’t as good as her fathers but they managed to garner the procession would start in about an hour or so, the girl brought over a carafe of wine and exited to the kitchen.

They were the only people in the restaurant and Arthur began to wonder why, their food arrived and Arthur got an answer to he's question.

The food was awful, they'd obviously been no care taken in it's production and it showed.

After a couple of mouthful's Kate felt her stomach contract, put down her fork and pushed the plate away.

"Wow, must be bad!" joked Arthur struggling on for a moment then conceding to the inevitable and doing the same.

"Yeah it is!" said Kate "Still we've been lucky up to now, never mind".

They concentrated on their wine and fell into easy conversation, after a while the girl returned to collect their plates, she made no comment on the fact they were hardly touched and Arthur asked for the bill.

They paid and walking through the bar stepped into the now cool night just as the procession was about to begin, there were hundreds of people lining the square, Kate guessed they must have come from the surrounding villages due to the size of 'Solaria', the precession begun.

Dozens of children entered the square from the route Kate and Arthur had entered a few hours previously, they were each holding a placard picturing various saintly figures.

Following the children were people of all age's including the really old holding banners flame-torches and drums, beating out a sounding rhythm that reverberated around the square causing the windows of the buildings to rattle.

Following these were street performers, fire eaters and tumblers both plying their art as they went. It was a true fanfare a celebration of colour and sound, the square had burst into life. The revellers joined the procession and followed the crowd around the square dancing and chanting at the top of their voices as they went, Kate and Arthur followed suit enjoying every moment.

Suddenly everyone went quiet and the people all parted lining the route from the entry into the square to the steps of the church.

The choir entered the square, young men and women dressed in red and white smocks holding candles and singing in the most gentle tones, a hymn Kate didn't recognise but thought sounded wonderful.

After the choir came a group of priests holding a large plaster Icon of the saint on a plinth. The choir stopped on the steps of the church and turned to face the crowd, their voices rose in volume, the priests placed the Icon on the floor before the steps and the choir finished, next the children rushed forward to cover the Icon in flowers and red banners, giggling all the while.

When the Icon was barely visible beneath the deluge, the children were hustled back into the crowd and quietened whilst the oldest looking priest spoke a long monologue in Spanish waving his hand in the sign of the cross as he finished, changing to the appropriate Latin.

Then a group of young men broke from the crowd and picking up the Icon walked in the opposite direction from where they'd come, the crowd parting to let them through. Now carrying incense burners swinging from chains and filling the air with rich-scented smoke the priests followed the crowd closing in behind, followed by the choir who once again began to sing. The procession headed out of the village and towards a nearby hill, torches were handed out among the procession and the singing of the choir spread. Although they had no idea what they were singing Kate and Arthur joined in, the sounds and smells filled the night air infusing it with the feel of fiesta.

When they reached the top of the hill the procession wound it's way to the entrance of a small church surrounded by fairy lights that cascaded from the roof and were strung through the nearby trees. The Icon was placed on the steps and after another blessing by the same ancient looking priest the crowd receded.

Only then did Kate see the long tables laden with food, someone lit a large bonfire and the party really begun. In a nearby shed someone had set up a table that served as a bar and set about serving the crowd, everyone was in high spirits and the cavorting Kate was sure could be heard from miles away.

A couple of hours later the party was still in full swing, Kate was about to ask Arthur if he wanted to go back to the bar when she spotted Carl through the crowd as she did he turned and made eye contact.

He came over.

“Hello you two!” he said, his face glowing with intoxication.

“Hi!” said Arthur.

“Hello” said Kate.

“Are you enjoying yourselves?” he asked.

“Yes it’s quite a party!” said Arthur.

“Yes it’s good fun” said Carl “Come, you must meet my friend’s”.

He led them through the crowd to a table under a tree. There were three people sat at the table, they looked up as they approached.

"Who have you got there?" asked one of men in a thick French accent.

"This is Kate and Arthur" he said motioning to the pair. "and this!" he said facing the man that spoke "is Frank" then indicating the others in turn "Clare and Morris".

The last two answered in unison with Spanish accent's. They made room at the table and Kate and Arthur squeezed in.

"So where are you from?" asked Frank.

"America" replied Kate "and you?".

"Can't you tell?" asked Frank.

“France?” ventured Arthur with a grin.

“That’s right” replied Frank over emphasising his accent “and these two are from E-Spain-a” he said hyphenating the E and A.

Clare gave him a playfully sharp look.

“How did you meet this one then?” Frank asked Kate indicating Carl.

“Last night” said Kate “,we had a good conversation”.

“Good conversation, with him!” said Frank feigning disbelief.

“Yes, occasionally I am capable of such things!” replied Carl with humour.

The night continued on like this with good natured jibes being thrown across the table, it wasn’t long before Frank took pot-shots at Kate and Arthur but they held their own returning the comments as fast as they were thrown. By the end of the night they felt as though they'd all known each other for years. Wishing each other a good night and swapping postal addresses they parted company. Kate and Arthur walked back down the hill as dawn was breaking over the now distant Pyrenees, colouring the sky with glorious hue's of mauve and violet, they stopped to take in the sight before moving on back to the bar and after waking the owner and securing the room till noon sank gratefully into bed.

CHAPTER 9

They woke just before lunch and after consulting the owner of the bar found they still had time to reach the next the next hostel before dark, they set off feeling a little worse for wear. The weather was again beautiful, the sky was a pristine blue totally void of cloud and the sun was high in the sky. Kate noticed a flock of birds flying overhead and dispite her heavy head couldn't help to notice the semi-visible sphere encasing each bird that seemed to touch the edge of every other bird in the V-like formation they made as they streaked across the sky.

"I wonder if they use those fields to stay in formation" she thought "and if they do, do they also use their fields in conjunction with the fields of the earth to navigate when they migrate?". "Perhaps" she thought on "but I do remember hearing once that birds use the magnetic fields of the planet to navigate, which must mean that these fields are one in the same or at least connected in some way, maybe there differing vibrations of the same energy!".

Arthur broke Kate out of her train of thought.

"Ive been thinking, what did you make of that ceremony we saw last night?" he asked.

"I'm not sure, what did you think?" asked Kate.

"Well, I reckon there was some symbolism in carrying that effigy up the hill" he said.

"Probably was, what did you see?" asked Kate.

"It'll probably sound silly but I couldn't help but think of the whole thing as a metaphor for life. You know like, the journey of. I mean the effigy entered the town or to follow my interpretation entered life, then after an initial celebration began the journey up the hill".

"I see" said Kate "carry on".

"Well after birth we began our 'trip' through life and for most of us it's an arduous task full of work. We struggle to reach a level of enlightenment, or at the very least a level that will allow us to cope with the demands life place's before us before we die. I think that when the effigy reached the top of the hill it symbolised finding true enlightenment or if you prefer death and rebirth, you know like rebirth into a higher reality" said Arthur.

"That's not silly, I can see your point of view and it doe's make sense but Ive never forgot what the visitors told me back in Vantage. Do you remember?" asked Kate.

"I think so, you mean the bit about ascending without ascending and bringing Heaven to Earth" answered Arthur.

"Yes exactly and we as a race need to be focusing on achieving this now before we leave it to late and suffer the same fate as the visitors did, after all that is what this trip is all about" said Kate.

"But how exactly can we go about that?" asked Arthur.

"Well we have to keep our lives joyful by removing or balancing with the parts or people that disturb us. To achieve that we must be able to stand strong in our own space, a good diet and healthy amount of sleep will help accomplish this. Remember the old saying 'we are what we eat', it rings as true now as it ever did!. Beyond that we need to keep an active mind and body through meditation and exercise plus the 'we are what we eat' proverb also applies to what our minds eat, I think this is neglected in modern society more than in the past due to the amount of distractions we now have in our lives and the immense amount of crap we let into our heads both consciously and unconsciously through such things as video games, tv and changing social trends, basically clearing your personal space to let the higher energy and aspects of your self remain prevalent in your daily life".

"I understand and agree with what your saying but it's still difficult to implement in life, you remember what our friend Mike said back in Vantage about the difference between knowing a truth and living it. How do we deal with the influences from our lower aspects without letting them take control, I know that it sounds simple but these lower aspects have a way of building up on you and taking you by surprise" said Arthur.

"Ah" said Kate "Well you need to learn to acknowledge the influences as they come as being your own baggage, try not to take others baggage on board as your own and initiate the following sequence. Take your awareness to your centre and affirm to yourself that you acknowledge the imbalance in question but are able too and will let it go with love, it may help to study a particular meditation to bring this in affect but with practise anyone can do it".

"Sounds almost too easy to be true" said Arthur "But I suppose that's probably why not enough people do it".

"Yes and their lack of belief actually stops or blocks the process" said Kate.

"Makes sense but what did you use the word affirm for that seemed very deliberate" asked Arthur.

"It was" said Kate "Affirmations are very important when trying to grow esoterically, Arthur do you remember when we were sharing Zen proverbs on the way to Cornwall at the beginning of this trip well affirmations are very similar if not entirely identical just as in mantras the affirmation works in the same way and must be repeated often enough to have an effect. I think I will explain it better if I just say one and you can figure out how it works, it should be easy to grasp. This particular affirmation relates to what we were just saying about clearing lower aspects of one's persona" Kate cleared her throat and spoke in a strong clear voice-

"I ACCEPT WHERE I AM IN THE NOW, BUT I KNOW I WILL GROW IN THE NOW".

"Wow" said Arthur "That sounded really strong, I think I understand how it works you have both confirmed and projected this affirmation into yourself and are willing it into reality by your own being!".

"That's exactly it, remember what Carl told us 'where we chose to place our focus is where we learn', like I said at the time, he did have some interesting ideas. Affirmations can be put together by anyone but it's best to keep them simple and to the point plus we need to make sure we understand entirely what we are willing into our reality. There's another proverb that jumps to mind at this point is 'Be careful what you wish for, you might just get it!'. Again something to think carefully about before using an affirmation!. Although sometimes all the affirmations in the world wont change some situations and at times like these we have to admit to ourselves that 'this is where I need to be' and every once in a while we need to go back to go forward".

"Life's full of contradictions isn't it" said Arthur with resignation.

"It certainly is" agreed Kate.

They settled into silence whilst they walked, each left to their own thoughts and conclusions as to what was said. A few hours later they reached the next village on the trail, Kate popped into the small store whilst Arthur booked them into the hostel. Kate caught up with him in the bar and taking the key said she was going for a shower, Arthur sat in the bar enjoying a beer.

Kate was in a state her mind was whirling, she couldn't believe it how could this have happened? "That's a silly question!" she thought "How's Arthur going to take this?, I don't think I'm ready for this!". According to the test kit she'd bought at the store Kate was expecting!. She didn't know what to do.

"No I couldn't be!, we've been careful. It must be a mistake that kit could have been in the store for years, No-I'm not pregnant!" she spoke aloud.

Kate took a shower and convinced herself she was just late, if she was honest at this point she would admit she'd been late since they left America! but this wasn't the case, she showered and using every ounce of will power she had dismissed 'it' from her mind. She returned to the bar and Arthur.

"Hiya baby!" he said on her arrival.

Her mouth twitched and she sat down wordlessly.

"Are you aright?" he asked "you look a little pale".

"I'm fine" said Kate "Just last night catching up with me!".

"Yeah I know what you mean, still this beers helping some!" he replied "Do you want one?".

"Er, no I'll have an orange juice please" said Kate.

They had a meal and enjoyed a walk around the village, they visited the local chapel and an open air market selling local goods to local people.

Arthur bought some fruit and a new handmade pair of leather sandals whilst Kate bought a couple of baggy tops and some cheese. After which they headed back to their digs to get an early night.

On reaching the room Kate slipped into one of her new tops and got into bed, facing away from Arthur. He kissed her lightly on the cheek and shrugging his shoulders turned over to sleep. The next day they set out early enjoying the feel of the dawning day and the cool crisp air, Arthur felt great this trip was really working out.

They were having wonderful insights and were getting along great, he loved the sense of affinity he seemed to have developed with the land, his thoughts seemed not to come from within his own head but more from the land and the wind, like these elements were just extensions of his own mind and with this self analysis came the most glorious certainty that he was completely connected!. He felt great!.

Kate on the other hand felt anything but, she couldn't purge the thoughts of pregnancy from her mind. She glanced at Arthur, he looked strong and capable. She knew he was a good man and she could do a lot worse. She also knew she loved him, but to bring a child into this world!. Dispite the insights and knowledge she was constantly gathering. Her more practical aspect had come to the surface, this world is an awful place it's full of war and warmongers and hate and fear. She stopped this train of thought, as she was thinking she could feel her energy pulling these reality's into her life. She made an effort to dispel the thought patterns and felt them lift. Again the thought of a child plagued her, she glanced at Arthur.

"Do you realise how far we've walked?" he asked.

"No, how far?" she asked.

"About three hundred miles!" he said.

"Really!" asked Kate glad of the distraction.

"Well probably not exactly but pretty much, yeah!" he replied.

"No wonder I feel so fit!" said Kate thinking of her soon to be large tummy.

"Arthur can we stop for a while?" she asked.

"Yeah sure, you feeling tired?" he asked as they sat on their bags by the side of the trail.

"No, not really. Ive got something to tell you!" she said.

"Sounds serious" he replied.

“I’m pregnant!” she blurted out.

Arthur looked stunned, his pupils grew twice their normal size and the colour drained from he’s face. All this happened in a split second.

A smile exploded onto his face and the colour returned instantly.

“That’s wonderful!, are you sure?” he asked.

“Pretty sure!” said Kate.

“Oh wow!, I’m going to be a dad!” Arthur was bubbling, he looked as though he were about to take off!.

Kate couldn’t help smiling dispite herself “So your happy then!” she said.

“Of course!, you?” he replied in a more serious note.

“Sort of, it’s just such a shock. I mean I never planned to have children but then again I haven’t planned most of the last few years, yeah I am kinda pleased, it’ll grow on me” she said.

“Yeah literally!” said Arthur laughing.

“Very funny!” said Kate laughing.

“How long have you known?” asked Arthur.

“For sure?, yesterday but if I’m honest I think Ive known since before we left America” said Kate “about five months I suppose”.

“Five months!” said Arthur incredulously.

“I know, I’m starting to show!. I think Ive been in denial!” said Kate demurely.

Arthur slipped his arms around her "Never mind!" he said.

They held each other close for awhile then set off again along the trial, the changing light of day urging their progress. They reached the next township by late afternoon and after a bite at a local cafe took to their bed, Arthur was still in a bright mood and dispite Kate's misgivings she couldn't help but join him in he's contagious exhilaration. He lay next to her in bed, asleep as soon as he's head touched the pillow. His hand unconsciously draped across her slightly swollen tummy.

Kate lay awake staring at the ceiling, now Arthur was asleep the optimism he'd procured to her had at first ebbed then left her entirely.

"He's not seeing what this really means!" she thought.

"Once this baby's born we'll have to settle down somewhere and get responsible" she thought on "Could Arthur handle that!, he loves to travel as much as I do. What if we break up, it's been known to happen, people get on wonderfully and have a child, then real life steps in and pulls them apart. No I cant think like that, I know he loves me and I know I love him and that's as much as anyone can hope for when having a child-it'll be fine" Kate consoled herself.

She tried to keep control of her thoughts and banish any negative projections but she wasn't winning. She continued to stare blindly at the ceiling. Her eye's drifted out of focus and she welcomed sleep, her half-closed eye's fell to the middle distance of the room. In the moonlight streaming faintly through the semi-drawn curtains she saw light flecks of colour and movement. She sat up and stared, the colour coalesced into form and the room took on a heavy feel, the air was thick with energy and she could quite suddenly see perfectly around the room. The form took shape and dimension. It was the white lady!.

"Child" she said, again with thought not words.

"Yes?" said Kate feeling the warmth and basking in the pure love emanating from this being.

"I feel your pain but you have no need for fear, yours and Arthur's child is a very special being. This soul will bring a lot of light to a world that most needs it!".

"How?" asked Kate dumfounded.

"How is not your concern at this time" she replied *"would you like to meet your child?, I feel the closeness of the soul".*

"Now? -Yes!" replied Kate.

The white lady dissipated and disappeared leaving Kate alone in the dark. A second later an enormous amount of heat and light entered the room, the energy once again coalescing into form but not that recognisable as human. Just the appearance of a body in the finest silver thread-like light. The only communication was that of incredible love. The image wavered and was gone.

Kate lay back and closed her eyes, she fell immediately into a deep sleep.

Kate and Arthur woke late and had a leisurely breakfast. Arthur thought Kate seemed distant somehow, every time he tried to engage her in conversation she seemed to try to listen but would then drift off into herself.

He decided to bring it out in the open.

"Are you worried about the baby?" he asked.

Kate looked him steadily in the eye for a moment before she spoke.

"Not really, well not anymore" she said.

"Not anymore?" prompted Arthur.

"I was" said Kate "but something happened last night, well I think something happened last night!".

Arthur thought for a moment.

"You were, why?" he asked.

"I was feeling fearful about what could happen between us when the baby was born" she said.

"I'd never leave you, you know I love you, don't you?" he said.

"I know but lots of people love each other and have a baby but it can change a lot between two people, it's a huge thing having a child!" said Kate.

"I'm aware of that and I admit it's a huge responsibility but I think I'm ready for that, I can't imagine spending my life with anyone else!" he said emphatically.

Kate took his hand and held it between her own "Thank you" she said "I love you too!".

“So what happened last night?” he continued.

“It was incredible!” said Kate “I saw the white lady!”.

“The white lady!” said Arthur “What did she say?”.

“She told me not to worry, she said our child was very special and would bring a lot of light into the world when the world most needed it!” she said.

“Oh wow!” said Arthur “I wish I saw her too”.

“It felt like a dream!” said Kate “I was half asleep but as I’m telling you now it’s making it all clear in my mind again, she also asked me if I wanted to see our child”.

“And did you?” asked Arthur excitedly “was it a boy or girl?”.

“I don’t know, it wasn’t that clear. It looked like a ghost!, but the energy it brought in with it was incredible. There was more love in that one being than even the white lady herself and everything we’ve felt so far just falls into nothing after that” said Kate her eye’s wide with remembrance and awe.

“Wow!” said Arthur “Still that’s evolution for you I suppose!”.

“Yeah, I suppose so!” said Kate.

They sat quietly for a moment, each engrossed in their own thoughts.

“I wonder what the white lady has to teach us” said Arthur thoughtfully.

“I don’t know” said Kate “but I can’t wait to find out”.

"Also, I wonder if it's such a good idea to continue on the trial. I mean you should be taking it easy now, shouldn't you?" said Arthur showing concern.

"I think your right but I don't want to return to America just yet, couldn't we find somewhere nice to relax for awhile?" asked Kate.

"I don't see why not" responded Arthur "our luggage is in Santiago so I suppose we could catch a train there and decide what to do next".

"Sounds good" replied Kate.

After breakfast they asked the owner of the cafe where they could catch a train to Santiago and got a taxi to the nearest town, which thankfully was only a few miles down the road. On arrival at the station they bought their tickets and settled down to wait for the train. After an hour and lots of sweets they boarded the train and made themselves comfortable for the three hour journey to Santiago, Arthur fell asleep and Kate taking out her notebook began studying the other passengers. There was a wide variety of people getting on and off the train, there were families and teenagers and of course the very healthy looking elderly that Spain seemed to have in abundance.

"It must be due to their healthy diet and good air" thought Kate.

One old man in particular took her interest, he was wearing an old battered Panama that had once been white but now had the appearance of used chewing gum and a flannel shirt with blue jeans. He looked strong, his sleeves were rolled to the elbow and Kate could clearly see the sinew and ropy flesh of his forearms, this man had a hard but healthy life.

His face belayed his age, furrowed and weathered he was easily in his late sixties but he stood straight and true like a man who knew exactly who he was. He glanced towards her and she felt he's questioning gaze touch about her eyes and head, satisfied with her honest curiosity he gave her a mild grin and returned to looking out the window. Kate was both thrown and impressed by the mans frankness and strength. She continued to survey the carriage looking at each person in turn but her eyes always returning to this man. He was a father figure for all men, something she felt all men truly aspired to be. She wrote her impressions of him in her notebook and putting it away looked out the window admiring the passing countryside.

"Everything's going to be fine" she thought.

Arthur woke shortly before they entered Santiago station, Kate looked over to where the man was sitting but he was gone. They left the station and got a taxi to the Hotel where their luggage was waiting, on arrival they were told by the receptionist in perfect English that their luggage would be brought up to their room.

The room was fantastic it was clean and bright with a huge double bed dressed with fresh expensive linen and to Kate's great pleasure there was an ensuite with a bath. Plus south facing French windows leading to a small balcony overlooking the expansive plaza below.

Compared to the hostels of the trail this was a palace!. There was a polite knock at the door, Arthur opened it to find a bellhop in the hotels livery carrying the luggage they'd sent on earlier, Arthur let him in and once the young man had put their belongings next to the room's wardrobe tipped him and showed him out.

Kate run a hot bath whilst Arthur began unpacking the bags.

"I can't wait to put on some clean clothes" he called to Kate.

"Yeah me too, better have a bath first though. Do you want to join me, this baths huge!" answered Kate.

"Silly question!" he replied.

They bathed and change, it was now getting on to dinner time so they went down to the lobby and asked the receptionist if she could recommend anywhere nice as they didn't want to eat at the hotel. She gave them directions and this brought them to a open aired restaurant on the plaza, after eating well and soaking up the bustling atmosphere they decided to explore the city.

They walked around the city for about an hour taking in the sights and smells of the local night life. After which they headed back to the hotel feeling tired but comfortable.

On reaching the hotel Arthur wanted to talk about their options but Kate feeling tired said they could leave that decision till the following day.

They woke early and ordered room service, over which they discussed what to do next.

“I’d like to go back to Britain, you know Cornwall again” said Arthur.

“Wouldn’t you prefer to go further abroad, somewhere a bit more exotic?” asked Kate.

"Sounds good" said Arthur "but I reckon we need to be in one place, somewhere there's decent hospitals. Plus you know in another couple of months or so they wont let you on a plane!".

"Yeah I know but if we have the baby in Britain you realise it'll have British citizenship don't you?" asked Kate.

"That's not a problem, we could apply for duel citizenship for him" Arthur caught Kate's eye "or her" he added hastily.

"That's true" said Kate "Yeah I wouldn't mind spending the next few months in Britain".

After breakfast they visited the Cathedral of Santiago, the official finish of the trail and saw the tomb of St James through the tiny grate behind the main Alter. When they returned to the hotel Arthur went up to their room and Kate made the arrangements to fly to Gatwick the next day, she also phoned ahead to insure a rental car would be waiting. On returning to their room she found Arthur sat on their bed making a racket on his bo-ruan, trying to regain something of what the man in the shop in Glastonbury had taught him-he wasn't doing a good job.

He gave up when he noticed Kate standing in the doorway looking pained.

At this she began to mockingly clap his prose.

"Yeah aright!" was he's only reply.

"No, honestly that was truly great!" said Kate feigning genuine pleasure.

"When we leaving then?" he said changing the subject.

"Early tomorrow morning, we'll have to leave here at five a.m. to make the flight from La Coruna. Plus Ive booked us a car at the other end" she replied.

"Excellent I'm looking forward to being around people that I can actually talk to!" said Arthur.

"Well thanks a lot!" said Kate laughing.

"Oh, your OK but I need to talk to someone sensible, you know like a man!" said Arthur confidently.

Kate didn't say a word she walked over to the bed and set about beating Arthur senseless with a pillow, him protesting submission then reaching for pillow himself and engaging in battle!.

That evening they went down to dinner in the hotel's restaurant and enjoyed a last Spanish meal before going to bed early to be ready for the next day's travels.

CHAPTER 10

They arrived at Gatwick airport just after lunch, after picking up the rental car they decided to drive down to Bath. Which located just outside Bristol provided them with a semi rural setting within the reach of the city.

They booked into a hotel in the town centre and settled in for the night.

The next day they decided to see the sights, Kate wanted to visit the Roman baths from which the town took it's name. She got a real sense of peace whilst walking through the passages that linked the various 'baths' together, the baths themselves were more like small lakes and Kate could all to easily imagine dozens of people relaxing around the pools living the Roman ideal.

"What a life!" she thought "shame like most elitist societies the down trodden were seriously down trodden".

"Penny for your thoughts" said Arthur returning from the gift shop carrying a small plastic bag.

"Oh, nothing really. I was just thinking about the lifestyle the people that were here in the past must have lived" said Kate.

"Yeah I bet it was great, lounging around and overeating, would've suited you to a tee!" he joked.

"Not really, I don't like the idea of the level of servitude involved!" she replied.

"Yeah I suppose, still nice to imagine though" said Arthur.

"Yeah, what did you buy then?" she asked changing the subject tactfully.

“Not a lot really, I got us a mug each and a couple of postcards to send home”.

After they left the Baths they ate lunch at a small cafe and spent the rest of the day wandering around the shops and taking it easy.

Arthur saw an advert in a newsagents window advertising a holiday cottage a few miles outside the town.

“What do you reckon?” he asked Kate indicating the advert.

“Well it’ll be cheaper than staying in the hotel and it would be nice to settle somewhere for a while, are you sure you want to have the baby in Britain it’s not to late to get a flight back to the U.S you know!” said Kate.

“It’s up to you really, I don’t mind either way but I still think we have something to complete with the white lady and I get the feeling that whatever that is it’s going to happen here!” he replied.

Kate couldn't help but notice the conviction in his tone as he spoke and felt her own awareness move toward the same conclusion.

"I think your right" she said.

Kate phoned the number on the advert and arranged a viewing for the following morning.

On seeing the property they were overwhelmed, it was perfect.

The cottage itself was set amongst a large garden edged with Apple trees a small lake and an expansive lawn leading from the cottage's big crazy paved patio.

The village the house was in was made up of mostly holiday lets and had a small rustic pub and post office.

They decided on the spot to take it, Arthur made the arrangements with the owner for an extended let, they moved in the next day.

"This is such a nice house, I really don't mind spending the next few months or so here!" said Kate as they were unpacking their cases that night.

"I know what you mean, it's so quintessentially English isn't it?" replied Arthur.

"Yeah, quaint!" said Kate.

They settled into a routine very quickly over the forthcoming months and became very comfortable with their surroundings and each other, they really felt like a couple or more to the point a family.

Three months after moving in to the cottage, the seasons moving onwards to winter Kate, now (in her own words) whale-like and wrapped in layer upon layer of wool. Left the house on her way to the post office to pick up the newspapers (one of the many little routines she had fallen into and in her present state about all she could manage). She called over her shoulder as she left telling Arthur where she was off to.

"OK, I'll make some tea" he called back.

She reached the post office a little more out of breath than usual and stopped to catch her breath before going in.

"Are you OK my dear?" asked a voice behind her. Kate turned towards the voice, it was Mrs Bushet the elderly post-masters wife.

"Oh, thank you, I'm fine though really" Kate replied.

"You don't look to well, come in and sit down for a mo, I'll make you a cuppa" offered Mrs Bushet "here let me help you" she said taking Kate's arm.

"Thanks" laughed Kate dispite herself, they must have looked a sight. Kate the whale being propelled into the post office by this tiny sparrow like woman with a blue rinse and a cheery demeanour. She allowed herself to be steered to a deceptively comfortable chair behind the sweet counter.

"You wait there dear, I'll go make us some tea" said Mrs Bushet disappearing into the back room.

"What's wrong with her Lizie?" asked Mr Bushet from behind the post counter "She's not, you know!" he added peering over his counter at Kate's wholeness.

"Don't be silly Dave, she's just a little puffed, that's all" called Mrs Bushet from the back room. "Still can't be long now can it dear?" she added returning to the shop carrying two steaming cups "Here you go, I put plenty of sugar in".

"Where's mine?" asked Mr Bushet.

"You know where the kettle is!" answered Mrs Bushet.

“Charming!” he replied.

Mrs Bushet returned her attention to Kate who was trying not to laugh.

“Got to keep him on his toe’s you know!” whispered Mrs Bushet conspirativly. “You don’t stay married for thirty years without a bit of fire!” she added.

“I suppose” said Kate.

“So how you feeling now then?” asked Mrs Bushet.

“A lot better now thank you, I was just a little out of breath” she replied.

“Where’s that young man of yours, he should be out and about not you. You should be taking it easy!” said Mrs Bushet.

“No it’s fine I need to walk and get some air at least once a day or I’ll go mad” said Kate.

“Well I can understand that” said Mrs Bushet “I’ll get your papers then shall I?”.

“Please” said Kate.

She finished her tea and after paying for the papers headed back to the house, she met Arthur half way coming in the other direction, his face bright red with obvious exertion, he skidded to a halt.

“Are you aright?” he asked breathlessly.

“I’m fine!” said Kate “I wish people would stop asking me that!”.

“You were gone for ages I was worried, I thought you might have gone into labour or something” he replied.

"Your sweet, but Ive got at least two weeks yet!, I was just a little puffed out and Mrs Bushet insisted I have a cup of tea and sit down for a while" said Kate.

"Good for her!" said Arthur, he slipped his arm around her waist and they walked back slowly to the cottage.

The tea Arthur made had gone cold so he made a fresh pot and brought it with some toast through to the lounge, the pair of them sat looking out the French windows admiring the garden sipping tea and falling in to the usual argument as to what they should name the baby when it was born, this was hampered by the fact that during the last three scans the baby had turned so the doctors just couldn't gauge the sex, Kate was certain the child had done this on purpose.

As they sat it began to rain, Arthur took the dirty crockery out to the kitchen to wash up leaving Kate watching the weather. The wind picked up whipping the rain against the glass and then whipping it away just as quickly, Kate fell into a deep slumber.

Arthur sat quietly reading the papers whilst Kate slept, he kept glancing in her direction making sure she was OK, he knew he was being silly but he couldn't help it. He laughed silently at himself and tried not to look so often.

Kate was dreaming-

She thought about the window, the glass like a veil between worlds.

Warm and comfortable within, whilst the storm raged without.

Nothing but the thinnest of barriers keeping the two separate.

She thought about her child, her body the veil between worlds.

Warm and comfortable within, whilst the storm raged without.

-was the storm so random or doe's it have purpose.

She laughs, it always has purpose and like rain on the wind the direction taken is always right, there is no wrong - it's all right!.

She wakes.

"Are you hungry?" asked Arthur standing.

"How long have I been asleep?" she asked.

"Only a couple of hours" said Arthur.

"Oh, what are you making?" asked Kate.

"Thought I might do some fish with vegetables" replied Arthur.

"Sounds great, I'm famished" said Kate.

Arthur nodded accent and headed out to the kitchen, Kate looked out the windows. It had stopped raining and the wind had dropped, the sky looked dark and dismal. Kate got up and went into the kitchen to help Arthur prepare the meal.

The next day was the very opposite of the last, the sun was shining and the sky was the clearest azure blue. Due to the rarity of this kind of weather at this time of the year Kate and Arthur decided to go out for the day. Arthur got out the car, they had got rid of the rental a couple of months ago due to the expense and bought a decent used car planing to sell it when they left the country. Arthur had to cope with the driving on the left thing due to Kate no longer being able to fit behind the wheel, much to her distress.

They drove out to Glastonbury to have a coffee and do a little people watching, Kate had her notebook out and was taking notes of the passers by Whilst they sat outside the Rainbow cafe, the waiter they'd seen here on their previous visit some months ago wasn't to be seen.

This didn't bother Kate or Arthur in the least, they were quite happy to remain anonymous. After they had a coffee and something to eat they walked a little around the town taking in the atmosphere.

"I think that I preferred it here during the summer, it just seemed to have a happier vibe about it then" said Kate.

"I know what you mean, even though the sun is out and people are obviously taking advantage of it, there's definitely an underlying element depression that just wasn't present during the summer" replied Arthur.

"Do you think that might be due to that S.A.D thing that was in the public eye not so long ago" suggested Kate.

"That's about not receiving enough light isn't it?" asked Arthur.

“Yeah, not getting the full spectrum affects peoples moods, it’s just one of the many things that’s a bit alternative in it’s thinking but are finally being recognised, or remembered” said Kate.

“It’s not really that off the beaten path where conventional science is concerned, I mean it’s always been known your can’t grow a plant under an ordinary light bulb. It needs a full spectrum to grow, ultra violet in particular. Why scientists would ever entertain the possibility that we as people are any different I’ll never know” replied Arthur.

“You know you can buy light box’s now as well, to dose up on the missing colours!” said Kate.

“That’s a good idea” said Arthur “I do think more emphasis should be placed on peoples moods and emotions, the areas of cause and effect need to be fully investigated”.

“Well that’s just common sense really, remember cause and effect also works on the level of instability or a problem on the emotional or mental level and will if left untreated show up on the physical. That's just the sub-conscious really shouting at the consciousness that there is a problem!" said Kate.

"Yes it's also very important to remember there is no separation between these levels, this rings true in so many different ways!" said Arthur.

"How do you mean?" asked Kate.

"As you know, there is no separation between you as an individual person and the very universe or cosmos or even the reality as you perceive it. Which at the end of the day is only our own and all creation's higher aspects that are the essence of the overall group consciousness, of which we all are part because there is no separation even our lower aspects are part of the Whole. The deeper effects of recognising this truth has such far reaching ramifications that it must be experienced to truly be explained!" said Arthur emphatically.

"I understand what you mean, we are the entire universe incarnate and the life force that is the make up of the reality is also completely incorporated within ourselves. This leads to the conclusion that if we can be at peace with our inner reality, without striving for control but at the same time being in control. Just allowing ourselves to move with the energy, then we as a race can be at peace both with our own selves and those around us, leading us to be completely in sinc with the exterior, I use the term loosely, world and in so doing we would be able blend and move our own reality's in a very literal sense. Which would in affect, bring heaven to earth! because this would completely eradicate all the earth's usual problems including hunger, war greed and envy because everyone would be creating everything they could ever need and this would in turn leave people free to work through their lower aspects and in so doing strengthen this new reality and keep it for ever moving onward and upward!" reasoned Kate.

"It sounds wonderful, doesn't it?" said Arthur "could you imagine living in this world. The quicker we achieve this level of evolution the better!".

“Yes and we have to hurry and begin to consciously work towards this goal” said Kate.

“Why did you say that?” asked Arthur.

“I’m not entirely sure” said Kate “I just really feel that time is running out and if the level of awareness is not reached soon people are going to be left behind and I don’t know what will happen if they are”.

“I shouldn’t worry to much about it, the universe always finds a way!” replied Arthur.

“Yeah, it does doesn’t it” said Kate “It brought us together after all and who would have foreseen where that supposedly chance meeting would take us!”.

“To the best possible conclusion” said Arthur stopping and taking Kate in his arms.

CHAPTER 11

A few days later Kate and Arthur were sat in the cottages garden enjoying the warmth given off by the outdoor heater, the dying light of the passing day. Each others company and the remnants of their evening meal, Arthur poured Kate another glass of grape juice and they snuggled closer together under the blanket on the swing-couch.

Earlier that day Arthur had set night lights about the garden to provide atmosphere for their meal, it looked stunning. The little electric paper lanterns stretched from tree to tree around the perimeter were glowing like miniature moons in the encroaching darkness around them, Kate especially liked the way they reflected in the pond's surface and rippled with the breeze.

Arthur took Kate's empty plate and placed it on the floor on top of his own and put his arm around her, they sat in comfortable silence each reading the contentment in the others aura.

Kate gazed out at the pond and her eyes drifted into the middle distance, something caught her eye.

"What was that?" she said aloud.

"What?" asked Arthur.

"Over there passed the pond" said Kate indicating.

"That looks like -" began Arthur.

Kate instantly came to the same conclusion.

"The lightness we saw in Tintagel!" she said.

As they watched the lightness came closer and took form, it was a little girl!.

"Hello" it came in thought-speak.

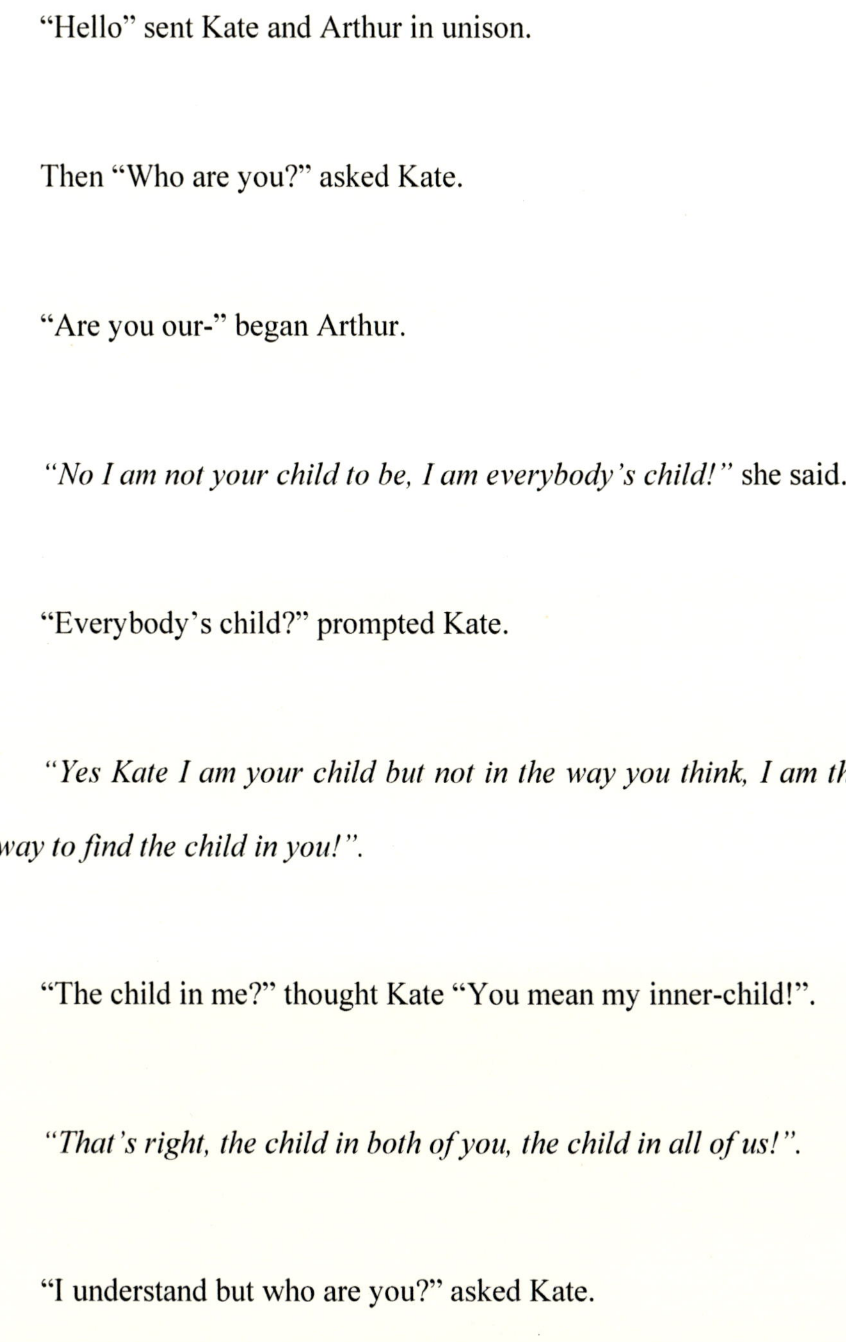

"Hello" sent Kate and Arthur in unison.

Then "Who are you?" asked Kate.

"Are you our-" began Arthur.

"No I am not your child to be, I am everybody's child!" she said.

"Everybody's child?" prompted Kate.

"Yes Kate I am your child but not in the way you think, I am the way to find the child in you!".

"The child in me?" thought Kate "You mean my inner-child!".

"That's right, the child in both of you, the child in all of us!".

"I understand but who are you?" asked Kate.

The image flickered and lost form falling in on itself becoming a small tornado of energy quickly coalesced into a new form.

The white lady stood before them.

"You!" thought Arthur "I thought we'd see you again!"

"And you were right my child. This is one of many expressions, I'm known to many different cultures by many different names and images. But you may call me mother or sister for this is what I truly am. Like you I am multidimensional, like you I exist on all planes of reality simultaneously but unlike you I am not in the dense matter of the physical and so I live in constant awareness of my wholeness. I am the soul of this planet".

"Mother earth?" asked Arthur.

"That's one of my names, one I knew you would understand and that is why I first came to you in this form but for what I have to teach

you now I must adopt a higher expression, that of the child. The highest expression in the universe for we are all truly children".

The white lady transformed into the child with such speed Kate and Arthur found themselves questioning whether or not the lady had ever stood before them.

"What are you going to teach us?" asked Kate.

"You are an expression between expressions just as I. We start at the trinity, the father, the mother and the spirit. The spirit is the child. I am in this world the mother and the cosmos will be expressed in the father. I the mother will lead you to the child and the child, the spirit within you will lead you home into the cosmos, the father".

"Why must it be expressed by the mother, father and child" asked Arthur not feeling comfortable with the religious connotations.

"These are the three main expressions of life for there to be life these three energies must be present in any form and for the true path of evolution these three must be present within you as individuals for you to truly connect with life and move forward to achieve that which has been promised".

"What has been promised?" asked Kate.

"To all questions, you already know the answers. But this one it is close to the surface in you".

Kate felt the answer bubble up through the layers of her being but she had grasped it the moment the child had answered.

"Heaven on Earth" she replied.

"Yes divinity in the flesh, we had this once but we stumbled on our path and lost our way but thankfully you are now all starting to remember who you are and why you are here".

“But what about those that choose not to remember?” asked Kate remembering her previous fear, for that was what it was.

“They will be given more time, I shall leave a shell of myself behind when I ascend. This planet will be but a shadow of myself but will be ample for their needs.”

“So you are going to help us connect with our inner child then?” asked Arthur.

“That is why I am here with you now, come join me in your minds eye. Come dance with me, trust me to guide you, come and play, come express the child within you!”.

Kate and Arthur instinctively closed their eyes and drifted into a trance like state.

The Essence of the planet was before them in her child form, Kate and Arthur looked down at their bodies, they too were children. They laughed and the laughter rang through them like the peal of small bells and running water, it was a cleansing sound. A sound of innocent's, a sound of purity, of joy, of pure expression. With none of the constraints of adulthood, none of the cage-like structure. Freed from this they felt the simple joy of being. They stood silent and their surroundings swam into focus, they stood on a beach. The Essence kneeling at the waters edge beckons them and they approach, she gestures them to kneel with her and willingly they obey. The child dips her hand into the water, looking intently Arthur and Kate follow suit watching the child's action with wonder and expectation. The child deftly twists her wrist splashing both Kate and Arthur in the face giggling at their shocked visage's she stands and runs though the waters break back down the beach. Kate and Arthur look at each other and are over come with their own gullibility, standing they chase the Essence through the surf. She standing a little further on watching their reactions throws her head back and laughs before running on. They catch up with the essence and kick the water at her and each other whilst running, Arthur trips over his own feet and crash's head-long into the water. Kate and the child stand over him with hands on hips laughing and jeering, he feeling indignant swipes his arm through the water creating a mini tidal wave that engulfs the pair. He jumps up before they can retaliate and runs up the beach towards the nearby scrub like brush. He turns the Essence and Kate poke out tongues before turning away and running in the other direction, Arthur laughs and pursues. They play for what seems like hours until each collapses on the beach in exhaustion like only children can. Arthur wants an ice-cream and three appear in his hands, he smiles and accepts the simple truth his eye's purvey, handing one to each of his friends they sit and feast each somehow managing to cover themselves in the sticky substance and falling into fits of laughter at the appearance of each others countenance.

They finish their ice-creams and wash themselves at the waters edge, with only a marginal amount of splashing. The essence speaks.

"It is time to return my friends, you have both strengthened your connection with the child. Remember this aspect is the only true master".

The beach swam into nothingness, Arthur and Kate opened their eye's, before them lay the garden just as they had left it.

The white lady stood before them.

"You have learned this lesson well, the child within you is now awake, be well".

The white lady disappeared.

Kate and Arthur did not question the experience they had that night, they took to their bed soon after they arrived back at the garden and fell pleasantly into a warm comfortable sleep. Each still holding the innocent feeling of lightness the experience had given them.

Over the days that followed Kate and Arthur found they were even more comfortable together than they had ever been before, neither of them would have imagined this possible. They were remembering the alliance's they made as children, alliance's so easily made and maintained-simple, honest friendship and love. Living within this state neither of them wanted to leave the cottage, the discussions and expanded awareness was so acute and insightful yet was communicated with such simplicity and openness. They felt themselves to be truly what they were, children of the universe. Eventually they were forced by necessity to leave their very happy bubble and venture out into the 'real' world to get supplies.

Arthur was waiting in the lounge, Kate was in the bathroom. She'd been in there for what seemed to Arthur an incredibly long time, he knew she didn't want to go. He felt the same but they couldn't stay in the cottage for ever, it just wasn't healthy. They needed to get out to see people and to integrate with the rest of the human race, they'd spoke in depth about this the other night and they'd both agreed on the dangers of becoming so involved with what was going on as to loose touch with, well basically- humanity!. So here they were about to drive into Bristol to go to a supermarket and do a weekly shop, the most normal thing in the world -so why was Arthur feeling so jumpy!.

Kate came down the stairs.

“Ready?” she asked casually.

Arthur felt her energy, she’d buffeted herself in and he could feel her distance.

“Yeah” he replied.

They got in the car and drove out the drive, Arthur was driving and finding it all very difficult. Everything seemed to be coming at him at such a speed and with such harshness he could barely keep his nerve, Kate sat quietly trying not to pick up Arthur’s energy. He railed his strength and poured it in to present, into being here and now. The speed and harshness dropped away a little, Arthur relaxed into himself and began to drive.

“Shall I put the radio on?” asked Kate a few moments later.

“Good idea!” he replied.

Kate turned on the car’s radio and it sparked to life filling the car with friendly noise. They spoke periodically and once again found that balanced space between them where they could truly be themselves. On arrival at the supermarket Arthur felt a twang of apprehension just as he were entering the store but quickly asserted himself to quell it and entered.

“These lights are awful” said Kate once they were inside.

“I know they really play on your eye’s don’t they?” said Arthur.

“Yeah and not just the two you can see!” said Kate “my third eye is pounding!”.

"In a good way?" asked Arthur, he too feeling the play of light across his brow.

"Harmless, I think but I'm not entirely sure if it's pleasant" replied Kate.

"Oh well it's an experience if nothing else!" said Arthur.

"Yeah I suppose so" said Kate.

They done their shopping as quickly as possible, Kate wanted to leave. She felt her energy depleting by the second, plus her ankles had begun to swell.

"I wonder why our energy's depleting so quickly in here" said Arthur, he too feeling his awareness drop.

"I think" said Kate "It's due to the advertising mostly and all the bright labels plus this is a synthetic environment".

"How would the advertising affect us?" asked Arthur.

"It's all pulling at our consciousness, in a thousand different directions at once. Kinda trying to fracture our awareness and leave us vulnerable to suggestion, it's really a huge infringement on our free-will as well as our human rights!" said Kate.

They made their way to the checkout and waited in line.

Kate felt her knees turn to jelly and she nearly fell to the ground, Arthur caught her just in the nick of time.

"Are you OK?" he asked.

Kate's eyes rolled back in their sockets and she went limp in Arthur's arms, he felt his bile rise in his throat and fear hit his heart like a sledge hammer.

There was the sound of running water, just for a second then Kate opened her eyes.

“I’m OK” she said “I’m having the baby!”.

Arthur was speechless, he looked down at his shoes. They were covered in liquid. Everything went blank…

The world jumped back into focus, he was on the floor and Kate was standing over him looking concerned.

“Are you aright?” she asked.

“I’m fine” said Arthur standing “what happened?”.

Kate smiled “You fainted!”.

Arthur steadied himself on the counter.

“Really?” he asked.

“Afraid so” said Kate with a hint of laughter.

“We’d better get to the hospital!” he said urgently.

They left the queue and walked passed the other customers, who cheered and laughed as Arthur staggered by trying to support Kate but in truth they were supporting each other.

“Can we leave that there?” asked Arthur motioning their shopping cart to the girl behind the counter.

“Yes of course” she replied “and good luck!”.

“Thank you” said Kate.

They headed straight to the hospital and booked themselves in, Kate was asked to wait in a small room next to the maternity ward. After a six hours initial labour Kate was taken to the birthing pool, they’d decided on a water birth some time previously believing it to be an easier transition into the world for the baby and a lot less discomfort for Kate. They both got into the pool followed by the midwife, a friendly young man with an easy manner and caring demeanour. Arthur sat at Kate's side holding her hand and trying not to look at what was going on beneath the water's surface, Kate was coping well she'd taken all the pain killers on offer and although obviously still in a great deal of pain was quite relaxed and comfortable with the proceedings, this confirmed to Arthur that women were definitely the stronger of the sexes. Two hours later a healthy baby boy was born, Kate was taken back to the ward whilst a doctor examined the baby to make sure all was well. A few moments later the midwife arrived with their baby, wrapped in a fluffy white towel the child looked like an angel, completely at peace and settled. The midwife passed Kate the baby and left them all to get acquainted, Kate and Arthur looked down at their child and he smiled benignly up at them, just for a fraction of a second the child's eyes had a look of extreme age about them. Kate and Arthur started in surprise and the child laughed, the moment passed leaving them thinking they'd imagined it. They just stared at what they'd done together and felt the pride of the new parents seep into their bones.

“What are we going to call him?” asked Arthur.

“I like James” said Kate staring adoringly at the new born.

“James it is” replied Arthur smiling.

After an hour of the most wonderful time of his life Arthur left Kate to sleep and after following the nurse down the corridor to watch her lay him in a crib. Arthur went to the nearest pay phone to call his parents back home in Vantage to tell them the good news, they were ecstatic after asking after Kate and the child’s well being, they made Arthur promise to bring the child home as soon as possible. He said he’d ask Kate and would let them know but as far as he could say that was already the plan. After much questions in regard to the baby he eventually put down the phone and returned to Kate’s room, the nurse had set up a camp bed along side Kate’s and Arthur sank gratefully into a deep slumber.

The following morning the happy family discharged themselves from the hospital and returned to the cottage, the baby gurgled contentedly in Kate's arms as they drove.

On arrival James, Kate and Arthur settled into life together. Arthur's parents were once again on the phone speaking sweet nothings through the receiver held tentatively to the baby's ear, James laughed down the phone to the extreme pleasure of Arthur's parents. Kate said she would phone her folks in a few days telling Arthur that since they had no idea she was pregnant it may come as some what of a shock and she wasn't quite feeling up to that just yet!.

Arthur thought it was a little strange that Kate had neglected to tell her parents but surmised she must have her reasons and since he was yet to meet them decided not to mention his misgivings to Kate.

The next couple of weeks were complete bliss for the young couple, dispite the early wake up calls generously arranged by James. They took it in their stride and welcomed this, the next chapter in their lives together.

CHAPTER 12

Two weeks further on James had settled in to regular sleep pattern and Kate and Arthur had acclimatised to it. Being stuck indoors for the past four weeks had really started to grind on Kate's and Arthur nerves, they decided to go out on a day trip. Kate had seen an interesting site in Avebury containing a circle of standing stones, not far from where they were on the T.V that she really fancy's seeing before they returned to America and dispite the feeling of mobilising an army they decided to check it out. The morning came, after waking at six a.m. they finally left the house and got in the car by ten, they congratulated themselves on their expediency and started the car. Or at least tried to, turning the key Arthur was greeted with the sound of silence, he tried again and again there was nothing.

"Oh no" he said "looks like we're going nowhere!".

"Your kidding!" said Kate "after all that!".

James gurgled and began to cry.

“I’m not giving up that easy!” said Arthur.

“What can we do?” asked Kate.

“I’m going to phone a cab, if we can get into Bristol I’m sure we can catch a train to Avebury”.

“OK” said Kate “if I have to spend another day indoors, I’m going to scream!”.

Arthur phoned the station and confirmed there was a train station in Avebury and a connection from Exeter, after which he called a cab.

Half an hour later the cab arrived and took them to the station, after an hours wait they caught a train to Exeter and missed their connection to Avebury at which point James decided this wasn’t fun anymore and begun to cry. No matter what they did he wouldn't stop until after another hours wait they finally caught their connection to Avebury and when an elderly lady approached them and began talking to James he finally stopped crying and started to enjoy himself once again. Kate and Arthur with sweat flowing freely from their brows couldn't thank her enough.

Eventually they arrived safe and sound in Avebury, it was three o'clock in the afternoon and Kate and Arthur were exhausted.

They stopped for a bite to eat at a pub adjacent to the station and after eating and asking the bartender directions began the short walk to the stone circle. To reach the site they had to walk across a car park, a few cars were parked in the lot and their owners could be seen walking among the large scattered stones in the middle distance.

The site itself consisted of a deep trench surrounding the first circle of stones, within this circle there appeared to be approximately twenty stones, they were made of granite and between ten to fifteen feet tall. Inside this circle there was another, smaller than the first but no less impressive, this circle contained ten stones also made of granite and about ten feet in from the first and of the same size.

As Kate and Arthur (carrying James in the travel crib) approached they couldn't help to notice the other people move away and begin to return to their cars. Kate felt a buzzing in the air, almost like the stagnant crackle of an old stereo speaker on stand by, she glanced at Arthur and he nodded accent, James had gone very quiet.

Arthur looked at the people moving to their cars and driving away.

"I think we're in for another dose!" he said with a smile.

"I think your right!" said Kate.

They picked up their pace and soon found themselves standing at the boundary of the first circle, they stopped.

The buzzing had increased and the air had taken on that heavy velvet like quality they had grown so accustomed to at times like this.

James was still very quiet, Kate glanced at Arthur and they both stepped into the circle.

Their heads began to swim and the world around them took on an almost false appearance, nothing looked real it all seemed to be made of synthetic materials. Even the grass looked like plastic and the stones look as if it were possible to pass a hand right through them. The air had changed in tone too, being late afternoon on their arrival at the site it now appeared much later, almost like dusk -it was very odd.

They moved on towards the second circle of stones, their feet feeling light as feathers and their movements smooth and languid like the flow of water but not constrained in any way but totally liberating almost as though the machinery of their bodies were functioning correctly for the first time. James was still very quiet.

On reaching the next set of stones they stopped once again. Kate could feel the invisible barrier spanning between the monoliths, she could also see a much smaller stone set in the centre of the circle. It had a large flat surface at waist height that filled Kate with dread and foreboding plus and this when recognising the emotion surprised her-guilt. She looked at Arthur and felt the projection of her thoughts feelings and conclusions passed to him in a split second, he caught the projection and mirrored the connection, they'd been here before!.

James was still very quiet.

Arthur wanted to turn and run, this one he didn't want to face. Kate picked up on this urge and Arthur felt her return the feeling.

They stood where they were for what felt like an eternity, then moving as one entered the circle.

Images assail them, their sexes are reversed, he is she and she is he.

They stand before the altar, for that was what it was. It was night, a clear night, the stars stood out in stark relief to the night sky. They were dressed in ceremonial robes, both in white with bold splatters of red across their chest's, no not red -blood!. Arthur's counterpart, in this life a woman shouts to the sky in an unrecognisable dialect, her head thrown back and a cruel looking knife held above her, blood dripping from the blade she finishes her call and smears the blood across her brow. Her partner moves forward and she wipes blood across his brow, he bows to her whispering in the same archaic tongue and steps back out of their line of sight returning with a young girl dressed in peasants clothing and looking terrified, she moves dumbly, propelled by the man and stupefied by some drug or controlling influence.

Kate and Arthur find themselves touching in on the girls energy, she's pure light, unfocused but pure and incredibly strong. Both Kate and Arthur feel the fear of their counter parts. The girl is placed on the alter, her arms and legs tied, the knife is raised, silhouetted by the moon, the knife fatally falls and the moon expands in an instant, obliterating the vision.

Kate and Arthur find themselves back in the present, they fall to their knees and weep. The imagery burning their inner sight and their hearts hurting with regret. They come to another realisation -that was James!, it comes so clear as if spoken on the wind and with such certainty as to purge their minds of all possible denial. Another thought follows, a memory told to them by a friend years ago in Vantage "The same souls always revolve around each other from life time to life time". Kate crawls to where Arthur sits cradling James, tears streaming down his cheeks, she holds on to them both and they weep. The tears and grief pouring from them, James remains silent

"Be still my children" Spoken, the words come from above their heads.

"Who?" says Kate raising her head, Arthur following suit.

Above them stands a man, Kate recognises him instantly. It's the man she'd noticed months ago on the train in Spain except now his wearing a flowing gown of pristine white and surrounded in rich golden light. He smiles at the recognition.

"You!" said Kate.

"Yes, I am the father"

"The father?" asks Arthur "are you God?".

"We are all God I am but the aspect of the father, present in all of us".

"Was" asks Kate, her voice trembling "That real?" indicating the vision.

"Search your heart, was it real?".

"Yes" answers Arthur "but passed".

"That's right it is passed, that was a previous incarnation of the three of you. Although not a pleasant one, you must remember to let go, the beings you just witnessed are but aspects of you. They are not who you are now, you have grown in many ways since that

incarnation as has your child" He indicated James, who gurgled happily in reply.

"Why are you here?" asked Kate already knowing the answer.

"Once again if you search your hearts, you will come to the truth. I am here to take you back to unity, I am here to unite the trinity within you, I am her to bring you back to a state of oneness, of wholeness, to guide you home back to completion, to set you once again on a path of progression beyond the limitations of this dimension".

"How?" asked Kate.

"The mother told you she will leave a shell of herself for those who are initially left behind, she did not tell you this has already happened, in truth she never left the now. You as a people did and created this shell of her, this reality in which to express your lower aspects but you two are now ready to come home".

Kate went pale "Two?" she asked "Which two?"

"Your self and Arthur, the little one still has work to do. Both on his self and for the good of your kind, fear not he will be fine and you will be able to guide him from the other side, come, take my hand".

"What and just leave him here?" asked Kate her bile rising.

"Yes, he will be well -look"

He gestured behind them, through the enveloping mist that Kate and Arthur had not noticed before they could clearly see a young couple walking towards where they knelt. Kate kissed James and took the mans hand, Arthur did likewise and the three of them disappeared.

CHAPTER 13

"Claire, can you hear that?"

"Here what?"

"That" he walked towards the sound, as he approached the inner circle of stones he could hear it clearer, Claire followed him.

"That's a child!" she said.

They picked up their pace and on turning around the first stone they saw the travel crib and James, crying. Claire picked up the crib and stared into the basket.

"How did you get here?" she asked James who stopped crying and gave her a grin "You don't think he's been abandoned do you Matt?" she asked her partner.

“There were no other cars in the car park” he answered “We’d better call the police!”.

CHAPTER 14

They stood watching, barely three feet from the couple. Kate could have reached out and touched them, it was strange she was aware of the feeling of loss and resentment at leaving James behind but at the same time there were more prevalent thoughts running through her mind. She could see the bigger picture, she could see James's path stretched before her. He was going to be fine and on completion of his journey he would return to her in the now, Arthur held her hand and they went to meet, knowing with complete certainty that time was linear only to the third dimension and had no ties here nor did death or suffering, this was the true Earth, this was the true Heaven, this was Heaven on Earth. They faded from the scene to join the rest of humanity and their son.

ADVANTAGE -PART 3

CHAPTER 1

Kate and Arthur followed closely James's progress over the coming years. He was first taken to the hospital where he was born, then to a temporary foster home, where Kate influenced the mind of the chief nurse to call him James and stood by him in spirit whilst the police searched for any leads as to the identity and whereabouts of his parents. After much deliberation it was decided he had been abandoned and his parents were not going to come forward. He was handed over to a care facility and became a ward of court. At first he was placed in a more permanent home then later due to his age was adopted by a caring young couple, who found they really like the name James and decided to keep it. They were called Tom and Angie Lotts and loved James like he was their own, during this period of James's life Kate and Arthur took a back seat in his consciousness to give him the space he needed to grow up well balanced and happy with his new parents, James's older/higher self standing with them in the forth dimension generally took the lead on all the important issues in the young James's life.

James had a happy childhood, growing up in an affluent area of surrey, just outside London and very far removed from the spiritual under tones of life. Tom and Angie were quite well to do and were happy to give James all he could ever need. He wanted for nothing and with Tom being a computer programmer he learnt all manner of interesting lessons and information on the workings of the computer brain, Angie on the other hand worked in sales and advertising giving James a good view into the workings of the human mind and it's responses to differing stimuli. Both these influences gave James a very balanced order of thought and keen insight into human behaviour, by the time he was sixteen he'd decided he wanted to be an entertainer. He felt this line of work would provide him with enough stimuli to keep his overactive (yet as his foster parents would add, exceptionally clever) mind interested .

"And besides" he surmised "the money's good as well!".

James had begun to take after his real parents, he had the same colour eyes and hair as Kate but his features were mainly Arthur's, as was his size and build.

During the summer break between leaving school and starting college, he worked as a red coat at a well known holiday campus.

Many well known entertainers had started their careers in this fashion because it gave a basis in almost every avenue of the business, he sang, danced, told jokes and presented many of the competitions for the people staying at the complex. Besides this he also had to serve tables and help in the kitchen's.

After this experience he felt fully committed to going for his goal and wanted to avoid any menial work at all costs. He started at college and studied Drama, made friends and settled into student life. The next couple of years were pretty uneventful, James studied hard and finished the course with an A level in Drama and the performing arts as well as in Maths and English, at his foster parents instruction.

Before going on to university he took a year out and worked his way around Australia gaining people skills and having a good time.

On returning to Britain he started a degree in the performing arts at Plymouth university and again settled into student life. After celebrating his nineteenth birthday at a local student hot spot he began to notice strange sparkles in the air and his perception of synergy whilst interacting with others began to increase, he found he could tell exactly what other people were going to say before they spoke as well as anticipating forthcoming events, sometimes this foreknowledge would stretch to days or even weeks before the event. Besides this he'd noticed himself having very strange thoughts and looking at things in an entirely new way, sometimes there seemed to be a voice in his mind but not really a voice, more his own normal internal monologue giving him instruction and opening new avenues of thought, it was all very weird. James decided not to mention these going's on to anyone as he didn't want to appear odd in the eyes of his peers. It all seemed to be broadening his perspective so he just took it as a part of growing up that no-one mentioned, which he thought was odd because it seemed to be the best part.

This ‘guidance’ led James to the university’s library where he collected books on psychology and self-awareness, these books highlighted and completed the ‘missing bits’ in his growing awareness and gave him the appropriate terms for what he was seeing, feeling and thinking making it all a lot easier to integrate into his consciousness.

He began to spend more and more time alone, gathering knowledge and understanding from what he now saw as his higher self, he also changed his diet to keep his energy strong and focused. Besides this he also started a meditation course offered by a local group and through this exercise found there were other people thinking along the same lines and having similar experience’s, although James kept relatively quiet about his own personal insights and tended to just touch the surface whilst talking to the other members of the group. He began to lose his interest in Drama and the arts, he found to his surprise that he was actually beginning to enjoy Maths and English more. The numerology involved in maths seemed so pure and defined it seemed to be the only constant in his reality at this time, everything else seemed to change on a daily basis, he began to wonder why.

Soon after the answer came but he couldn't grasp what it meant, the answer he received was 'change is growth', he flipped this around in his mind for a while and gained deeper insight when he reversed it -'growth is change', as he thought this he got an image of a flower opening and understood that everything needed to be in a constant state of motion in order to develop, like building layers, the latter insights didn't make the former any less true but gave a more defining truth.

One lunch time after another painfully false Drama class James entered the cafeteria and after buying his lunch sat at a table opposite a young woman with her nose buried in a book, James took in the cover, it read 'Today's Psychology'.

“Are you studying Psychology?” he asked.

“Yes” she replied “are you?”.

“No, Drama mostly” he said.

“Oh, what’s that like?” she asked.

“Not bad but I think I’m going off it!” he replied.

“Why?, is it hard work?” she said.

“Not really, it just seems so false to me now” he said “I mean I’m still enjoying dance and the singing but the acting’s getting me down, I feel I’m wasting my time with it”.

“How so?” she asked putting down her book and leaning towards him across the table.

"I don't see the point in projecting myself into other characters when I'm still learning who I am" he said.

"Sounds to me like you should be doing psychology" she said.

"Maybe" he replied leaning back in his chair.

"Or maybe not" she said "I'm finding my course really confining, back in college it seemed a lot more open to interpretation but now it just feels as though I'm being programmed and that's not why I chose to study the subject".

James leaned back towards her as she spoke, when she'd finished he extended his hand across the table "James" he said.

"Kate" she replied taking his hand.

James felt a bolt of electricity shoot up his spine.

"What?" asked Kate sensing an odd response.

"Nothing, someone just walked across my grave, that's all" he replied.

"That's interesting you should say that" he continued "Ive been thinking that a lot of subjects seem to be like that, I mean an education is meant to serve you not the other way round".

"You mean like work to live and not live to work!" she said.

"Yeah, it seems to me that far too much emphasis is placed on what we do as opposed to who we are, the important thing in life a far as I can see is that you express yourself" he said.

"I know exactly what you mean, it's like we're not given enough time to develop as people, it just seems to be about what are you going to do" she replied.

"Yeah, I'd like to be able to take more time finding out who I am but I suppose that's more of a social thing than anything else. It's a real shame there's not a degree in self development that also offers a viable career for the future" he said.

"That's why I chose Psychology, you know the 'physician heal thyself' bit, but it's hard trying to apply the things we're taught without going to far into yourself and creating problems that in truth just aren't there" she said.

"Yeah I think that's one of the main problems with Psychology, perhaps Philosophy would be better" he said.

"But what would you go on to do with a degree in Philosophy?" she asked "I mean it's not like we live in ancient Greece where something like that is respected enough to provide for you is it?".

"Mores the pity!" he replied.

"It's just like being an artist if your recognised then it's great but if not then your in for a pretty hard time and with today's world I think we're encouraged to go for the safer options in life, which is why so many people end up doing something they hate for a living and spent their lives in misery. Which of course they take out on those around them and so the cycle continues" she said.

"Yeah" he replied "I know what you mean, I think we need to scrap the way our society is built at the foundations and start over, for one thing to much emphasis is placed on money and material gain. Surely we've come to a point in our civilisation that we can do away with that particular part of it all and focus more on the important things in life".

"Like self development" she suggested.

"Yeah exactly" he replied.

Kate went on to expand on what exactly could be developed on the human experience in her view and James put in a few ideas of his own, still not sharing most of what he thought, being worried about what she would think of him if he shared the conviction he held with some of his more outlandish insights.

They parted company promising to get together again at some point to follow up their conversation. James continued with his study's for the next three years over which he had more insightful conversations with his peers, he found that many people felt the same way about a great many things but he could see that most were content to live out their lives without actually taking their ideas beyond conversation. This he had trouble reconciling with, eventually he accepted that most people just didn't feel as strongly about these ideas as he did.

After he finished his degree's in Drama, English and Maths. Doing rather well, he decided to stay on in education and study Philosophy and science. He felt this was the best suited environment to pursue his now fully developed passion for self growth. He truly loved opening new areas of knowledge previously unknown to him and expanding his mind, many people viewed him as self absorbed but he took a differing viewpoint and thought that most people around him placed far to much of themselves in what was going on around them as opposed to what was going on within them. He found the two intimately connected and repeatedly noticed a very definite reflection of his inner environment to his outer one. From this he eventually grasped the concept of 'no separation', that being between himself and the rest of reality, with this realisation came an almost euphoric sensation of oneness with the world around him, this sensation very quickly became addictive as well as a practical method of measurement for the correctness of other forthcoming insights, he began to trust this form of divination more than his own profound sense of logic. Through this his awareness began to grow at an even more accelerated rate, by the time he was thirty he had begun to communicate on a regular basis with people that had passed over and higher beings in what he had learnt to call spirit, he would often be walking down a street or even just sat at home when someone in spirit would quite literally pop up and talk to him. He even learnt to guide them through to the next world when they were lost for whatever reason, pretty soon he started to notice colours drifting around people that were directly connected to their thought forms, he would even watch these thought forms go right out of peoples own space and pull towards them whatever they desired, the effectiveness of this corresponded to the person in particular's state of clarity at the given moment, which correlated to their general level of balance. He decided to dedicate most of his time to investigating this most exciting area of what he termed metaphysics.

He turned his attention to his own level of clarity and much to his distress found was not as clear as he thought. He discovered the lower more primeval areas of his persona, those dedicated to domination of others and petty competitiveness, he spent more time alone and in meditation making a very conscious effort to keep his mind from drifting and thinking over much on unimportant issues. As he did so he began to discover how much more effect his thoughts had over his reality due to their increased power. He found it difficult holding this mental stance in every day life but as he developed his space and learnt to let go of the trivial he found it got easier and more importantly, it didn't have to be difficult.

One hot day in June whilst relaxing in his local park and watching the people go about their busi-ness, he felt the familiar touch of his higher self about to communicate with him. He cleared his mind and sat awaiting the usual stream of information when instead he felt vague image's flitter in his minds eye, these image's became clearer as he shifted his focus and began to show people, most importantly a man and a woman. James knew he was adopted and that he'd been found in a field somewhere, it had never really bothered him for some reason. He was happy with the parents he had and had never wasted any time wondering about his real folks, until now.

As the image's poured into his mind he felt an overwhelming amount of love for these two people and knew instinctively who they were, they were his real parents!.

Kate and Arthur stood before the portal, they'd watched James's progress with interest. He done well, they were not surprised at the speed of his growth standing next to his older/higher self made it very clear how evolved this soul actually was and what was planned for the expression living on the third dimensional planet they now viewed, this information they had garnered from the higher self existing far beyond even their plane of existence, this was the god-head or to put it another way the combined higher self of creation, the nucleus of the cell.

James watched the image's with fascination, he looked like his parents and was about the same age. He briefly wondered why they'd chose to leave him and received a speeded up video like answer giving him all he needed to know, his mind reeled from the concept of ascension and broke the connection instantly. He walked back to his room trying all the way to re-establish the link, on arriving home and putting on the kettle the imagery returned. This time he accepted the idea of ascension and the imagery expanded showing him the pyramid like structure of the dimensions leading to the point then shooting out the other way to form a hour glass like shape, this then both spinning and twisting round on itself to create at first a circle then a sphere which then revealed itself to be just a cell in an even larger body, the enormity of what he saw almost blowing his mind but at the same time exciting him beyond all measure, 'the possibilities are endless' he thought.

He then glimpsed a figure standing between the first two, this person very much resembled himself and was in fact his higher self. They smiled at each other across the dimensions. James felt other dimensions and levels of consciousness link with him and this higher aspect of himself, spanning outward like the threads of a web he found himself present on all these other levels simultaneously each aspect living independently yet still dependent on the others, again the concept of no separation broached his mind and he felt himself expand filling every possible space the universe provided -every expression in the cosmos was a part of his own celestial body like the fingers of his hand he could move it all without thought just impulsive reflex.

Yet it occurred to him, he was still sat in his little room. he heard the couple living below arguing. The contrast made him laugh and concerned for his sanity as well as his ego he pulled away from his connection, closing down the doorway's for now and relaxing back into himself he began to feel more human and centred. He thought on the experience and could sense the connections still in place.

"Well I've done it now!" he said aloud.

CHAPTER 2

The next few days were difficult to say the least, he had to constantly remind himself to remain in the present. The attraction to allow himself to drift into his new found perception was almost impossible to resist but resist he did and to his great pleasure it became easier to walk between the worlds.

He also realised his control over his own reality had grown in bounds, it felt as though he was surrounded in a warm bubble that stretched tendrils far out into the universe and kept his multidimensional selves in perfect sinc, each consciously now playing their role as part of the whole that was both himself and the entire universe, he finally understood what exactly the Buddhist's meant by nirvana, he had found true enlightenment and the really amazing thing was he didn't even have to work that hard. When he was hungry -he ate, when he was tired -he slept, when he was bored -he played.

Everything else just sort of fell into place teaching him at every turn, he just moved with the teaching's, taking them on board and allowing them to show him the way. The only real difficult part was keeping his ego in check, every time he let his guard down in this respect the whole comfortable structure would collapse and he would have to start again. Even this he got used to, when it happened he would just think "Oh well" and move on, this action in itself helped him work through the ego.

One morning whilst watching tv, he saw the pyramids in Egypt and felt an overwhelming attraction to them. He called his foster parents and they sent him the needed funds. He set off a week later.

He got to Cairo in the early hours of the morning and after a nights rest at a local backpackers stop headed out to the pyramids which by this stage in the city's development were situated in the suburbs, it seemed strange standing amongst the houses looking directly at the structures, almost like what it must have been like when they were first built. Images came to mind, himself standing in the kings chamber within the great pyramid. He blinked and the image faded. Picking up his bag he walk towards the towering monolith. On arrival he was greeted with the automatic weapon of a guard standing at the gate telling him he couldn't enter due to maintenance, fortunately the guard was open to bribery and quarter of hour later he was entering the main corridor leading to the chamber.

The energy hit him like a wall, his perception span out of control and he had to stop and lean against the rough wall to steady himself and regain his thoughts. When he felt back in control of his faculties he walked on. As he approached the kings chamber he's persona fell away leaving him naked and vulnerable, this would have worried him but in this case it felt correct and he remembered being here before, a long, long time ago facing this same initiation but he remembered last time he failed.

"Not this time!" he resolved and moved forward entering the chamber.

Something was wrong, whatever was being done here it wasn't maintenance. He could feel false energy structures forcing back the energies trying to come through this site. The government was worried they would lose control if they allowed this to be released amongst the populace and had set up psychic barriers, James smiled to himself and felt his energy rise, he felt the connection to his multidimensional selves and felt them working with him. Knowing the correctness of his next action he still paused and asked the cosmos for permission, it came instantly with a sense of approval for his caution.

His solar plexus opened like never before, energy came spiralling out with a force so intense he braced himself against the wall. Golden tendrils of light spilled from him enveloping the chamber and connecting with the stone itself, then reaching beyond the stone to the true structure, a structure of pure light within that of the stone. The correlation between this and his own body was not lost on him. Energy soared through the light body of the structure and met with his own, blending and spiralling out down through the Earth and out into the atmosphere was released into the mass mind of mankind. The psychic barriers dissipated like night before dawn and it was done.

James collapsed and sat on the cold stone floor, after a second he felt totally grounded and overflowing with life force, he centred the energy and stood up. He turned to leave and his energy dipped, there was more to do!.

The initiation was not yet complete, he lay on the floor across from the stone sarcophagus and closed his eyes, colour swirled before his eyelids, them all went black and the stars appeared, floating amongst them he suddenly shot faster than light to a certain star where he once again connected to the multidimensional self, pulling the aspects into one linking him to the God head, he viewed the cosmos with the wonder of a child he was in the warmest place he'd ever known, the feeling was incredible he'd never known such sureness of being and he didn't want to leave -ever.

This he now knew was where he'd once failed and with every piece of willpower he possessed he returned to his body and opened his eyes once again laying on the cold stone floor, after a moment he stood and walked out the chamber feeling cold shaky and rather sick but very pleased with himself.

CHAPTER 3

Back in Britain a few days later he reflected on his experience and wondered what was next. A few days later he got his answer, again whilst watching tv he saw a documentary on Peru and the machu pecu, an ancient Aztec city and decided to go, he had enough money left over from his Egyptian visit to buy a return ticket and set off. He arrived in Peru and after spending the night in a nearby town set along the trail towards the ruins.

As he walked he received many visions of himself in past lives living in the area, the site of the ruins was in fact, he garnered from his visions a highly spiritually advanced city before the Aztec's moved in. They just picked up on the energy and utilised it for their own ends, he knew what he had to do. The energy pathways surrounding the site needed cleansing as the Aztec's were very much into blood letting and the stigma this left on the ground still remained to this day.

As he entered the city he had to force the image's of sacrifice from he's mind. This once again took all the will power he could muster. He headed for the tallest structure that remained in the city, this being a large stepped stone pyramid. As he reached the steps he was over come by a sudden stabbing pain in his stomach, he stopped and clutched his abdomen. James laughed at his own obvious ingrained fear of the place and what had gone on here and once again stepped on the first step of the pyramid, only to be stopped by the same stabbing pain. He took a deep breath and resolved to make it to the top, again the pain hit him and he stopped.

He felt his guidance laughing at him.

"What's so funny?" he asked out loud.

"why do you think you have to climb the largest structure here to complete your task?" came the answer whispered on the breeze.

"Ah" thought James "Ego!".

He looked around him and saw a small partially ruined stone hut off to the left.

"There" he thought.

He sensed approval and moved towards the structure, his energy began to rise as he entered. He sat on the floor and took a deep breath, immediately his mind reached out to the surrounding leylines, filling him with dread as the blood letting hit him. He reached below this touching on the true nature of the pathways, that of love and he opened his heart to it letting it fill him and returning it to the Earth creating a circuit with himself between the two poles. He had to sit in this state for over an hour before the immense amount of blood and suffering began to break down, soul after soul stood before him asking to be released back to the light, they'd been here a long time and helping them return home filled James with incredible warmth and a steely determination to finish the task.

After which he opened his eyes feeling tired but satisfied, the pathways below his feet now glowed with pure clean life force. He returned to the nearby town to relax in a hot bath and let go of the days work. He returned to Britain two days later.

CHAPTER 4

After these recent experiences he resolved himself to the work the universe had set before him and began actively awaiting instruction.

None was forthcoming, he watched documentary's on tv and scanned the news papers daily waiting for something to leap out at him.

He began to get frustrated and this wasn't helped by the fact that his abilities seemed to have deserted him, he still picked up on peoples synergy and could still generally tell what they were thinking but that unnameable elusive sense of balance that had so far aided him at every turn seemed to have diminished. He applied his intellect to the problem but this only made it all the harder to regain what had been lost. Deciding he wasn't getting anywhere by this course of action he let it go and resumed his daily routine once again.

Forcing his mind back into his study's and relaxing into the norm he found some of what he'd lost returning and he realised his error, he'd been over focused, even became a little obsessed with it all and had forgotten to live.

He immersed himself back into the third dimension once again and in so doing found he could activate the higher portals of his mind whenever he chose. This he thought seemed to be a more practical way of living with his abilities and he started to view himself more as a bridge between worlds helping people to connect with their higher selves. At first this was done on a totally sublime level as far as the people involve were concerned but eventually with a select few he could operate on a more conscious level. He found this invigorating and it gave him a fresh out look on what he was doing.

He became more and more relaxed with who he was and noticed that when he was in this particular space he was more in tune and more able to work with his energy.

He decided to take classes to share what he was learning with others, he reconciled any misgivings he had about this venture by thinking that people would either think him mad or that what he was saying would resonate with them opening their own higher portals so they could begin to remember who they were and more importantly who they are now.

The classes went well and people seemed to understand most of what he had to give and would approach him after a session to ask him to expand on some of the harder information to grasp. He felt happy with his life at this time, he was doing what he had grown to love and felt it was beneficial to humanity as a whole, it felt like towing the line.

The people that attended his talks began to grow, better yet they were learning to enlighten themselves which James deduced was the best way because in truth we all had our own special part to play. After doing this work for a few months James realised that the universe had shown him he's next task after all and found the irony amusing, the universe it seemed was not without a sense of humour.

He began to meet people working on the same level as himself and developed relationships with them, this aided him during some difficult times and helped by the simple fact that he was not the only one doing this work. Things were going really well for James until one workshop he was taking some years later when something totally unexpected happened.

He was standing in an auditorium talking to well over a hundred people when quite suddenly a huge wave of energy entered the space, lifting everyone present into an elevated perspective. The energy continued to build moving about the room in a circular motion, taking the people higher with each turn. James urged everyone to move with the energy. This they did and the energy multiplied ten fold, a few people left the room at this point not able to hold this vibration of energy. The rest on the other hand began to visibly illuminate, to James standing facing them their skin had become almost totally transparent. They was a load POP followed by complete darkness then dazzling white. Everyone in the room was still there but the room was not.

Something was coming, something huge, suddenly they were engulfed in rainbow, information flowing through their brains. Each of them had a golden shadow standing behind them, the shadows closely resembled the person before them. They were merging!, it became clear. They were merging with their higher selves in the physical!, at this level.

The feeling this brought was unimaginable, suddenly their minds were completely free of all noise, they were overcome with an extreme sensation of love and oneness with each other. Their minds connected and acted as one, doing so one piece of information rose to the forefront.

They were continuing the journey of the soul but now at a much higher level, they had transcended the third dimension and now stood in the forth, James could sense his parents nearby. The journey is the completion of self , to unite the aspects with the nucleus, the God head.

Their shared mind wobbles as someone throws out a thought.

-"Then what?"

The answer comes simultaneously from within their circuit as well as the dimension itself.

"This nucleus it but an extension of another yet higher existence, from here they will once again scatter themselves as was done in the third dimension but this time it will be done amongst the varied levels of consciousness found in this higher 4th dimension and they will as in the third dimension grow through every expression of life on this level. Until on completion where they will enter the next level of levels, the fifth dimension. On this the never ending quest for perfection that is the universe".

-Life is about the journey not the destination, live in the now!.

The Daily Paper….

Over one hundred people

Vanish into thin air!!

Yesterday at a lecture on 'Alternative Psychology' given at an arts centre in South-west London over one hundred people supposedly disappeared into thin air. This reporter was first at the scene, an eye witness who attended the lecture gave this statement- ' I was enjoying the talk on meta-physics when things went weird, I started to feel light headed and stepped out side for a breath of air. As did a few other people, when we went back in everyone else had just sort of vanished!'.

The Daily Paper then asked Chief Inspector Wigan, the Officer in charge of the current investigation what progress they had made, he had this to say- 'At present our inquires have led us to believe this is some kind of prank organised by an unknown party but to what end we have been so far unable to comprehend, we at the metropolitan police would like the people involved to step forward and stop wasting police time. As well as the unnecessary anxiety they're causing their relatives'.

This reporter will stay on the case until the issue has been resolved and a logical explanation has been found to this mysterious occurrence.

About the Author

After he finished his schooling, Robert felt there was more to life than what he had been taught so far.

He decided to travel, extensively around Great Britain and Europe. In so doing had many mixed experiences and met manifold people from various walks of life, providing him a keen insight.

Now at twenty five and finally doing what he always felt drawn to do. An intriguing, innovative and thought provoking story has emerged.

With this his first novel complete, Robert's very interested in what you the reader will make of his work...